THE MIRROR
of
MONSTERS
and
PRODIGIES

THE MIRROR
of
MONSTERS
and
PRODIGIES

A NOVEL BY PAMELA DITCHOFF

COFFEE HOUSE PRESS   MINNEAPOLIS

Segments of "Prodigal Voices" were published, in *Chicago Review*, Vol. 37, 1991.

Segment on Homer published in *This*, Spring, 1995.

The characters in *The Mirror of Monsters and Prodigies* are drawn from history; the events and customs of their periods are a matter of record. The majority of official documents, personal correspondence, newspaper articles, film reviews, and references to published works are nonfiction. The character's voices are fictionalized accounts spoken from the imaginative conclusions of the author's research.

Quotations from the film *Freaks*, © 1932, Turner Entertainment Co. All rights reserved. Used with permission. Excerpt from "A Woman Young and Old" reprinted with permission of Simon & Schuster from *The Poems of W.B. Yeats: a New Edition*, edited by Richard J. Finneran. Copyright 1933 by Macmillan Publishing Company, renewed 1961 by Bertha Georgia Yeats.

Coffee House Press is supported, in part, by a grant provided by the Minnesota State Arts Board, through an appropriation by the Minnesota State Legislature, and by a grant from the National Endowment for the Arts, a federal agency. Additional support has been provided by the Lila Wallace-Reader's Digest Fund; The McKnight Foundation; Lannan Foundation; Jerome Foundation; Target Stores, Dayton's, and Mervyn's by the Dayton Hudson Foundation; General Mills Foundation; St. Paul Companies; Honeywell Foundation; Star Tribune/Cowles Media Company; Beverly J. and John A. Rollwagen Fund of The Minneapolis Foundation; Prudential Foundation; and The Andrew W. Mellon Foundation.

Coffee House Press books are available to the trade through our primary distributor, Consortium Book Sales & Distribution, 1045 Westgate Drive, Saint Paul, MN 55114. For personal orders, catalogs or other information, write to:

Coffee House Press

27 North Fourth Street, Suite 400, Minneapolis, MN 55401

Library of Congress CIP Data

Ditchoff, Pamela, 1950-

The Mirror of monsters and prodigies : a novel / by Pamela Ditchoff.

p.   cm.

Includes bibliographical references (p.).

ISBN 1-56689-035-7 (pbk. : alk. paper)

I. Title.

PS3554. 1839M57 1995

813'.54—DC20   95-18247

                                                          CIP

10   9   8   7   6   5   4   3   2   1

All the same, books do serve some purpose. Culture doesn't save anything or anyone, it doesn't justify. But it's a product of man: he projects himself into it, he recognizes himself in it; that critical mirror alone offers his image.

—Jean-Paul Sartre

The Mirror of Monsters and Prodigies

Turn these pages carefully; they're made of glass. They are fragile. They can cut and shatter. Some pages are ancient, older than the mirror books of the Middle Ages that sought to reflect the factual world, *Speculum Mundi*, or to serve as a moral guide, *Speculum Disciplinae*; far older than the prognostic Renaissance mirrors, *Mirror Uranicum*, or fantasy books of imagination, *Mirror of Fancies*.

This is the mirror cracked, the fun-house mirror, the other side of the looking glass—the mirror of monsters and prodigies. Within these pages voices and images of a cryptic culture are sustained in glass and ink. They will speak to you with the tongues of gods and legends, sages and idiots, kings and fools, artists and critics, holy men and profane women, exploiters and victims. You will see with their eyes.

Keep in mind, you can't gaze into a mirror without your image mingling its own nature with that which is contained within the frame. You will see their eyes watching you watching them.

The purpose of this book is not to save or to justify, but to propose that you reflect a bit longer before deciding which images are truly monstrous.

ANCIENT VOICES

OLD KINGDOM EGYPT, 2500 B.C.

TISRET

My beloved, Knumhotou, is the smallest man in the world. You don't believe me? The gold bracelet I wear on my upper arm once encircled Knumhotou's neck, and the belt of beads he wears to secure his linen, I strung for myself as a collar. You may search throughout the vast lands of Pharaoh Pepi and you will not find a man small as my beloved, because he is more than a man, he is honored by the gods.

This is what I believe. We know the world was made by the Sun God, Ra, and that Ra called into being all the other numerous gods. Khnum, the ram-headed god, was assigned the task of fashioning men from the clay of Mother River upon a potter's wheel. When Khnum grew weary and closed his eyes, Bes, the most diminutive god, laughing, lion-headed dispeller of evil spirits, crept on his tiny feet to the wheel and fashioned one man in his own likeness before Khnum awoke. That man is my beloved, Knumhotou.

Knumhotou is Guardian of the Royal Wardrobe, born in a noble house of Egypt, cousin to Hapsut, first wife of Pharaoh Pepi. The pharaoh depends on Knumhotou to select the finest linens and girdles to adorn the royal body; his jeweled collars must glorify Ra, and the leather of his sandals must be tender upon the pharaoh's feet.

My beloved's quarters are near to the pharaoh, within his private rooms, between the harem and the robing chamber. Oh, I have seen the envy in the eyes of the harem women, shining black as obsidian when I pass by. Even though they are blessed by receiving the seed of Pharaoh Pepi, who is the Son of Ra, his seed is scattered among them like milkweed on the wind. I have seen their eyes turn soft as butter for Knumhotou, but he does not look upon them. I

3

alone am honored with the love of Knumhotou, Son of Bes.

My small room is at the east end of the servant's quarters. I am servant to the Keeper of the Cosmetics, Hotah. Hotah the Huge is the name I say in my head. His rooms hold caches of bread and cakes, beer and wine, fruit and sweets. His breath reeks of sour poultry. Such a fuss he makes with his fat fingers in the royal chamber, smudging kohl pots, waving bowls of perfume about while I stand behind Hotah with my palette of colors, deciding which hues will best complement Pharaoh Pepi according to his garments of the day. I mix the colors for his eyes, for his cheeks, for his lips, and Hotah takes up brushes to apply them. Finally, Hotah grunts to his plump knees and lifts the royal mirror for Pharaoh's approval. He has not once been displeased, and Hotah's bulk quivers with pleasure at the sound of Pharaoh Pepi's praise.

Tisret praises Knumhotou as we ride in his boat among the rushes where the water is still and smooth. Our happiness overflows, and Mother River doubles us within her body to partake of our joy. He plucks blue lotus blossoms to lay in my lap. Knumhotou whose mouth on mine is honey, no harsh, groping hands holding the back of my skull, wrapping my braids in a knot, gritting teeth and grunting in my ear, heaving flesh up and down along the length of my body. Knumhotou's hands explore with delicate caresses, his strong legs hook behind my knees, his nostrils like butterfly wings between my breasts, his manhood a ripe plum, abundantly juicy, nestling in the nest of my love. I am content. I am more content than the fish resting among the papyrus reeds.

So revered is Knumhotou that a tomb decorated by royal artists, furnished with woven rugs, chests of ivory and gold, vessels of alabaster and silver, has been prepared by Pharaoh Pepi for my beloved, as close to his own great tomb as Knumhotou is to the pharaoh's heart.

QUEEN HAPSUT

Mourners gather below the Balcony of Appearances—listen, they speak my husband's name, and to speak his name is to make him live again. My tears bathed his feet as the priests made him ready, opened his mouth so he may eat the delicacies and drink the wines that fill his house of death; so he may speak words of praise to Osiris.

Draw back the shades and behold their numbers. Soon the priests will lead the procession with smoking incense and prayers. I must take my place behind my nephew, Pharaoh Pepi II, beside my good sister, second wife of Pepi, mother of the new pharaoh. Behind us will walk our cousin, Knumhotou. He knows the funeral path well.

Each evening as Ra begins his journey to the underworld, painting the sky in red and purple, Knumhotou visits the tomb provided him by my husband, where his beloved Tisret rests. Mother of his son, she who died giving birth, but was three times blessed: with the love of one favored by the gods, with a son from his seed, with a son likewise favored by Bes. Inside the tomb, in a niche in the wall, next to her sarcophagus, is a carved effigy of Tisret. Knumhotou purifies the tomb with frankincense while offering prayers to the dead; he takes the effigy from the niche and divests her of garments. He cleanses her with rainwater, bathes her in perfume, clothes her in fresh raiment, and most tenderly sets her back in place.

Knumhotou is easy to find among the crowd; he's the man no bigger than the child Pharaoh. See him there, attending to Pepi's raiments as he did for my husband. The boy tickling the Pharaoh's chin is Rahn, Knumhotou's son. The two boys are as close as grains of wheat upon the stalk. I have no son; my womb is barren as the Western Desert. Oh, that my soul were setting sail to the islands of Osiris, accompanying my husband to the realm of the dead.

KNUMHOTOU AND RAHN

"Father, why are we different from the others? Is it true we are touched by Bes?"

"What man can presume to know the whims of the gods? Every man is different from every other man, and the same."

"No riddles tonight, Father. You know what I mean. Pepi and I are the same age. He's grown into a man. I have not."

"Rahn, you're twelve years old, time enough left to become a man. Do you wish to be taller?"

"Sometimes I wonder how things would look if my eyes were level with other boys' my age. I'd be better at games. If my legs were longer, I could run faster, and in a crowd, I wouldn't need to move to the front in order to see."

"I'll tell you a secret, Rahn, for you to remember always, to share with your children. Where you stand has little to do with what you see. Without Ra's light, nothing exists to man's eye. Cover your eyes. . . . Now you see only darkness. The banquet hall has disappeared."

"But I hear the harp, the flutes and drums, and I smell the food. I can touch you with my hands."

"So your ears and your nose tell you I'm at your side. What does your mind and your heart tell you?"

"That you're talking in riddles, Father."

"Remove your hands and open your eyes. You do not see the dancers, the musicians, and the pharaoh."

"I don't?"

"You see light reflected from the Ba, from their bodies. You cannot see their Ka. Even Ra cannot penetrate the Ka, which is the soul and substance of a man. The brighter the light, the more the black of the eyes close to hide the Ka."

"Has anyone ever seen a Ka?"

"Your mother—she could see into my Ka, with her mind and her heart. Rahn, your eyes are like a mirror held to your mother's face."

"I'm not sure I understand, Father, but I will remember."

"You're a good son. Now, let me give you some useful advice. Climb a hill if you want to be taller. Everything is related to perspective. Think about the animals that share our land. Which are the largest?"

"Horses and oxen, lions, the crocodile."

"The horse must carry men on his back, oxen are beasts of labor. Lions are strong, but they cannot escape the pharaoh's spears and arrows."

"If they hide in the tall grass, they can."

"Yes, when they make themselves smaller, like the crocodile lying in the river rushes with hooded eyes. And what creature is most plentiful in Pharaoh Pepi's land?"

"Birds?"

"There are many varieties of birds. Look at the servants standing beside the banquet tables. What are they doing?"

"They're fanning the food with palms."

"Why?"

"To keep the insects . . . insects! There are more insects than anything else."

"Look to your feet, there's a grasshopper; how large we must appear to his eyes. The smallest creatures are the greatest in number, and who knows, Rahn, what type of men live in other lands? There may be a land where men are no bigger than that grasshopper, or a land of men so large they could stand with one foot in the Great Sea, the other in the Red Sea, and straddle the land of Sinai."

✧

SETHUR'S OMINOUS REPORT

I told them we saw giants there, and that we twelve were as grasshoppers in their sight! We laid down the fruit we had taken in Hebron: the cluster of grapes carried on a pole between two men, the pomegranates and figs, large as my head. Aaron rejoiced, "We have come unto the land Yahweh promised, and surely it flows with milk and honey, and this is the fruit of it."

Caleb shouted, "Let us go up at once, and possess it, for we are well able to overcome it."

I was struck dumb! I should have reminded him of the commandment Yahweh gave to Moses on the mountain of Sinai: "Do not covet your neighbor's house nor anything that belongs to your neighbor."

How did we come to know the giants who dwell in Hebron? After we made camp in the wilderness of Paran, Yahweh commanded Moses to send forth men to spy out the land of Canaan, southward into the mountains, one man from each tribe. We twelve were to find if the land was fat or lean, wooded or bearing fruit, if the cities were tents or strongholds. We came first upon Hebron, where the giants dwelt, and we spent forty days among their clan.

Upon return to our encampment, Caleb excited the people to go up and claim the lands of Anak. I waved my arms and protested,

"We cannot go against these people, they are giants, their cities are grand and fortified with stone walls. The men are of great stature, sons of Anak; and we are as grasshoppers in their sight. They will crush us beneath their heels, as they crushed the three who did not return with us."

Caleb's eyes held mine but a moment before turning away. He knew I was bearing false witness, that the sons of Anak do not dwell in walled cities, that they did not crush the absent three, and though they are twice as large as the men of our tribes, no son of Anak would raise sword or shield against any man.

SONS OF ANAK

We first saw them several days ago when they arrived in the plains of Paran below our hills. My brother Jebu and I were herding goats from the south pasture when we were startled by a deafening din. We followed the sound and saw people numbering in the thousands, small and bony, exhaustion plain in their posture. The few wagons, pulled by beleaguered oxen, clanked with utensils and squawked with caged birds. Behind them trotted herds of thin, protesting sheep. By nightfall, their torches were like stars upon the valley floor, a sight which caused me to feel as if the earth had slipped away and I was floating in dark water between two nights, one reflecting the other into eternity.

In the morning, Jebu suggested we go down and greet them with fruit, bread, and wine, but I thought it best to observe from a distance for a time. On the first day, several men erected a pavilion in the middle of the camp, formed with yards of blue, purple and scarlet cloth. They carried a large gold chest, supported on four gold poles, into the pavilion and set it upon a gold table. With the front draping left open to the sun, the interior blinded us and threw spears of light into our hills.

On the third evening, our clan gathered in the common house to discuss the newcomers. We were interrupted by voices, which rose in collective anger. To determine the cause of their distress, we walked down to a grove of acacia trees, beside a pond where the valley view is clearest. The people crowded around an aged man who wielded a wooden staff. So intense was their discord that it worried the sheep. They broke from their corral and toppled four lanterns, setting fire to nearby tents.

When the flames raged enough to draw the people from their anger, their screams rose higher than the flames. "Moses," they implored, "help us."

Jebu and I pushed aside the stones that hold the pond. Water coursed down the hillside and extinguished the flames. The people fell to their knees murmuring before the old man.

On the fourth day, Jebu observed a group of men being sprinkled with water by priests. He guessed they were holy men from the garments they wore: embroidered coats and girdles in colors of gold, blue, purple and scarlet, breastplates and staffs of gold. The other men removed their clothing and the priests shaved all the hair from the men's bodies. Each shaven man departed to return with a young bull and a sack of grain. The priests placed the grain inside the pavilion. They slit the necks of the bulls and collected the blood in jars, which were taken inside. They slit the bull's bellies and removed the fat and carried it inside also. After much commotion from within, the carcasses were hauled to the edge of the camp, where they were burned.

On the seventh day, their voices rose again in anguish: "Oh, for a few bites of meat, or the fresh fish, cucumbers, melons, onion and garlic we had in Egypt." One man held aloft a piece of gum resin, which falls from ash trees at night, and he cried, "Day after day, manna!"

No wonder they complain. This resin is used by our clan as a purgative.

They were hungry and we had much to share. That evening we released half our pigeons into the camp. Such a scampering of delight; we couldn't help but laugh! At the sound of our laughter, they turned their heads toward our hills, palms held upward as if expecting rain. Alas, their hunger was so fierce, they didn't cook the birds sufficiently and several people took ill. Some died. Heavy with remorse, our clan decided to intervene no more.

These people are hungry, yet lambs, bulls, and doves are slaughtered for the pavilion, and sacks of grain are given to the pavilion. If I had not seen it built with my own eyes, I would think a voracious monster dwelt within. Forgive me, it's unjust to compare their customs to ours, as if we are the ideal for all to emulate. Oh, but here is gladdening news. Jebu tells me twelve men climb our southern hill at this moment. We must hasten to prepare a proper welcome.

THE THREE DEFECTORS

one: Twenty years my father labored in Pharaoh's brick pits, bruised to the bone from building the treasure cities of Pithom and Ramses. I still see his face, swollen and stern with disease as he pitched a rock at my feet. I didn't want to leave him. I begged him to let me stay. I cried and tore my hair, but he would not weaken. "The next rock will strike your head" were his final words to me. Months ago he was left in the wilderness of Shur, expelled according to the laws of Yahweh because he had leprosy. Yahweh commands us to honor our parents. Is it right then to leave those we honor to starve alone in the wilderness? Aaron said if the disease touches one, it will touch all, and sacrifices must be made for the preservation of our people. Here, in Hebron I met Talman, the ancient grandfather of Jebu. His legs and arms bore circular silver scars. When I questioned him about the curious marks, he told me he'd caught leprosy as a young man after traveling to Moab and sharing his water skin with an unfortunate woman. "How can this be?" I asked. "Leprosy is certain death." Talman said the disease will not spread if contact with the wounds is avoided. The body will heal if bathed twice daily and select foods and herbs are eaten.

TWO: There's plenty to eat here; no one is hungry in the land of Anak. When we twelve scaled the mountain, we reached a wooded plateau. Following a path through the trees, we came upon a clearing where a huge stone table sat, longer than the Pharaoh's ships tied end to end. The table was laden with fruits, vegetables, breads, and foods we'd never seen. We knew a table of that size must belong to giants, but we were so hungry, we couldn't resist. We climbed upon the great slab and began to feast. Then we heard them approach.

THREE: The ground trembled and we were shaken from the table as flies shaken from a horse. Our mouths stuffed with bread, we prostrated our bodies upon the ground. What use running? They could catch us easily. Stories of the Anakian giants' cruelty have been told among our people for ages.

TWO: But the giants called out, "Welcome, friends. Rise and partake of the food we've prepared in your honor." I lifted my eyes and beheld a man's foot that stretched the full length of my arm. Turning my head, I looked into a forest of hairy limbs. The giants numbered near one hundred men, women, and children. As I stared, a huge hand was offered palm up, and I extended my quaking hand.

When he lifted me to sit upon the table, and likewise my companions, I feared we would be eaten, that the glow on their faces was anticipation of a hearty meal. Our fears were quickly eased as the giants sat on the ground about the table and bade us to enjoy the fruits of their labor.

THREE: To the west are gardens that rival the pharaoh's own. Next to them are arbors of grapes and groves of figs and pomegranate trees. They have flocks of goats, but do not eat them. From the milk of the nannies they make a soft white food that tingles the tongue. When their animals die, the skins are used as blankets. They do not cover themselves with clothing.

ONE: Yet they are unashamed.

TWO: Here there is neither shame nor guilt.

ONE: Look about you, look into the ample, generous faces of the Anakians, see how they live in harmony, and tell me that God is not with them. Theirs was an ancient race before the flood. I may have forsaken my tribe, but I have not forsaken my God; I worship Him beside these giants who have become my brothers, who praise Him by revering His earth and all His tribes.

THREE: At times we hear words from the encampment, and always the sons of Anak hear, for their ears are large and their hearing is sharp. Bless Sethur—after he spoke of the giants, how we three were crushed as grasshoppers under their heels, the people wept and wailed all night, crying, "We wish we had died in Egypt rather than be taken into this country ahead of us. Yahweh will kill us there and our children will become slaves. Let's go back to Egypt. Elect a leader to take us back." In the morning, Moses called the

13

tribes together and told them Yahweh had appeared to him, enraged by the faithlessness of his people. As punishment, they will wander for forty years in the wilderness before reaching the promised land, one year for each day the twelve spies were in the lands of Anak.

TWO: We'll be gone well before then. A party of Anakians are preparing ships on the shores of the Great Sea. They've traveled many times to avoid conflict and to find new lands. Talman is the clan's guide; destinations are revealed to him through the liquid sleep of dreams. Talman's dream vision is an island in the seas north of Egypt and west of Assyria.

THE ISLAND OF CRETE, 800 B.C.

FARMER OF KNOSSOS

That's quite a tale, friend. Your voice is good and loud, but the plink of your strings is lost on these ears. I'm becoming deaf as a stone. Oh-oh, my wife's scowling. She thinks me a dolt, griping about my ears to a man deprived of sight. Woman, you can see Homer is a man of learning and good nature. Please, sit at our table, and we'll repay your entertainment with a meal.

Now, I'll tell you that your story of giants sailing for an island out of the land of . . . where did you say? Sinai, yes, Sinai, tweaks this old Cretan's head. Have you seen—curses—have you *heard* our wild goats bleating? They're everywhere! An ancient story tells of giants who sailed to Crete from the east bringing wives, children, and goats. They were named Triamates by my ancestors, and they lived in hiding for many years. Then one day, so the story goes, two men were traveling to Iraklion and came to a strange village where fierce dogs

14

guarded each house. The men asked a woman of the village for shelter. She said she'd fetch her husband and left them with her son, a boy as big as a man. As they waited, one of them noticed the boy had a third eye on the back of his head—the mark of the Triamates. When questioned, the boy let on that his mother had gone to get the rest of the clan to slaughter and eat the travelers. The men escaped by killing the boy and feeding pieces of his body to the guard dogs. Then they gathering up men from throughout the country and returned to kill the monstrous inhabitants of the village.

Some folks around here claim there's one giant left, living in a cave on the cliffs to the south, but I don't put much stock in gossip—stories to scare little children, keep them from wandering into dangerous places.

PRUDENCE

I congratulate you on finding my home—not many do, and fewer still cross the threshold. Have you always been blind? Only a blind man or a fool would brave these cliffs. The noise you describe that led you here is my brother, Polyphemus. Your ears are true—he is very large and very miserable; he hasn't had his wine today. Shall we strike a bargain? I'll tell you about my brother if you'll play as I talk.

Ah, your music begs my feet to dance. How long has it been since I danced? I can't remember. No, I can—since Polyphemus was born. Father said he was a curse from the gods, who were angered by an old man indulging in pleasures of the flesh. Polyphemus emerged from my mother's womb disfigured; a huge baby, nose spread across his face, his mouth a gaping hole, and his left eye absent. Despite his gruesome appearance, Mother loved him and kept him hidden from the eyes of everyone in the village. Monstrous babies like Polyphemus are thrown into the sea, which is where they belong. She made Father dig a grave behind our house. For a month's passing she'd go to the grave at high sun, when the villagers took their meal, and loudly lament her stillborn child.

As he grew, it became harder to keep him secret; he was a demanding and selfish boy. In the black of night while the village slept, Mother would take Polyphemus into the countryside, where he'd run and run with wild goats. This nightly ritual kept Polyphemus asleep most of the day, but it wore down my mother, and she died when he was ten years old. Instead of grieving her death, Polyphemus raged, threw plates against the wall, smashed chairs, ripped my mother's robes into tatters and tied them to his body. Neither Father nor I would take him out at night for fear he'd wake the village. So he paced the floor, bleating like a goat, grating our nerves raw. Finally, Father told him the tale of the Triamates, warning that the villagers would tear him to pieces if they ever caught sight of him. Though Polyphemus was just a boy, he was larger than my father and duller than goat dung. That tale always sent him whimpering into his closet.

At age sixteen, Polyphemus fell in love with Althea, a village girl. Concealed behind rocks on a hill above her cottage, he'd watch her herd goats for milking. This was a peaceful time for Father and me because Polyphemus quieted his anger and spoke softly. For the first time since Mother's death, he took care of his appearance, even though he dared not show himself to Althea. Unfortunately, our peace was short-lived. Althea was struck by Eros in the guise of a beautiful boy. When Polyphemus saw them together on the hillside, he let out a great bellow, lifted a boulder and hurled it at the lovers. The young boy pushed Althea away, but his body was crushed by the stone.

We had to flee the village; Polyphemus brought us to these cliffs that hold many caves. He chose one large enough for the three of us and rolled stones in front of the cave's mouth. That was a portent of the gloom that has remained with me all my days. One need not be blind to live in perpetual darkness. But who can live in a cave and not go mad? I could not, so during the following year, Father and I built this house.

After Father died, Polyphemus holed up in that cave day and night with his goats. I could've gone back to the village, but what good awaited me? The shine had gone from my raven hair, my bright eyes were streaked with red, my smooth olive skin had turned pale and ashen, my round figure gone to bone. When I was of marriageable age, Father drove all my suitors away, fearful that they'd discover Polyphemus. After Mother died, Father was vicious to any man who set foot on our doorstep; he meant to keep me in his service. Too late I found myself too old for wife, too old for mother.

I leave platters of food, and jugs of wine outside the cave. Polyphemus eats and drinks and raves. When I die, he'll die also, and be glad for it. Now, do you still want to visit his cave? Don't say you go without warning. Take the jug with you; if he allows you inside, I'd advise you to keep a clear head—no matter that your eyes cannot see, wine is the glass of the mind and what it reveals of Polyphemus may well terrify you more than if you beheld his beastly face.

HOMER'S FIRST NARRATION
ON THE CYCLOPS

Prudence set me upon the path with a jug of wine. I followed the pitiful sound higher and higher, cleaving my body to the cliff, gulls screeching round my head, the sea thrashing below. Locating the source of the howling, I touched a boulder that blocked the cave entrance. His voice vibrated my fingers through the thick stone. I called, "Polyphemus, Prudence has sent me with your wine."

"Go away!" he roared.

"I'll wait until you're ready to receive me," I replied, and sat on the ground. Out of habit, my fingers idle, I began plucking my lute. A

17

rush of wind ruffled my hair as the boulder was dragged inside the cave. I was seized by my shoulders and snatched from the ground.

"No music!" Polyphemus growled and shook me as a fox shakes a rabbit. He stopped suddenly and set me down. "Your eyes have no light," he said. "They're white as goat's milk."

"I am blind. I cannot see," I stammered, stumbling to control my weak knees.

"Why are you here?" he demanded. "To steal my goats?"

"I'm a storyteller. I travel great distances playing music and gathering tales to tell. I've brought your wine. Would you like to hear a story?"

Polyphemus prodded me inside and rolled the stone back in place. He took my hand and led me to a fire. The cave was warm and dry, and the floor had been swept clean of debris. For many hours, seated before the fire, I told him tales of my travels. He didn't speak a word of question or comment. My throat grew dry, and I asked for a taste of wine. I heard goat hooves scraping and impatient bleats. Polyphemus rose and the squeak of a gate followed, the soft trickle of grain falling upon stone, and a comforting rumble from the deep well of his throat.

He returned to the fire; I felt sparks rise as he added wood. I asked if he had a story to offer. After a long moment, he spoke: "I wish to die. If I take my own life, the gods will deny me my mother's embrace. No man has yet come to the entrance of my cave who didn't flee. I hold a stake of olive wood, hardened by fire. You will thrust it into my belly."

"I cannot, Polyphemus," I said.

"If you refuse, I'll keep the stone in front of the entrance until you consent."

"If I kill you, how will I get out?"

"I'm strong enough to move the stone before I die."

"What if you are not? What's to become of your goats? They will die slowly of starvation."

"I'll release them now." Polyphemus rolled the stone aside and opened the pen. When hooves clattered near my ears, and I felt oily wool brush my cheek, I grabbed the horns of one large goat and wrapped my legs around his belly. Down the cliff face he dashed in a clatter, nostrils fluttering with the promise of sea grass, me hanging on like death, teeth jarring, muscles straining, bones groaning.

The goat halted abruptly when he reached a patch of green. I dropped to the sand and thanked Zeus for my deliverance. Even at that distance, with my heart and the tide pounding in my ears, still I could hear Polyphemus weeping. Would that he'd raged and showered me with rocks, which is what my listeners will do if I end this tale with a weeping giant. No, in my story Polyphemus will be more terrible than in his youth, a monster to make heroes tremble, a Cyclops from the race who helped Vulcan forge the thunderbolts of Zeus in the depths of Mount Aetna, rather than a slave confined to a cave in the cliffs of Knossos, mourning his unbreakable, invisible chains.

THE ISLAND OF SAMOS, 500 B.C.

AESOP AND DIECHO

We were both slaves a year ago, both purchased by Xanthus the Philosopher. Now Aesop is guest of the royal palace in Lydia, preparing a journey to Babylon financed by King Croesus. I'm still in Samos, slave to the insatiable desire of Erista, Xanthus' rattle-boned shrew of a wife.

I'd seen her at the market two days before I was sold. Her eyes gleamed like sesterces when they fell upon me. Her fingers dug into Xanthus' arm, and she pulled him aside and whispered in his ear. The next day, Xanthus returned, his purse fat with coins, students at his heels. Three new slaves were brought to the block, one of whom

I'd never seen the like. Aesop. His coloring was dark, his nose flat and without bridge, his lips hung swollen as if stung by a swarm of bees. These features were set in a long, gourd-shaped head and his squat torso curved to the left. His belly preceded the rest of his body, which sat on legs with knees opposing one another.

Xanthus approached the block and the slave on Aesop's right waved to him and boasted, "Buy me, I can do everything." The slave on Aesop's left leaned forward and said, "Buy me, I can do anything." With experience you can spot a soft touch and easy taskmaster. Although Xanthus is tall, his shoulders curl forward and his long white arms dangle like wilted flowers. Aesop choked with laughter, holding his round belly, his mouth wide open and gasping. The students, curious about the cause of his merriment, pressed Xanthus to inquire. Xanthus blinked his large eyes in confusion, then asked Aesop what services he could perform. Aesop replied, "Nothing at all—my companions, who can do everything and anything, have left nothing for me to do." Xanthus laughed, as did the rest of us near enough to hear the little monkey's witty reply. Aesop continued, "Which shall you choose? To doubt everything or to believe anything are two equally convenient solutions. Both dispense with the necessity of reflection." Xanthus purchased Aesop and off they trotted, engaged in serious conversation.

Xanthus returned early the next morning before the market opened, looking sheepish, and without his entourage. He purchased me privately. Upon arrival at his fine whitewashed home, I noticed a curtain drawn back. Erista's dark eyes and hawk nose peered from behind it. I saw Aesop also, squatting in a vegetable garden, humming to himself as he pulled weeds. Xanthus eagerly went to speak with him, leaving me on the stoop. Thus my work began.

On nights when Xanthus wasn't away, which were rare, and I was reprieved from the labors of the mistress' bed, Aesop entertained me with stories. He has remarkable talent for telling tales. He told me of the greeting *he* received from Erista. You see, the day Aesop was bought, she'd sent Xanthus to market to purchase me. Aesop knew from Xanthus' plodding feet as they neared the house that something was amiss. Erista danced from her bedroom, draped in gauze, hips thrust forward, nipples taut, her lips wet. When she saw Aesop, she screamed, "Is this a man or a beast?" Then she loosed her rage upon Xanthus, who turned to Aesop with pleading eyes. Aesop said, "From lying at the mercy of fire, water, and a wicked woman, good gods deliver us." That he chose to quote a truly revered philosopher was a jab wasted on Xanthus.

Aesop usually is not so blunt; he veils his intent in animal parables to reveal the truth of human nature. Being so offensive to the eyes, if he offended the ears as well with undecorated truth, he'd be struck dead. I don't have Aesop's wit. I have beauty and long for the day I'm old and wrinkled, sent out of the rich houses into the fields to labor.

Born to a court slave in Athens, I was put on the blocks at age ten. The man who purchased me collected beautiful young boys. When one of them slit the master's throat as he snored contentedly in the boy's arms, we were all sold to pay the master's debts. Since then, I've been in as many households as there are months in a year. My masters and mistresses clothe me in yellow silks, bid me bathe in perfumed oils, and mount gleaming, silver mirrors beside their beds. I hate my image, which is so unlike me that their praise of it mocks me. What deception wins, cruelty must keep. Beauty perverts; in order to justify their lust, they idealize me, and when I disappoint them by offering my heart, I'm sold again.

Aesop too was born a slave, in Thrace, an object of jest and disgust, likened to beasts, and he has won the respect and admiration of kings. I miss his stories, but I'm happy for his good fortune. I picture him, at King Croesus' side, telling the fable of Aesop and Diecho, which he might title The Frog and the Cistern.

21

ERISTA

Good riddance to the croaking toad—big mouth forever flapping. Aesop made my husband look the fool, as if Xanthus needed any help. Praise Zeus for sending the eagle, otherwise Xanthus never would have parted with Aesop. During our Spring Festival, an eagle swooped down and snatched from the altar the ring that bears the seal of Samos. A short time later, a slave appeared with the ring, claiming it had been dropped into his hands by an eagle in flight. The citizens took this event as an augury of calamity to the state and turned to Xanthus for interpretation. Of course, he had no idea, and he put them off by begging time for deliberation.

My husband, the great philosopher, will gladly pontificate for hours on the nature of government, things celestial and terrestrial, to a herd of sycophantic boys. However, this official request sunk Xanthus into a depression so deep, he threatened to swallow poison. Who was close by, listened at doorways, ready with a solution? Aesop. He has a way with animals. I'd wager he trained that bird to steal the ring and deliver it to his own hands, then put it into the hands of the slave along with words for his mouth—just as he put words into Xanthus' mouth to present to the Council.

Does it surprise you that Aesop convinced Xanthus to say the augury was best interpreted by a slave? And consequently Aesop was summoned to explain the omen? Ha! Aesop said only if he were free would he be qualified for the function of interpretation. The Council granted his freedom, and Aesop spoke thus: "The eagle represents royalty, and dropping the seal in the hands of a slave portends loss of liberty; a fierce prince has his eye on Samos."

Sure enough, within days, Croesus of Lydia demanded a tribute from Samos, and without such, war was eminent. You know as well as I that these slaves have networks; gossip is thick as honeycombs between them. Aesop, with his big ears so low to the ground, would've learned of Croesus' plan weeks ago.

Where is Aesop now? A lap-dog in Lydia, petted and pampered by Croesus, while Xanthus is as impotent as a dead fledgling in the nest, and Diecho's cup is nearing the dregs.

AESOP'S CRIMINATOR AT DELPHI

I did it . . . put the cup in Aesop's pack, but I didn't know the purpose, I swear. If only he'd kept still, if he'd kept his lips quiet . . .

I keep quiet. I know my place. I'm servant to the priests who interpret the inspired words of the oracle, Pythia. At dawn I rise and in silence follow the priests, who follow Pythia to the fountain of Castalia. There she bathes before donning her crown of laurels. Then we climb the slopes of Parnassus to the temple of Apollo. I help the lady into her three-legged chair, which straddles a chasm in the rock face. She closes her eyes and inhales deeply. Multitudes await the moment her body will shake and her mouth will utter the divine words of Apollo. None but the priests can understand and interpret her words. Many people come from distant lands to put questions to the oracle. I've heard countless answers, and I can make no sense of them, but I'm a stupid boy, and I don't ask questions.

I see hundreds come and go through Delphi, and rarely do I remember a face, unless it's a lovely girl with an inviting smile. But who would not have noticed the deformed creature perched on a rock, watching the oracle for days and sniffing the air like a hound? His vigil ended, he sought out the eldest citizen in Delphi, who happens to be my grandfather. He remembers the time before the oracle, before Apollo's temple was built, before the people came. He told me vapor has always risen from the oracle's chasm. As a boy, he'd seen sheep, grazing near the chasm, fall to the ground and twitch violently. I warned Grandfather against talking about those days to strangers, but he's old and doesn't fear much.

I learned from whispers in the Temple, that the deformed man was called Aesop, a freed slave renowned for his wit and wisdom. He'd stopped at Delphi on his way to Babylon. The magistrates were eager to hear him speak, and urged him to address the people. His good words about the oracle, repeated on his travels, would bring many more believers to Delphi, their purses rich with tribute. Aesop agreed, but his speech was his downfall. He said: "The curiosity that brought me to Delphi is akin to people standing by the sea who observe a thing far from shore. At first they think it could be a wonder, but when it reaches shore, proves to be a heap of weeds and rubbish." The citizens were outraged, and the magistrates' faces flamed red. I should have guessed they would plot revenge.

As Aesop readied to leave Delphi, I was sent to his quarters with orders to slip the gold temple cup into his pack. He was apprehended outside the city, charged with sacrilege, jailed, and condemned to death—sentenced to be thrown from a precipice of Parnassus. After the judgment was proclaimed, Aesop waved his arms, screwed up his face, frightening the magistrates into silence, and said: "A rabbit, fleeing from an eagle, took sanctuary in a ditch occupied by a beetle. The eagle flapped the beetle aside and devoured the rabbit. The insulted beetle planned a revenge, watched the eagle fly to her nest, then continually climbed there while the eagle hunted, and rolled the eggs out of the nest. The eagle appealed to Zeus, who allowed her to lay her next clutch of eggs in his lap, but the beetle contrived a way to make Zeus rise from his throne and destroy the eggs unaware. Zeus, upon hearing the beetle's case, found the eagle to be the aggressor and acquitted the beetle."

The citizens pondered this; Zeus's name had been called. But Aesop didn't stop there, didn't keep silent. He sputtered, "Don't flatter yourselves that oppressors of the innocent shall escape divine vengeance." He turned his long head, found me in the crowd, and gave me a wink. I wanted to throw myself off a precipice! Surely he knew I'd put the cup in his pack.

Up the mountain, I followed the procession, and though Apollo shone brightly overhead, I shivered at Aesop's piercing shouts as he was dragged toward death . . . *an old man, spent all his life in the country . . . wished to see the city before he died . . . friends loaned asses that knew well the road . . . a terrible storm . . . asses fell into the pit, crushing the old man . . . with his dying breath said, miserable bastard I am, to die by the lowest of beasts . . . and my fate is worse . . . in the hands of ignorant, corrupt, drunken, blind . . . no conception of humanity or honor . . . gods will not suffer my blood unavenged . . .*

His cursing diminished with each thud against the rocks. A mob stood at the precipice edge, peering down, and nearly jumped out of their skins when Aesop's echo screamed—*blood unavenged.* Then there was silence, a silence deep and eternal as the grave.

THE ROMAN EMPIRE, 5 B.C.

OVID

Gravitas, gravitas, gravitas. I am a dangerous old man. Stay hence, far hence, you prudes. I'm in exile here, on the damned edge of the Black Sea, to preserve the dignity of Rome. Augustus, revered one, silences the voice of individuality and fosters the poetic propaganda of Virgil and Horace's odes to rural life. Yes, Horace lives the simple country life—with ten house slaves! He can't tolerate the noise of Rome, the pungent odors, the congested streets, the beggars; these offend his delicate nature. I am sick with longing for Rome. This solitude resounds like seashells pressed to my ears.

For love I was exiled, *The Art Of Love*. Augustus considered the book a bad influence on society, immoral, nongravitas. However, not until his granddaughter sought me out with her generous praise and uninhibited gratitude was I exiled. She was as well, but to a gentler community. Pater familias, Augustus!

Lucian is my only family. I think of him often and wonder how he fares in the house of Caesar. The cruelest blow, to deny me the son who shared my life most of his twenty-odd years and take him under the emperial wing. Shall I tell you how I met Lucian? One day while walking to the baths, I saw a babe lying by the road, staring at me with intelligent hazel eyes. It's yet a common custom to abandon unwanted children—girls or deformed boys. Compelled by the infant's expression, I approached and was about to unwrap the swaddling when he said, "I'm hungry. Have you food to share?"

Remarkable, indeed. When he smiled, showing a full set of teeth, I offered him my bread and sausage. Obviously, this boy was not an infant. He threw his wrappings aside, stood up on sturdy, well-formed legs, and gratefully accepted the meal. He shook my hand, the little diplomat, and introduced himself as Lucian. He said he'd not grown in the past two years. His parents, poor and frightened of being cursed, turned him out at the age of five. We talked until the sun was high over our heads, and I came to realize Lucian was unique and deserving of a better life. I lifted him into my arms and thus established responsibility for his upbringing.

Lucian proved to be a bright student and a fine companion. I sent him to the Litterator, where he learned reading, writing, and mathematics. He spent a short time with the Grammaticus, but teasing from the other boys drove him into the streets, so I instructed him at home in history, geography, and astronomy. Smart as he was, he rarely opened a book. The boy was forever cleaning, chasing dust with his small broom, scrubbing floor tiles, tending the hearth. Before Lucian came, I confess, I couldn't find a thing when needed. My method was to purchase more than necessary rather than waste time searching. Lucian eagerly ran errands and haggled like an Arab at market. To practice oration, he'd read my newly written work, which gave me a fresh ear. Oh, and the ladies loved Lucian. The moment he'd enter a room, the women would open their arms to him. "Come, precious darling," they'd coax with honeyed voices. But he'd blush and run from their advances. "Lucian," I'd say, "you'll be a wiser man if you learn to view the world through a woman's eyes."

With the years, Lucian's height increased no more than a hand's length. Do you know, Augustus wears shoes with padded soles to give him a taller appearance? I raised Lucian to accept his uniqueness as a gift, and he was good-tempered in my presence. But at times I observed him alone, staring at his image in the fountain pool, his expression dark and brooding.

What expression does he wear for Caesar? I suspect the reason I've not heard from Lucian is that my letters are confiscated. Ah, it's annoying to be honest to no purpose. To ease my loneliness, I work on *Metamorphoses,* a volume reflecting upon love as the agent of change.

LUCIAN

My parents would be gratified to see me, confidant to Caesar, robed in regal attire, dwelling in Augustus' grand country estate. This is the life they had planned for me, had begun by sending me to the most learned men in Rome. I was engaged in lessons with the poet Ovid when tragedy struck. My parent's villa was consumed in flames. They both perished.

I fondly remember how Mother carried me on a velvet pillow, kissed my cheek, and called me her tiny king. She commissioned a marble statue of me, and the artist said he'd never seen a more perfect model possessed of such delicate symmetry. Alas, the statue was destroyed in the fire. There, on the pedestal, is Augustus' replacement crafted in gold. Examine it closely: the likeness is true, and clearly shows that I am not from the same genus as the pygmaios of the arena.

My parents' wealth and belongings burned with the villa, and I was left with nothing. Ovid offered me shelter, and I stayed with him fifteen years. I'm grateful for Ovid's charity, but I was never content in his house, forever longing for something I couldn't identify. Here, with Augustus, I have found my true home. Allow me a comparison, and you'll understand. Civilitas is Augustus. I've often remarked upon the divine power of his gaze, and this pleases him. He is greatly pleased when a man whom he looks upon keenly lowers his eyes as if looking into the light of the sun. Augustus is wealthy, but frugal. He enjoys simple foods, especially green figs, and he avoids wine. Although he must frequently host dinner parties, we two eat a small meal beforehand and thus stay alert to conversation at the party table.

One would think Ovid a rich man the way he handled money, as if it burned his palm, giving to any friend or beggar offering a sad tale. He entertained too much. When he'd saved enough, he'd organize banquets of jellyfish and eggs; sow udders stuffed with salted sea urchins; roasted fallow deer in onion sauce; ham boiled with figs and bay leaves; dormice stuffed with pork and pine kernels; fricassee of roses wrapped in pastry; and plenty of wine. Ovid could not sit still at the table. He hopped around from guest to guest, his face jerking this way and that, laughing, singing, kissing women. These parties lasted into the early hours, but Ovid would be up with the sun, off to the baths, leaving a disheveled, snoring woman in his bed.

Augustus does not bring guests to our estate, not prattling boys nor giggling women; his wife and her son prefer Caesar's quarters in the city. Civilitas. Augustus sleeps late and avoids the baths. Understand, he suffers from dreams that wake him in the night, and I'm close at hand to whisper comforts. He says my voice is soothing as a bee's buzz in clover. The Emperor is afflicted with rough spots of skin that itch intolerably, which I relieve with a scraper and poultices of sand and reeds. I also singe his legs with hot nutshells to make the hair grow softer as he likes. Augustus diverts his mind with fishing and games. He enjoys playing dice and marbles with young boys and will send me ahead to find groups at play, paying attention to those who are attractive for their pretty faces, especially Syrians and Mauritanians.

Caesar's agents routinely collect pygmaios from throughout the republic: black men from Egypt, brown men from Syria, pale men from Gaul and Germania. These men are assigned to the arena, fitted with armor, and engage in battle against cranes, ostriches, or women. I'm the only small man to live as companion to Augustus, but I'm as different from the pygmy gladiators as Augustus is from Ovid. Tomorrow is a games day; go to the arena and see for yourself. Their limbs are short and clublike, their legs bowed, their heads overly large with bulging brows and ungracious expressions, and their lips perpetually drawn downward.

ACHILLIA

Up or down? Since Augustus will be absent from the games, we'll look to the dainty thumb of his wife, which is at the moment digging roast beef from between her teeth. Tonight the Romans provide a banquet for those who fight on the morrow, and see how they eye us, appraising as they would livestock, placing bets. My opponent is one of Augustus' legion of tiny men. He's seated on a stool between the African and the Syrian who toys with his food.

I recognize my opponent. We called him the Little Lamp Man. When I was a girl, he visited our village, selling lamps and oil from his wagon. He let the children hitch rides, and he once told me the light of my yellow hair shone brighter than all the lamps of Rome. I'm comforted to know he cannot recognize me.

In my fifteenth year, Roman soldiers invaded our village. Though they were four times our number, we fought, and fought fiercely. Survivors were taken as prisoners, tied together with rope and marched to Rome, where we were put on blocks for sale. The march did not exhaust my anger. Whenever I was pulled from the cells, I punched and kicked and bellowed, I spit in the faces of the fat marketers. I never was pretty by Roman standards, and scars from the whip added to my unattractiveness. Fine with me—who will buy an ugly, unruly slave, her face mottled with bruises, her teeth and nose broken sideways? My sole value to the Romans was my hair. Look to the head table and count them: one, two, three Roman noblewomen with long, straight, golden hair. They're wigs, wheat and honey tresses of slave girls from the north countries. One of those shining heads of hair may be mine.

A few months after my capture, Arius, a trainer of the gladiator school, visited the slave market with an eye out for fighters. With my shorn head and short temper, he mistook me for a man. I spoke as few words as possible on our way to the gladiators' quarters. When we entered, those muscled necks turned to appraise Arius' purchase. One gladiator removed his helmet, laughed scornfully, and said, "It's a wiry boy you've brought us, Arius." Quick as a rabbit, he was upon me, grasping with his great arms, hefting me off the floor, pressing my body in a grip so tight the breath was forced from my lungs. He set me down, his eyes filled with merriment. "Arius," he shouted, "you should handle the goods before opening your purse," and he ripped open my shirt.

I got the last laugh—my sharp knee to his soft loins. How the gladiators roared! I ran to Arius and pleaded to train as a fighter. He was reluctant, but the men were on my side. Arius went to Augustus, who relished the idea and encouraged him to find more women gladiators. Arius eventually did add more women to the school, but I alone had the opportunity to train with the men; no woman has beaten me.

30

If I win the battle, and the Empress turns her thumb down, I'll be spared taking the Lamp Man's life. A giant bird will be loosed on him and the spectators will howl with laughter. Though he may suffer a few wounds from the bird's sharp beak and foot spurs, his sword assures his victory. If I lose, I'll be given to the praetor who has donated the most money to the games. I must not lose. Better a beak to my opponent's thigh than my body pierced between the thighs by a praetor's skin sword.

Dignity is at stake for both of us, but the reason I will win is my lack of alternatives. Augustus cherishes his tiny fighters, and gladiators who please the Emperor may eventually buy their freedom, set up a shop, or return to their homelands. My home is gone forever, a ruin, haunted by mourning spirits. Women slaves are never granted freedom in Rome. My only alternative is prostitution. You can put your money on me.

Joerd, Mother of Earth, spare us—the Empress's pet poet has his eyes on me. Now he stands and clears his cursed throat.

How can a woman be decent sticking her head in a helmet,
denying the sex she was born with?
Manly feats they adore, but they wouldn't want to be men.
Poor weak things, how little they really enjoy it!
Hear her grunt and groan as she works at it,
parrying, thrusting;
see her neck bent down under the weight of her helmet.
Look at the rolls of bandage and tape,
so her legs look like tree trunks,
Then have a laugh for yourself, after practice is over,
armor and weapons put down, and she squats over the vessel.
Ah, degenerate girls, tell us,
whom have you seen got up in such a fashion,
panting and sweating like this? No gladiator's woman,
nor a painted whore would ever so much attempt it.

✧

FALLA

Aye, aye, aye, just a moment longer, and I'll be all yours. This idiot's nearly done. If he hadn't drank so much wine, his prick would be stiffer. Hear him! Carabas laughs as he squirts. What a treasure. Most men are too proud to laugh when a woman holds him inside her—passion threatens to even the odds. Get off now, I've got a paying customer. Here, Carabas, don't forget your crown, and pull the drapes on your way out, that's a love.

Hand me that basin, dear. I'm the cleanest whore in all of . . . what's the matter? Oh, if you want a man, go down two streets . . . You want to talk?! Charge is the same. Sit down then and pour me a glass. That one, Carabas? Wanted to show me his finery. Looks like a king, eh? King of the Jews is what the revelers dubbed him. Dressed him up, took him to the governor's house, and made a scene. Lots of people in Alexandria hate the Jews, and they're mad at the governor for being soft on them. Roman soldiers think it's real funny, they don't like the governor much either, and they took to Carabas, bought him food and drink.

We've known each other a long time. Won't tell you any sad stories about my youth because there aren't any—I chose to be a whore. But when Carabas was a boy, he was locked in a gloottokoma, a chest that hinders a child's growth, then they're sold or made to perform tricks; a lucrative trade. He escaped after three years— three years in a box! That's why he's so short and his back's humped and he drags his right leg. Had my share of bad treatment, but I never been locked up; I'd lose my mind.

One thing he learned in that box was how to make money. He'd listen to the shysters and watch through the bars, committing every scam to memory. Oh, it pays to be an idiot. I've seen him at work, picking pockets smooth as you please, lifting bread from under the baker's nose, cuddling up to ladies' bosoms and stealing their jewels, spouting gibberish, taking the fists and kicks as cheerfully as the coins people throw him.

Carabas speaks clear enough when he's counting his percentage of my business. Brings me customers; knows I can't afford to be particular anymore, and he knows they're all the same to me: short, tall, fat, thin, young, old, male, female, dark, fair, Roman, Egyptian, Macedonian, Greek, Jew. They look at me and all they see is my cunt. They all want the same thing—to feel satisfied. They look at Carabas and all they see is his hump, and they feel satisfied.

Warned him not to go with the soldiers tonight; they're Pilot's men, traveling south to Jerusalem, but he's soused and figures he can work this King of the Jews bit for a fortune.

CARABAS AT GOLGOTHA

An unnatural blackness at midday. Lightening rends the skies, and the gods weep. When the storm's over, I'll run if I must back to Alexandria. I've had enough of Jerusalem. Falla warned me not to come, but I was drunk with festivities and possibilities. Wine flowed like the Nile on the way to Jerusalem; Caesar provides well for his soldiers. And I provided them a good show; nothing whets the appetite of bullies like the dullness of a fool. Once, I put on a helmet, took up a sword, barked ferociously, then squatted on a shield and shit in it. They rolled with laughter. In daylight I played the fool, and at night I lifted coins from their belts while they slept.

Jerusalem was ripe for picking, elbow to elbow crowds, merchants lining the streets, filling the temples. I was in a Jewish temple, changing the Roman coins I'd acquired, when a man came in and tore the place apart, knocking over tables, shouting, "My temple is a place of prayer and you make it a den of thieves." I asked the money changer who the man was, and he said, "A prophet from Nazareth who claims to be the Messiah."

The next day, a crowd was gathered outside the temple, and this fly smelled honey. The prophet was addressing priests who demanded to know by whose authority he'd thrown out the merchants. The prophet said, "I'll tell you if you will tell me, was John the Baptist sent from God?"

The priests said they didn't know, and the prophet refused to answer their question. Instead, he told them a story about a man with two sons who told the eldest to work on the farm. The son said he wouldn't, but later changed his mind and went. Then the father told the youngest son to go, and the son agreed but did not go. "Which of the two was obeying his father?" the prophet asked.

"The first," the priests answered.

I'll have to remember this story for Falla. The prophet said, "Publicans and whores will get into the kingdom of God before you. John came to you in righteousness and you wouldn't believe him, but the publicans and whores did. You saw this with your own eyes and refused to repent, so you couldn't believe."

Another priest said, "We know you're honest and teach the truth regardless of the consequences, without fear or favor. Please tell us, is it lawful to pay tribute to Caesar or not?"

A clever trap; I listened for his reply. He asked the priest to show him a coin, then he asked, "Whose image is this and what name is stamped upon it?"

"Caesar's," the priest answered.

The prophet said, "Then give it to Caesar and give all else to God."

I don't need to tell you there was laughter at the priest's expense. I'd gladly relieve their pockets of coins. Who is more needy of gold, Carabas or Caesar? The prophet lost me there; I turned my attention to my trade.

A few days later, the soldiers I'd traveled with found me and dressed me again in kingly robes. They set me on a donkey and led us up a hill, yelling, "Make way for the King of the Jews." People lined the trail; some laughed and touched my hump, but others wept bitterly. At the top of the hill I saw the prophet and two other men nailed to crosses. Over the prophet's head was a sign: JESUS, KING OF THE JEWS.

Fucking pig Romans, sons of bitches crucifying men and leaving them to die slowly in tortured pain, in hunger, in humiliation. Until the prophet spoke, I kept up the game. Recalling the tales of Saturnalia, I knew the fool king could be next to die. When the sky darkened, I was able to slip away and find shelter in this cave.

Nobody could ever get to me, nobody! I've heard every possible taunt and curse, they run off my hump like the rain on these rocks. His words seized my head, my own words falling from his tongue, the terror remembered, the sound of the lock, the sight of my father's back. "Father, why have you forsaken me?"

THE KINGDOM OF LUSITANIA, A.D. 400

RICCHAR

She carried lilies and lay them upon the altar. I truly thought she was an angel. Her skin was whiter than the lilies, her hair yellow as marigolds, her eyes bluer than violets, and her mouth pink as a rosebud. Brother Bernard hastened to greet her; royal heritage was obvious in her attire and her manner.

Princess Wilgefortis' visits became frequent, and she was moved to accept the true religion of Our Father. With each visit I grew more enamored with her grace, her dignity, and her faithfulness. So too did my anger and frustration grow, for she would at times enter the church, her face wet with tears, begging our forgiveness for her foul smell. To discourage Wilgefortis, her father, King Euric, ordered dung thrown upon her as she walked to services. Here in my vest, next to my heart, is the blood-stained kerchief that fell from her sweet hand one day as she prayed through battered lips. Euric, a Visigoth, a heathen Arian, tried to beat the faith from her.

Oh, that I were as steadfast as she. How I admired her, how gentle her voice when she spoke to me. What chance had I? Son of a farmer, indentured to the priest, and she a princess. God is gracious with His miracles, for as a flower seeks the adoring light of the sun, our love blossomed, and with God's grace, we pledged our troth. When King Euric learned of this, he promised her in marriage to Agila, Visigoth King of Sicily, also Arian, a political alliance. The wedding day was fixed and Agila traveled toward Lusitania. Wilgefortis told me to fear not, the wedding would not take place, and God willing, she would be my wife.

King Euric prepared a royal welcome for Agila: soldiers, musicians, and subjects filled the courtyard with jubilance, red and white banners danced in the wind, caged doves cooed their songs, dozens of tables were laden with meat and cakes. Wilgefortis, dressed in red and gold satin, her beauty modestly veiled, sat on the throne beside her father.

When Agila stepped forward to claim his bride, she spoke thus: "Were I to weep all my days, never could I shed enough tears to wash the grief from my heart, for I have resolved to keep my body for Christ, pure from the touch of man. Christ, the immortal, promised me paradise for dower, and now it is my lot to be made the wife of King Agila. In place of unfading roses, I have, not for adornment but for disfigurement, the roses that fade."

Her piece spoken, Wilgefortis drew aside her veil to reveal a beard as red as blood. My heart leapt to my mouth. Agila raised his arms to cover his eyes. Wilgefortis spoke further: "And whereas by the fourfold stream of the Lamb I should have donned the shawl of purity, this regal robe hath shown itself a burden, not a glory. Unhappy I, whose lot should be Heaven, but who, on this day, am plunged into the abyss. If this is my fate, why was not the first day of my life also my last? Would I had entered the gates of death before I was nourished at the breast! Oh, that the kisses of my dearest mother were showered upon me in my death."

King Euric, trembling with rage, jumped to his feet and shouted above the hooves of Agila's retreating horse, "By Woden, you shall join your mother and your Christ!"

PRINCESS WILGEFORTIS

Father, I beseech thee in the name of Jesus Christ Our Savior, please reveal all to Ricchar. I would dispatch a letter, but the king keeps me locked within my chamber, denying me even the comfort of dear Ingrid. Hammering spikes sing through the courtyard; they form the cross to carry me to the arms of my Lord, to the embrace of my dead mother the queen.

These are the words I would speak tenderly in Ricchar's ear: I raise my eyes to the Redeemer's hands, pierced for the lives of humankind, and I look no longer on my royal diadem, for my mind's eye gazes upon His crown of thorns. I abhor the grand estates of my father, stretched far and wide across Lusitania; I desire only the lands of Paradise. Loathed are these regal chambers when I behold the Lord seated among the stars. My beloved Ricchar, the earth is naught, naught also is the life men enjoy. Rather we should seek the life not closed by death, not wasted by disease or cut short by accident. Therein I will abide in eternal bliss, dwell in a light that set not and, greater than this, translated to the angelic state and in the very presence of the Lord, enjoying every fresh contemplation with indissoluble joy.

I do not fear. I dress for death, not in the layers of costly cloth threaded with gold sewn for my marriage to King Agila, but in the simple white gown I chose for the wedding of Wilgefortis and Ricchar. I will not wear the nuptial jewels sent from Sicily, nor will I cut the hair from my chin though Father threatens to beat me if I do not. Should his guards restrain me to shave my face, I will struggle; they may slip the knife and deny King Euric his pleasure in watching my crucifixion.

I pray you forgive him, Father.

INGRID

The Valkyrie took Wilgefortis as she breathed her last upon the cross. Riding Thor's lightning through the sky, mounted on white stallions, shields flashing, spears held high, came Woden's virgin warriors, choosers of the slain. Wilgefortis' shorn head lifted, her spirit quit that broken, bloodied body, and rose, shining and whole. As I watched, the clouds parted to reveal Bifrost, the rainbow bridge. The Valkyrie embraced my darling Princess and carried her across the bridge to Asgard. Bless Woden for this vision, a gift to an old woman who keeps the faith.

Not all of us have forsaken the beliefs of our ancestors. Long, long ago our tribes were driven from the northern forests. My great-grandmother told me of her grandmother's journey south to the Black Sea, and of her own journey to Lusitania. Here, Visigoth tribes lived peacefully, side by side with Romans—when a mouse sleeps within the mane of a lion, he does not squeak. The Roman Emperor issued an edict declaring freedom of worship throughout his lands, but his preference was for the Christian faith, so my family kept the old ways in private. Many of our people forgot the legends of Woden, did not pass them to their children, whose children desired to be more Roman and practice the Arian religion.

To the east is an orthodox church, to the west an Arian, to the south a temple. Rulers and religion! No matter which king rules the land on which I dwell, my spirit belongs to Woden. If not for kings and priests, my Wilgefortis would be resting her dear head in my lap.

She was a newborn babe when her mother passed on, and King Euric sent for a nursemaid. My son Tibor was a plump and greedy little suckling, already on his feet, and I had plenty of milk to spare. I'd bore five sons, and dreamed of having a daughter. I hurried to the castle, and they put the tiny princess in my charge. Such a delight she was, a cuddling and quiet babe. Then, when Wilgefortis reached her first year, Loki must have snuck into the nursery while I slept. Bright red hairs appeared on her chin! I was afraid if the king saw her whiskers, the blame would fall on my milk. Ach, I hated to pluck them, see her darling face wince, her blue eyes water. And they came back thicker, I had to use my knife to cut them from her face. To keep her from wiggling, I'd sing Grandmother's songs.

Don't you know, secrets are harder to keep than wind. In Wilgefortis' second year, Euric entered as I shaved her little chin. I was so intent to take care that I didn't hear his footsteps. I dropped the knife, fell to my knees, and said a prayer to Woden. The king yanked me swiftly to my feet. "A good and faithful servant keeps her tongue from wagging lest she lose it," he growled. "My mother suffered from this same affliction. And I forbid you to fill my daughter's head with old tales."

Did you hear Euric's oath when my darling bared her face to that ugly Sicilian? Woden! He called on Woden. By thunder, he'll never see Valhalla. I fart on Euric and leave this cursed place for the forests of my ancestors. My bundle is light, yet it holds a treasure more precious than the Nibelungen hoard. I found it this morning, beneath the bed, wrapped in her white shawl, with a note pinned on. It read: *For the two people who have loved me, to keep my memory with love, one for each, my dearest Ingrid and my beloved Ricchar.* I unwrapped the shawl to find her golden braids within.

SISTER BASIL

A prize relic. Hair from the beard of the virgin martyr Wilgefortis. I assure you it's gold as the sun though over one hundred years aged. But I'll not show it. Don't take offense, you know well an authentic relic is worth more than the most precious gem. Over relics, treaties are signed, and oaths are sworn. A relic's magical properties cure disease and injury. One cannot be too cautious on the road; thieves will knock you over the head to steal relics. Impostors in clerical dress peddle pig bones as those of saints! On my way to Lusitania, I came upon village fairs where fakery abounded, an incredible assortment of blasphemous relics of Our Lord: His swaddling clothes, His teeth, drops of His bloody sweat, a piece of bread chewed by Him, a basket used at the miracle of loaves and fishes. The genuine relic I carry was presented to me by Leander, Bishop of Seville, in appreciation of my arduous journey.

Gracious, it's good to be back in the land of the Franks. Followers of the Holy Roman Church are at peril in Hispania; there's danger around every turn, even for nuns. The risk was worthy of the reward and the pleasure it will grant the abbess at Poitiers. Abbess Luebovera is a devout and holy lady who has suffered much.

Because of the scandal at Poitiers, I began this journey two years ago, directly after the trial. Massive grief, sprung from the seed of the Devil's sowing, was brought by Clotild, a nun at St. Hilary and the daughter of King Charibert. Clotild incited a number of our nuns into rebellion and seized the lands of the nunnery. Then she ordered a band of evil-doers to break into the monastery and abduct the abbess. Afterward, they returned and set fire to an empty cask, making a beacon by which they could pillage the monastery.

At news of these events, bishops from each Frankish kingdom met in Poitiers to end this rebellion by the sanction of ecclesiastical law: bishops Gregory of Tours, Ebregisel of Cologne, Gundegisel of Bordeaux, and Maroveus of Poitiers. Whereupon Macco, then count of Poitiers, by royal order put down the rebellion by force, and Clotild was brought to trial. I traveled there from Amboise to lend my spiritual support to Abbess Luebovera.

When the bishops were seated in the sanctuary of the cathedral church, Clotild was brought before them. She showered abuse and accusations upon the abbess. She said that a man clothed in nun's robes was in the monastery, and that this person regularly serviced the abbess. "There he is!" she shouted, and pointed to me. I stepped forward and said that I knew the abbess only in name and had never exchanged a word with her inasmuch as I lived more than forty miles from Poitiers. I spoke plainly, "I am unable to do a man's work, and for that reason, I chose to serve God in the only manner possible to me."

As their eyes reflected doubt, I turned my back to the audience, faced the bishops, and lifted my habit to the waist. Save for Bishop Gregory, each man's face betrayed his discomfort; Macco's hand went between his legs.

Clotild was excommunicated. I could have remained, but news of the trial spread throughout the kingdom, and my shame begged distance. What began in shame ended in glory. With this relic in hand, I now comprehend the divine purpose of my journey.

ABBESS LUEBOVERA

Hair from the beard of Saint Wilgefortis has the power to overcome lewd advances of men. Not that I have such need. Still, it is an exceptional gift. Wilgefortis was the daughter of a Lusitanian king, a heathen Arian who arranged her marriage to the king of

Sicily, not knowing that Wilgefortis had taken a vow of chastity. She prayed for deliverance, and her faith was amply rewarded with a beard, which grew overnight and repelled her prospective husband. Her father was so angered that he crucified her.

Divine providence that Basil, a man who appears to be a woman, has brought me a holy relic from a woman who took on the appearance of a man. I was sorry when Basil left our region; his Christian works were many times those of the nuns at Poitiers. The humiliation he suffered on account of Clotild! How she discovered his secret, I still do not know—I didn't know myself until the trial. Even after Basil revealed himself to the bishops, Clotild made every effort to defame my character, saying, "What sort of holiness can this abbess claim, who makes men eunuchs and keeps them about her after the custom of imperial palaces?"

I answered that I knew nothing of this matter. Clotild was about to continue when Reovalis, a physician from Tours, came forward and spoke: "When this man was a boy, he had a diseased groin and was regarded as incurable. His mother sought the holy queen Saint Radegund and begged her to have the case examined. The queen summoned me and asked that I assist, which I did by cutting out his testicles, an operation that I'd seen performed by surgeons at Constantinople. The boy was restored in good health to his anxious mother. I never heard that the abbess knew aught of the matter."

My daily prayers since have included Basil's safe return, and my prayers have been answered threefold: he is safely returned, he has brought a sacred relic, which I will in turn present to Bishop Gregory of Tours. The bishop is a great personage, a scholar of Latin and Greek who has committed to paper the history of our Franks, of the saints and martyrs. Following his appointment as bishop of Tours, he set about restoring the cathedral of Saint Martin, making it a fit place for worship, and renewing the goodwill of his people. I must admit, I'll be happy to sit with him. He's a gracious host, cheerful, full of questions, and greatly enjoys company as he does not travel much outside of Tours.

Gregory owns a collection of relics, many inherited from his distinguished and noble family. The relics most treasured, those of Our Lady, the Apostles, and Saint Martin, Gregory wears about his neck in a gold case fashioned as a pea pod. But this is not the reason I choose to give Bishop Gregory the relic of Saint Wilgefortis. Gregory is set apart from others, as is Basil, as was Wilgefortis . . . he's as small as a child. I cannot presume to understand the glorious mysteries of God Our Father, but the holy scriptures assure us that God has made us all in His image.

GREGORY, BISHOP OF TOURS, SAINT MARTIN'S CATHEDRAL

Abbess Luebovera has retired after an evening of pleasant conversation. I'm too excited to sleep, so I write a while. Is it coincidence that I had begun writing the history of the Visigoths when the abbess arrived with the relic of Saint Wilgefortis? Hair from the beard of Saint Wilgefortis . . . it glows in my candle's light, as yellow as the flame. Only God knows what powers the relic holds; all holy relics protect and fortify the place or person who possesses them. I have witnessed this on several occasions, and have personally benefitted by their magical powers. I've never been robust of health; in fact, it was an illness in my youth that set me upon the righteous path. In the tomb of Saint Martin, I was cured of a purulent fever by the agency of a candle. When I am troubled by my stomach, I find relief by rubbing my abdomen with the end of the hanging cloth of Saint Martin's tomb, and for swollen tongue, I lick the rail of the tomb. I have beheld miraculous cures for those who drink water in which fragments dusted from the tombs of saints are steeped.

Before my succession to the cathedral church of Tours, it had been ruined by fire. During the rebuilding, I learned from a priest far advanced in years that relics of the martyrs of Agaune were hidden in the church by my predecessors of old. I discovered the reliquary in the Treasury of the church. Alas, the relics had fallen into decay. However, while I was examining them, the church custodian told me there was a hollowed-out stone covered by a lid, but what it might contain, he did not know. He brought it to me and I found within a silver casket containing not only relics of the witnesses of the sacred legion, but others of divers saints, both martyrs and confessors. After some exploration, we found other stones hollowed in the same manner, and within . . . go quietly now and close my door.

I've noticed your eyes on my books. Do you read? Yes, well we both know only the scriptures and works of Christian writers are to be studied; contact with pagan literature can be of demonic influence, and we ought not relate their lying fables lest we fall under sentence of eternal death. Tell me honestly, if you were to find rolls of ancient papyrus hidden in hollowed stones, alongside holy relics, would you not be curious to read them? Ha! I see the twinkle in your eye.

Come closer, for the walls have ears. I'll relate the writings of a Roman called Lucian. Lucian was a very small man, like myself. His language and script were both of excellent quality, due to his teachers. Lucian's education began when he was taken in by the poet Ovid, then continued after Ovid's exile through life at the court of Caesar Augustus. At the time of these writings, Lucian was in his old age, and able to reflect deeply upon his life. While in the company of Augustus, Lucian had access to the great libraries of Rome, and his quest for knowledge was devout. He discovered scrolls from Greece and ancient Egypt, which told stories of other small men who distinguished themselves in one way or another.

Have you heard the tales of Aesop? Naturally you have. Lucian describes him. Did you know he was a small man, deformed of frame? But his mind was keen; he saw clearly into the hearts of men and exposed the truth therein. For his truthfulness, he was thrown to his death from a precipice on mount Parnassus. Lucian also wrote of a tiny Egyptian man, Knumhotou, who tended the wardrobe of a pharaoh. He includes drawings from Knumhotou's tomb that depict his size, his occupation, how beloved he was to the pharaoh. Lucian wrote that in his own youth, Augustus sent forth agents throughout the Roman territories to collect small men, pygmaios, he called them. These men fought as gladiators in the arena with women and giant birds as opponents! What fascinates me is that these men came from divers lands of the empire and beyond, which causes one to ponder. Could it be we small people are a race unto ourselves? A race as ancient as the Anakian giants from scripture?

But I must return to Lucian's story, for it is engrossing and lively. Upon Caesar Augustus' death, his stepson, Tiberius, was crowned emperor, a depraved and brutal man who suspected treachery at every turn. Lucian wrote that not a day passed without execution, not even on sacred and holy days. Many were accused and condemned with their children, or even by their children; no informer's word was doubted.

I regress a moment in the tale to a day when Lucian attended the games with Emperor Augustus. On that day a pymaio was engaged in battle with a woman called Achilla. She lost the match, and Lucian asked Augustus if he, rather than the patron to whom she was promised, might have her. Since Augustus was most fond of Lucian, he granted his request. Lucian explained in his writings that the woman, even in defeat, showed no sign of weakness. Her gaze was as level and calm as Augustus'.

Their relationship was uneasy at the start; Achilla was all bristle until she learned Lucian wanted nothing from her save her company and conversation. Similar in age and both without the loving care of parents, a bond was struck. Barely had their friendship begun to grow when Augustus died, and as I've said, Tiberius was an evil man who surely would dispose of Augustus' favored slaves. Their departure from Rome needed to be swift. They hastily boarded a ship bound for Alexandria.

Lucian wrote of his despondency aboard the ship; he was wretched ill from the waves. Achilla took tender care of him, but his thoughts dwelled upon the poet Ovid, who had loved him as a son. With heavy heart, Lucian thought of Ovid's journey by ship into exile, and of his own cruelty in ignoring Ovid's letters, knowing well his loneliness. Nearly ten years the poet spent lamenting his yearning for Rome. He sent two books of verse there, hoping for forgiveness from Caesar, but forgiveness did not come, and the old poet died in exile. Lucian was humbled thinking on this. He would arrive in Alexandria just as he was when Ovid took him in—without money, without a home.

Lucian was so weak upon docking that Achilla carried him from the ship. Although Achilla was a strong young woman, she was frightened as a lost child, not knowing where to turn in this strange city. Lucian wrote that they must have looked a sight— a tiny, pale man wrapped in the arms of a large, quivering woman. But no one took notice of the pair, even though the port teemed with people. As darkness fell, Lucian regained his strength and began to wonder if it had been wise to leave Rome. He turned to Achilla and saw that tears had wet her face. He was searching for words of comfort when a figure approached them from the shadows with a sound like wind rustling dry corn husks. Lucian described the man as beastlike: his back was curved and bore a large hump, his face was scarred and ruddy, his eyes frightening in their need to roll upward, and although his clothes were clean, he reeked of wine. He offered his hand to Achilla, and Lucian was greatly surprised to see her accept. The man said, "My name is Carabas. Come, I'll give you shelter."

Carabas took them to a dwelling on the edge of the city where he lived with his wife, Falla. Lucian described her as so full-bodied that her flesh rolled beneath her gown in waves as she walked. She was slow to laugh, but when she did, birds fled the trees. So was born, Lucian wrote, a family, which lived in harmony for many years. Neither Lucian nor Achilla desired a spouse, finding satisfaction in their work. Lucian began a school for orphans. Achilla was content to work their land, which she nurtured into a bountiful garden. Since Achilla shunned the city, Falla happily and profitably sold the produce at market. Carabas would accompany her, then dash away, returning hours later with his pockets full of coins, his breath smelling of wine, and kiss his wife.

When Falla died, followed shortly in death by her husband, Achilla and Lucian buried them side by side on a hill above the garden. Lucian and Achilla lived into old age as beloved brother and sister. They were, as Lucian wrote, four separate people, each inflicted with a burden—two of the body, two of the soul—who, joined together as one, formed a body whole in spirit.

MEDIEVAL VOICES

THE MYDWYFE

After the birthing, I tended to the infants in a manner befitting those of noble birth. First off, I bathed the babes in warm water; my hope was they would dispart in the tub, but as I worked the limbs to chase out evil humors, I felt a band of flesh like a lamb's liver stretched between the girls' hips. With salt and honey, I comforted their bodies and lay them on a bed of rose leaves mashed with salt. I dipped my finger in honey and cleansed their gums and palates, then filled my mouth with wine and expelled two drops into each little mouth. Lastly, I wrapped the babes in an ermine skin and placed them in Lady Chulkhurst's arms.

She wanted to put them to her breast, but with the girls joined side to side, she could feed only one while the other squawked. The Lady looked up at me, her eyes wet and pleading like a little girl's who can't reach her dolly on the shelf. I took the bundle and lay the girls upon the bed, feet toward the baseboard, heads in their mother's lap. Lady Chulkhurst smiled, spread her arms wide, and leaned over the babes until her nipples silenced the bleating mouths.

"Bless you, Anne," she said. "How brightly shine their eyes, how pink their complexions, how sweet their dispositions."

I heartily agreed, for the two baby girls were uncommonly fair. Then the Lady asked me: "Did you not tell me some time ago of a ewe raised by your husband's brother in Lord Oto's fief that birthed a two-headed lamb?"

"Yes, my Lady, so I did," I answered, wishing to my bones I'd not told her this while she was with child. The old priest of Kent possesses a list of causes for unnatural births and what good or evil those births portend. And 'twas but two months ago our

King William was struck down by an arrow while hunting in the New Forest. The hair of my arms stood upright as I awaited the lady's riposte.

"I recall, you reported 'twas a year of abundant crops," she said.

"Most abundant in my memory, Lady," I said.

"And what became of the lamb?"

I had to think on my answer keenly. My husband's brother had been surprised and delighted when the good crops were attributed to his lamb. People journeyed from divers parts of Kent and beyond, bringing money to touch its twin heads. Soon enough though, all had seen the ewe, which ate with both heads, twice as much as any one sheep. He had tried to breed her, but every lamb slipped from her womb too early and bearing one head only. My husband's brother said her mutton was tasty and rich as duckling. "She lived a long life, Lady, and bore seven lambs," I lied.

She sent me straight away to the priest to arrange for christening on the morrow, as the devil's partial to tiny undefended souls. Afterward, when the priest had hurried from his vestry, I prayed to the Blessed Virgin for forgiveness in telling a lie and for keeping from the old priest the condition of the babies. He'd been awaiting the announcement with great anticipation. Lord Chulkhurst promised a generous donation to the church upon the birth of his first child.

LADIES ADELE, ELEANOR, FRANCINE, BEATRICE, AND CAROLINE

"Scandalous—five maiden godparents, and the whole of Kent as witness."

"Sister, five were required: one to hold the body, one for each leg."

"Such sweet arms and legs. They're beautiful girls; Mary resembles Eleanor and Eliza takes after Caroline."

"No, Mary takes after Adele, Eliza does favor Caroline."

"They both are the image of their mother. Did you note her demeanor at the christening?"

"What of the priest! Oh my, when Diana unwrapped the babies, he would have dropped his jaw into the fount."

"I was most proud of our sister and happy to be godparent to Mary and Eliza. She was joyful and gladdened to have our company."

"Our brother did not wear a joyful expression."

"He cannot be blamed. Imagine, Beatrice and Caroline, if instead of being born moments apart, you had been joined together in our mother's womb. A heavy burden to bear, which our sister and her husband carry with dignity."

"I say courage! Lord Chulkhurst commanded the entire populace to attend."

"Did you hear his words to the congregation?"

"That his subjects are bound to love what their lord loves and loathe what he loathes and never by word or deed do aught that should grieve him."

"And as he loves his daughters, so should they be loved by his people."

"But was it not too hard when he held them aloft for all to see the terrible cord that binds them?"

"Your youth betrays you, Sister. Our brother displayed the wisdom of Solomon in doing so. The unseen holds the greatest fear and that which is withheld breeds contempt. We pledged as godparents to keep the girls seven years from water, fire, horse's foot, and hound's tooth, now, likewise the people will watch over them."

"What think you of the priest's talk of signs?"

"Everyone knows King William was murdered, knows well the church's loyalty to him, and it's doubt in the new King Henry. The priest's meaning was clear when he decried William's death occurring on the second day of August, and that two months to the day, the two girls were born."

"Lord Chulkhurst was not pleased."

"He has much on his mind since Henry wears the crown. Who knows what demands the king will make of his lords?"

"To procure more knights."

"To act as judge against another lord."

"To choose a new husband for a widow."

"Gather more tolls and taxes."

"Remember, our brother was required to hold King William's head on each occasion of his crossing the Channel, lest the king turn green with sickness."

"I heard of a Norman lord obliged on Cristemasse to make before his king: unum saltum et siffletum et unum bumbulum—a leap, a whistle, and an arse expulsion!"

"Please, quit your giggles and think on our sister, Diana. She'll want our aid and our assurances."

"I wonder if the girls will be able to walk attached so."

"How will they sleep?"

"What of gowns?"

"If one should find romance, how will a man make a wife of one and not the other?'

"You speak too soon. Let us pray they will survive to welcome the new year."

ELIZA CHULKHURST

My tears are for Houdain—I miss my little dog sorely. Percival, our tutor, sworn to secrecy, delivered him in a basket to my love. Now I wish I had not sent him, could contrive to bring Houdain back to my embrace. But that I could see through his eyes, be a flea on his whiskers, or even better, exchange my spirit for his, I would be eternally content. If Mary were awake, she would accuse me of courting witchery.

I sent Houdain with a letter tucked in his bow. Shall I recite the words? I know them by heart: Dearest, I send you this little dog called Houdain and beg of you that you love him and keep him well, as he has been brought up gently. Know my love that I should like to call you a thief because you have stolen my heart.

The flower of knights, the most courteous and kind knight ever to wield a sword, the meekest and the gentlest that ever ate in a hall among ladies, this is my darling. Father holds him in high regard for his bravery in the battle at Bremule. My father was a knight in his youth; with age he suffers from yellow humors and does not ride or hunt. The business of governing occupies his hours. He knows naught of my love; only Percival has a hint. Perhaps too my Auntie Adele; she was last to marry and hence spent more time in my company. As with my other aunts, she lives far from Kent, and soon will have her hands full with children. I should like very much to be a mother one day.

Oh, I do miss my sweet dog. Tristram called his dog Houdain, which he left in the tender care of his lover, Isolde the Fair, as a remembrancer. Have you read their tale? I care naught for stories of battle, but enjoy the tales of Guenever and Launcelot, the tragic Lady of Shallott, the fairy queen Morgane Le Fay, and the enchantress, Viviane. My favored reading is *Lais* by Marie de France, a volume Percival brought. The verses are full of adventure and romance. There's the story of a knight enamored of a lady. She meets him every eventide at her window, where a nightingale sweetly sings. Her husband grows suspicious. The lady protests: "Husband, 'tis a nightingale disturbs my sleep, nothing more, the song enchants me." Thereupon, the husband orders the bird killed. The lady wraps the poor dead bird in gold embroiden silk and sends it to her knight. He encloses the nightingale in a silver mirrored casket and nevermore parts himself from it.

Would I be parted from my sister? You may as well ask a blind beggar what it's like to see. What good to think on it? True, I wished to exchange spirits with Houdain, for then I could sit in my beloved's lap, look upon his handsome face, feel his hands caress my skin, and sleep at his side. A flight of fancy. I did not even sign the letter; simpler to mend neglect than to quicken love.

What make you of this note? Percival placed it in my hand the day after I sent my letter. He said 'twas spoken by a Grecian poetess: As an apple reddens on the high bough, high atop the highest bough, the apple pickers passed it by—no, not passed it by, they could not reach it.

PERCIVAL

~~My love for my mistress 'tis so gentle,~~
~~soft as her hand on the stringed instrument.~~

~~My love for my mistress, Eliza,~~
~~'tis bright as the sun arising.~~
My love for Eliza, my sweet mistress,
'tis a love I long to express.
~~I serve her so timidly, am so humble,~~
~~like a bee in the roses a-bumble.~~

So timidly and humble do I serve her,
yet I know I do naught to deserve her.
~~I do not ever tell her of my longing,~~
~~thus my agony I am prolonging.~~

~~Her father is lord of this fief,~~
~~so my heart will have no relief.~~

Her father, a lord within his castle.
I am but a servant, a vassal.

How can I hope to be her suitor?
She sees me only as her faithful tutor,
and thinks dreamily on brave knights,
clods who can neither read nor write.
She knows not the sorrow in my heart,
even though she is quick and smart.

My love for her, 'tis chaste and pure.
Lovely Eliza so demure.
For lovesickness, alas, no cure.
I will be strong, I will endure,
for one day Cupid will be merciful
and join the hearts of Eliza and Percival.

MARY CHULKHURST

You may run your fingers along his breast, he's quite tame while
hooded. Are not his feathers softer than silk? I should like to offer
a morsel of fowl, but Father forbids me to feed him lest he lose his
taste for the hunt. I call him Grendel—see how he turns to his
name. We best not tarry, my sister's not fond of falcons.

Yonder are the stables, but Father does not allow me access
there. He says horses are terrible beasts that would trample me

underfoot. Still, I dream of riding one day. I remember as a small child how my aunts joined the hunt, beautifully attired in flowing garments, a falcon perched on each of their gloved hands. Saints' bones, I feel Eliza tremble. We'll go indoors, dear Sister. Have you heard the tale of Bayard? A horse of incredible swiftness, given by Charlemagne to the four sons of Aymon. If one son mounted, the horse was of ordinary size, but if all four mounted, his body elongated to the proper length. A bright bay with a silver star on his forehead, his body slender, his head delicate, his chest thick with muscles, his shoulders broad, his legs straight and sinewy, his mane falling over his arching neck—he rushed through the forest with defiance. 'Tis said by some Bayard is still alive and his cry can be heard in the Ardennes on Midsummer Day. I should like to hear that sound.

Here we are; let us sit by the fire. Yes, this is quite an exquisite bench. 'Twas carved for us special by the woodcarver, Johnson. Father provides us with all our needs plus sundry entertainments, and a tutor who instructs us in writing, language, Holy Scripture, the stories of saints, and sometimes legends. Like Eliza, Percival is partial to chivalric tales. I do so enjoy the troupes of jugglers, tumblers, minstrels, puppeteers, and storytellers, especially in winter. The stories of a lad named Rayer were my favored. Now he serves King Henry as jester and entertains on the other side of the Channel. 'Twas Rayer told me the tales of Bayard and of Bradamante.

Christ's blood, I would be Bradamante! The virgin knight of the white plume and shield, niece of Charlemagne, beloved of Rogero. That I could live her adventure in the grotto of Melissa where Merlin's spirit hovered and informed Bradamante that she would be the mother of heroes, great captains, renowned knights, princes wise as Augustus. She sounded her horn to call the hippogriff, a prodigy which seemed to pass the bounds of possibility: a winged horse with the head of an eagle, claws armed with talons. In her quest for Rogero, she encountered towering giants, cunning dwarfs, people bearing semblance to animals.

Ah, we each have our dreams. Do I dream of being separated from my sister? Recall Eliza's answer; my answer is, one born blind cannot image all to be missed.

MINSTREL'S CAMP

Gather round the fire and you shall hear
a song that's certain to bring you cheer.
On invitation this merry troupe went
to a fine castle in the region of Kent.
The Lord's generosity is renown
among us who sing from town to town.
Artfully I composed the verse
with flattery sure to fatten my purse.
Through rounded lips my song began,
"The Lord is a most distinguished man,
a knight who has shewn great bravery,
truth, honor, and courtesy."
With pious expression I continued my story
and praised each battle that brought him glory.
'Tis plain enough, truth be told
the Lord is now both fat and old.
He would have a better chance
of raising his pecker than raising a lance.
When I finished with praises of war,
I sang of his goodness to the sick and the poor,
how esteemed is he in people's eyes,
that he is modest and he is wise.
I sang lustfully and I sang long
and was well rewarded for my excellent song.
But good friends, you must realize

the Lord's daughters are the greatest prize.
Now, I've had occasion to report
the ugliness of King Pepin the Short.
He and his wife, Berthe au grand pied,
begat Charlemagne, fifteen hands high.
I've seen many wonders of this world
but nothing compares to the Chulkhurst girls.
They are a most identical pair
possessing two heads of chestnut hair,
two sets of eyes of emerald green,
complexions white and smooth as cream,
lips and cheeks of cherry pink,
waists as narrow as two minks.
Ah, but the gods have pulled a joke,
the girls are like oxen in a yoke,
joined at the hip by flesh or bone,
impossible to romance one girl alone.
Some men may claim the girls a beast,
for my eyes they are a sumptuous feast.
You know me a reveler full of sin,
I would welcome a bedden the twins.
I can but imagine the bliss—
four wet lips for me to kiss.
My fingers twitch with happiness
at the thought of four plump breasts.
Gladly I would plant caresses
underneath those noble dresses.
With arses like a sultan's cushions
they would offer the liveliest pushen.
Down on my knees, I pray to God,
bless me with a second rod,
that I may satisfy and content
the incredible, inseparable sisters of Kent.

THE SEAMSTRESS

"As we came together, we shall also go together," Eliza admonished the physician, when upon Mary's death he suggested their cord be cut. She knew death was certain one way or the other, though the knife would shorten her pain and join her more swiftly to Mary in God's Kingdom. Thus, for a few hours, Mary's soul flew free. That was Eliza's true design. I know this because I was present—not for Mary's death, but afterward, when Eliza summoned me. Her breath labored, death shaking his rattle in her throat, she bade me sew dresses of sky blue, white lace at hem, cuff, and collar, just as their mother wore to her grave. How could I hide my grief? I wept openly as she brushed her sister's hair and spoke to her as if Mary could hear, "How is it then to ride across heaven on the bright bay stallion?"

Thirty-five years ago, I was but a girl, brought to Kent by Lord Chulkhurst to sew his bride's trousseau. Crossing the Channel, I swore I'd return home when the job was done, but there were always more gowns and hats and purses, and the time flew faster than my stitches. Lady Chulkhurst and her five young sisters were gay as spring lambs, Lord Chulkhurst a steadfast shepherd.

Then the girls were born. I remember the first garment I sewed for them, a bunting cut from a single piece of cloth, drawstring at the bottom to keep their little feet warm. As they grew, I had to be clever and use trial and error methods. The pattern that proved best was to fashion two dresses full of skirt, leaving the inside seam open on both. The girls slipped them on, and I measured the distance from floor to hip. Then I sewed material around their joined flesh, like a loose sleeve. Finally, I sewed the end of the sleeve to each dress, which would lay disguised between the skirt folds. In addition, I padded the inside shoulders, as when the girls walked, their shoulders rubbed together. To aid in comfort, Mary wrapped her left arm about Eliza's waist, and Eliza her right about Mary's.

My thoughts seldom turned to home. To view Chulkhurst castle from without, the stone walls appear cold and foreboding, but within, in those happy days, girlish laughter chased along corridors, up stairways, and into every dark corner; woven tapestries brightened the rooms, their beauty matched only by the rolling meadows of spring wildflowers. I admit, 'twas love for the family kept me here, and for my Paul, gamekeeper to the lord. We were wed in the castle with all my girls present. Eleanor married shortly thereafter and moved to Northumbria.

Six children came for Paul and me, but my lady Diana was not so blessed. After the twins' birth, four male infants in three years passing fell from her womb before their time, and with the last, she joined her maker. Lord Chulkhurst was broken, and he traveled to ease his heart. The sisters, good godparents, kept their promise faithfully, and when Eliza and Mary reached seven years of age, their aunts married, one by one, and went to their husbands' homes. Lord Chulkhurst sent the girls to convent school, where young ladies of high standing receive education. This ended when one of the nuns spied several girls circled about Mary and Eliza; they'd hitched up their skirts and were examining their affliction. The abbess reported the incident to Lord Chulkhurst, and he withdrew Mary and Eliza from the school, though they protested heartily.

Lord Chulkhurst died when the girls were twenty-five years old, and after his death, they rarely ventured out. No, not out of shyness, I think, but because there was no need. To understand Mary and Eliza, imagine gazing into a mirror. At first glance, the image appears to be exact, but in truth 'tis exactly opposed. The image is most familiar, but look again—the left hand is truly the right, words appear in backward order. Still, you have no trouble deciphering the meaning.

Mary and Eliza left me a wealthy woman. I should never need to sew another stitch. They also bequeathed twenty acres of land to the church with the instruction that income from the property be used to provide cakes to the poor on Easter Sunday.

BARTHOLOMEW FAIR BEGINS

CHARTER OF 1133

In the name of the holy and undivided Trinity, I, Henry, King of England, William of Canterbury, and George Bishop of London, to all Bishops and Abbots, Counts, Barons, Justices, Gentlemen, and all men and faithful citizens greeting, grant to Rayer the Prior and the regular Canons, their Hospital free of all authority beyond Episcopal usage, defend all the rights of Rayer and the Canons, and forbid that any one molest Rayer. I grant also my firm peace and the fullest privileges to all persons coming to and returning from the Fair of Saint Bartholomew; and I forbid any of the Royal servants to impede any of their persons, or without consent of the Canons, on those three days, to wit, the eve of the feast, the feast itself, and the day following, to levy dues upon those going thither. And let all the people in my whole kingdom know that I will maintain and defend this Church, even as my crown; and if any one shall presume to contravene this our Royal privilege, or shall offend the Prior, the Canons, clergy, or laity of that place, he, and all who are his, and everything that belongs to him, shall come into the king's power.

JOHNSON WOOD-CARVING SHOPPE, 1175

Grandfather Johnson carved this cake mold in the year 1134. You can read the date across the maiden's skirts. That's the year they died. At the top are their names: "Eliza and Mary Chulkhurst." You can barely make it out. Yea, the writing is backward; if you were to hold it before a mirror, the words would be plain. Because the mold is pressed image-side onto the bread and cheese cakes before baking, the words must be carved backward so they'll come out of the ovens frontward.

This mold has been much used and is cracked with age. I'm carving one afresh for the coming Easter Sunday. A difficult task, to match grandfather's precision. Even though worn, you can plainly see the sisters' faces, the seven points of their crowned head-dresses, the lacing of their smocks. Hands are nigh on impossible to carve into a piece of wood this small. That's why the maids' hands rest behind their skirts, well, the two hands—they had only two between them, joined as they were at shoulder and hip.

I know Easter is three months distant, but I'll take good time and honor my family trade. The wood is oak, cut to the size of my open hand, a knuckle deep. I've shaved it smooth and flat on all sides, lest a splinter worry the baker. My knives are sharper than my wife's mother's tongue. 'Tis a fine thing, the maids providing for cakes for the poor. Father told me a priest ordered the sisters' image pressed onto the cakes. Why do you imagine the priest did so? Forgive me, I have moments to ponder such questions in my trade; my hands act on their own while my head takes flight. I understand feeding the poor on Easter as a tribute to our Lord Jesus who fed the multitudes and sacrificed his blood and flesh for our sins. 'Twas not the maidens' tribute well served before their image was pressed onto the cakes? Did the church want to display the benefactors of the cakes? To what purpose? The sisters can receive no gratitude, nor have they descendants to do so. Or is it to serve as example of generosity to the church?

A pity the Chulkhurst sisters didn't live to benefit from the Fair at Bartholomew's. 'Tis said that wondrous miracles are performed there under the guidance of the monk Rayer, who founded the Priory in honor of the Apostle. Since Rayer has been prior, many and innumerable have received miracles. A crippled man was carried in a basket to the new altar of Rayer's Priory and lost all crookedness and straightway recovered the use of his limbs. A woman's tongue could not be contained in her mouth and Rayer touched it with relics and painted a cross upon it with holy water. In the same hour it went back between her teeth. Last year at the high festival of Saint Bartholomew, a blind boy was led into the church. As he entered, he fell down to the earth, and there awhile turned himself now this way, now that way. Then he rose up, blood running down his cheeks, declared that for the first time he saw his parents, and called sundry things distinctly by their proper names.

The Chulkhurst cakes are well-liked and grow in number each year, as does the congregation. I put a question to you, if you had a bodily affliction, would you have your image pressed on cakes for the poor after your death? Perhaps the priest was fond of Mary and Eliza and wished only to remember them thus. Grandfather's mold depicts their smiles as most endearing.

POOR BOY, EASTER, 1570

Ain't right, ain't right always sendin me. Got better things to do. Ain't enough I work my arse to a bloody sweat six days a week, the old lady gotta send me to the damn church today for cakes. Let Peter flop his sorry body up to them church ladies, fancy clothes and "Oh, you poor soul" goddamn faces. Shit, make their fat knees buckle—what I'd give to see it.

My brother Peter look like a goddamn toad, swear to God. He got arms just stick off the sides of his chest, and his legs are about the size of my finger so his body sits on his feets. No neck to speak of, and goggy eyes. He ain't right in the head neither, but he don't cause no trouble and he's happy when I'm around. Ma keeps him inside. I told her she damn well better if she spects me to keep bustin my balls to feed the two of em. Woulda been nice if one of our fathers woulda stuck around. Fore I was big enough to work, Ma'd send us out together; I'd heft Peter on my back. Then he'd want to go all the time with me, grab onto my leg and ride my foot. You know, I didn't mind much neither till I had to start takin whacks and stones from boys in the street. None of em say nothin no more, I beat the shit out of em. Just makes my piss of a life a whit easier keepin him inside.

Now the old lady's naggin bout takin him to some damn fair in August at another damn church to get him cured by a miracle. I ask her when did she git so bloody holy? Hasn't set foot in a church far as I know, but she been sendin me for these cakes every goddamn Easter since I could walk. Lookit the things—two grinnin girls growed together at the shoulder. What the hell they got to smile about?

AMBROISE PARE, PARIS, 1573

Numerous reports from fellow physicians on the monstrosities who gather at Smithfield in London to be cured at Bartholomew Fair prompted me to attend in hopes of gaining material for my text, *Animaux, monstres et prodiges*.

As royal physician to Queen Mother Catherine de Medici, I took precautions to conceal my identity. I'm a surgeon of renown, and a French Catholic. Elizabeth is queen in England, and under her reign, rood and church images are victims of the martyr fires. To be sure, the incident in Paris is fresh in her mind; two thousand Huguenots massacred by command of the King and Queen Mother Catherine. Elizabeth had for many years sent aid to these Protestants, with her eye on Calais. Moreover, there is the issue of Henry, Catherine's middle son, and the nuptial negotiations which went afoul of late. Henry is eighteen years Elizabeth's junior, and a good bit prettier. He wears more face paint than the queen, more perfume, and more jewels. His liaisons with women are reported to be surpassed in decadence only by his assignations with the Princes of Sodom, his preferred companions. Hardly a match for the Virgin Queen. At any rate, Henry rejected her, announcing he'd not marry

66

her for she was not only an old creature, but had a sore leg.

I did observe Elizabeth in attendance at the fair. She was accompanied by several maids, her dwarf companion, a Mrs. Tomysen, and two giant porters. I do not consider dwarfs and giants as monsters or prodigies, those being that which goes against nature and stir fear and amazement. Queen Mother Catherine has many dwarfs at court, though her efforts to breed them have not been successful.

Not an easy task making my way through the reveling musicians and dancers, performers and booksellers, stalls stacked with woolen, kerseys, linen, and leather, dodging the coming round of oranges, apples, nuts, and beer. At last I arrived on the church steps, where the afflicted had gathered, some to be cured, most to beg. There was a man seeking alms because of a diseased arm, which he exposed to passersby. I tossed a coin his way, and as he bent to retrieve it, the decomposing member fell to the ground. He fetched it up with two good hands. Fakery is despicable. Much to my disappointment, the great majority of afflicted I encounter at fairs are fakes.

Still and all, I know the mysteries of God are wondrous. Did not Jesus Christ restore sight to the blind? Can any man doubt the existence of sorcerers? Moses expressly condemned them in the books Exodus and Leviticus. Likewise there are certainly demons and devils in the air, on the earth, and within man himself. This was the sad condition of a boy I observed at the fair who sat squat against the church wall with a woman I took to be his mother, for she was on her knees in prayer. I guessed his age to be twelve years, but this was difficult to discern as his posture was that of a frog, and in every other way he resembled such, with flipperlike, webbed extremities. I could see no hope for the boy.

I have found thirteen causes of monsters, which will be elucidated in my book. The first is the glory of God. Second, his wrath. Third, too great a quantity of semen, which produces joined twins

67

or parasites. Fourth, too small a quantity, producing headless creatures and half-men. The fifth, imagination. Sixth, a narrow womb. Seventh, an unbecoming sitting position of the mother, who, while pregnant, remains seated too long with her thighs crossed against her stomach. The eighth, by blows struck against the stomach during pregnancy. Ninth, by hereditary or accidental illness. Tenth, by rotting or corruption of the semen. Eleventh, by the mingling of seed, as with dog-headed or pig-headed boys. The twelfth, by the artifice of wandering beggars. Thirteenth, by demons or devils. And let me not forget the influences toward monstrous births caused by the configuration of the planets.

✧

THE ISLAND OF HVEEN, DENMARK, 1576

PROCLAMATION OF HVEEN

We Frederik the Second, King of Denmark, etc., make known to all men, that We of our special favor and grace have conferred and granted in fee, and now by this open letter confer and grant in fee, to Our beloved Tycho Brahe, Otto's son, of Knudstrup, Our man and servant, Our island of Hveen, with all Our and the Crown's tenants and servants who live thereon, with all rents and duties which come therefrom, and We and The Crown give it to him to have, enjoy, use and hold, without any rent, all the days of his life, and so long as he lives and likes to continue and follow his study of astronomy, astrology and mathematices, but he shall keep the tenants who live there under law and right, and injure none of them contrary to the law or by any new impost or other unusual tax, and in all ways be faithful to Us and the Kingdom, and attend to Our welfare in every way and guard against and prevent danger to the Kingdom.

Actum Fredriksborg, the 23rd of May, anno 1576.

FARMER OF HVEEN

Troll of Carlshoga, the children call Jeppe. Scares the devil out of them. Jeppe got that name on account of two things. First, he lived in the Castle Carlshoga ruins on the southeast side of the island. Nobody knows how he came here or where he came from. Some say he's descended from the first people of Hveen. Others say he's not human, but a thing bewitched, cursed to guard the castle for eternity. Second, he's strange to the eyes. This high he stands, to my hip, and his head is overlarge, with nary a hair. I wouldn't venture to guess his age; his face is like an old man's. Though he keeps to his own self, his tongue goes constant. Babble, babble words, but every once in a while, he speaks clear as a bell, and what he foretells comes to pass. He knocked on my door early one morning and told my wife to stay inside 'til sunset. Best not challenge a Hveen wife, good as an invitation. She rode out on the big geld, and a rabbit spooked him. She's buried in the Tuna cemetery behind Saint Ib's. Oftentimes, I find myself talking to her as if she were here. Not so odd, talking to yourself, specially if you hear voices, as I wager the troll does. And if those voices foretell the truth to come, you might babble to keep from spilling it out. We older folks respect him and leave him to his ways.

Our ways have changed since the coming of Squire Brahe. I guess that's plain as the nose on my face. By the by, have you taken a gander at the squire's nose? That castle yonder, right smack in the middle of the island, belongs to the Squire Brahe—Uraniborg he calls it. Mighty grand, eh? Those copper roofs can blind a man when the sun's bright, and there's holes in them so the squire can look at the stars with his instruments. Every one of those buildings belongs to him: workshop, windmill, paper mill, the orchard too. Planted most of those three hundred trees my own self. I know the squire's a respected man with big ideas, but that doesn't excuse his hot temper and ill treatment of us people. "Tenants," we are, on our own land, and by the king's decree, at the beck and call of the squire. We built his properties, leaving our farms to be worked by wives and children. As if that weren't enough, the squire asked King Frederik to send an order stating the tenants were not allowed to leave the island because Brahe required more labor.

Would a one of us wish to leave? Would not every one of us celebrate the squire's departure? Before his arrival, Hveen was as close to God's original plan as a land can be, spread out flat and green atop white cliffs, under His watchful eye, His breath, powerful and clean, pouring over the grasses. The quiet that comes from man's contentment fell sweet on His ears. Our livestock grew fat and plentiful on the good grazing and the fresh pond waters. Ships would pass by our high white cliffs on their way to busy ports, leaving our Eden untouched. Now the squire's buildings scar the land, and ships bring people to Hveen from foreign ports; they come to gawk and bluster at the Squire's grand accomplishments.

The Troll left his ruins to live in the new castle, where the squire has dressed him in a green velvet suit and a hat topped with copper jingle-jangle bells.

URANIBORG APPRENTICE

"Junker Paa landent," Jeppe shrieks, and we know it's time to get back to business, as the master will land on the island momentarily. How does he know? There's no logical explanation. Don't bother asking Jeppe about his gift, he speaks only to Junker Paa. Brahe enjoys telling the story of their meeting. When Uraniborg was under construction, the skilled work was performed by artisans brought to the island, while residents took up the heavy labor. The men of Hveen grumbled over the extent of their work, and Jeppe, standing close by, advised the master to give them plenty of strong beer; the complaints ceased. Since that time, Jeppe has been a fixture at Uraniborg. His primary duty is to cut the master's hair, which he does artfully to conceal his baldness. The long moustache and beard are trimmed by Brahe himself. His objection to sharp objects near his nose, or rather what's left of it, is well-founded. During a duel with Manderup Parsbjerg, Brahe lost the better part of his nose in a disagreement over a mathematical point. He crafted a nose of gold, painted it, and adjusted it to a natural appearance. In his pocket he carries a box filled with a glue of his invention that he applies when the nose becomes wobbly.

I conjecture Jeppe performs another service for his master, though no one speaks of it. Whenever Brahe is commissioned to draw an astrological chart, he and Jeppe disappear behind closed doors until the job is done. Don't mistake me—Brahe is recognized as one of the great astrologers and has drawn the charts of King Frederik's three sons. His knowledge is unsurpassed on configurations, directions, and the twelve houses of the zodiac. However, he dislikes spending time on astrological matters, wishing to confine himself to the wondrous course of stars.

Apprentices have come from throughout Europe for the privilege of studying under Brahe's guidance. I've been here as long as any; some complain about the master's impatience and cannot keep up his pace. Problems are the breath of life to him: how to improve the sights of his instruments, how to drain a field or increase the yield of the orchard; he oversees every aspect of life at Hveen.

Brahe thought this island ideal for observations, secluded enough to keep visitors from interrupting his work, yet near enough to Copenhagen to obtain books and materials. Uraniborg could not be kept secret, however, and visitors come by the boatful to see the marvelous instruments, or to be able to boast they've met the master. Although disgruntled, he's not without a sense of humor. Throughout Uraniborg's structures, he has installed various contraptions and devices beyond the understanding of visitors. He takes pleasure in pressing a button hidden under his study table, which signals, by connecting cord and bell, pupils elsewhere in the building to come to him. At the same time, he whispers their names and tells the dupes, after the pupils arrive, that his voice carries through walls and over space.

More than a few royal persons have come. King Frederik visited often before his death; young King Christian comes less frequently. Most enjoyable to Brahe was the visit from King James upon the occasion of his marriage to Christian's sister, the Princess Anne. Included in the royal party were the king and queen, the queen's ladies-in-waiting, the king's page, and a giant porter named William Parsons, who took peculiar delight in grabbing students, one under each arm, and carrying them along as if they were feathers. Long and learned conversations passed between Brahe and King James, and the wonders of Uraniborg were revealed to the king. In appreciation, he gave the master two of his pet mastiffs.

The only visitor Brahe welcomes with open arms is his sister, Sofie. For a period of several months, she was a constant guest at Uraniborg. Her mind is nearly as fine as any man's. She fell in love with an assistant, Erik, and they became engaged. Both were impassioned of alchemy, which proved to be their downfall. Erik left the island in a state of financial ruin. Despite her brother's strong objections, Sofie left shortly thereafter to find him. Jeppe was unusually jubilant for days after their departure.

KIRSTINE BRAHE

Do you know the feeling of comfort when in the company of one who brings out your natural self? That's how it is with Jeppe and me. We don't talk—not together leastways, not much. He talks all the time, but so softly near me I don't make sense of it. We have a kinship I ken in his face. The face is the mirror of the soul.

Women study men's faces, which reveal more than their tongues. Tycho's face is cramped with purpose, his brow ever furrowed, his eyes squinted and lined, seeking out error, peering into lenses, gazing at the stars. When they fall upon me, I do not see the look of reverence he wears for the instrument that once belonged to Copernicus. I'm not troubled by this; I'm well aware of the reasons Tycho took me for his wife. He told me, upon proposing marriage, that he wished for a companion and helper by whom he might beget many children, who would look after his house, look over the servants and kitchen, not bother him nor be in his way, not nag him to take her to court in Copenhagen or to give her dresses and jewelry. I'm also aware of the scandal our marriage caused; a nobleman wedding a bondwoman was a disgrace to Danish nobility, excepting Uncle Steen and sister Sofie. Sofie told me, her eyes atwinkle, the talk in Copenhagen was a philosopho with a metal nose couldn't get a noble young woman to wed.

In the letters Tycho writes to Sofie, he addresses her, "My Urania" and signs them "From Your Apollo." He holds her in high regard, and when last he spoke of her to me he said, "In themselves women possess great gifts, which are due to the influence of the moon and Mercury, which likewise causes most of them to become excessively talkative. My Urania is the exception to the rule." Might I be envious of Sofie? Once you lay eyes on her, you long to be close to her. Her face, her figure, her gestures, the sound of her voice, everything about her has a natural beauty. She belongs to nobility, but she does not put on airs. Upon our marriage, Sofie instructed me to keep certain conditions, that my children would be legitimate heirs: to carry the key ring on my belt for three winters, to openly share my husband's bed and board, to behave as a faithful, honest wife, dallying with no one else, and to bear him children. As you can see, the last I've done well. This one in my belly is the fifth.

I do miss Sofie sorely. So many men about! When she was not

working with Tycho, she sat in the kitchen and kept me company or played games with the children. I think it will be a long while before she returns, and a long while before my heart eases on the matter. Greed, one of the seven deadly sins, the root of our troubles. Ach, Sofie's smart, she knows chemistry and astrology; she even invented a pill, a tincture, and a powder that have cured many people of various ills. Alas, alchemy was her passion—she longed to devise a formula for producing gold. When she met Erik, who had a similar passion, her woman's heart got the better of her.

This is what happened, Tycho knows nothing of it. Last August, I took my bucket for washing and walked through the orchard toward the west pond. Oh, then I heard sounds of terrified crying, angry shouting, and splashing. My heart pounding, I ran to the pond, fearing one of the children had fallen in. There I saw Erik pushing Jeppe's head under the water. Sofie was in the water too, without a stitch of clothing. She was weeping and pleading with Erik, who seemed not to hear a word she said. He shouted at Jeppe, "Tell, tell!" From the pond's edge, I heaved the bucket, which knocked Erik on the head. He released Jeppe and took off running. Sofie carried Jeppe, choking and spitting, to where I was. Soon as he recovered, he ran off too.

I found Sofie's dress and helped her into it because she was standing still, looking first in the direction Erik had fled, then in the direction Jeppe had gone. When finally she looked to me, she said, "Through tattered clothes small vices do appear; robes and furred gowns hide all. Plate sin with gold, and the strong lance of justice hurtless breaks; arm it in rags, a pigmy's straw does pierce it." I thought she'd lost her senses, but then she explained the events that led to this tragedy. A few weeks before, Erik had gone to Tycho's study to retrieve a book, and he saw Tycho's journal lying open on the desk. Therein Tycho had written on the subject

74

of alchemy and the secrets Jeppe had shared with him. He wrote that after much consideration, he thought it improper to unfold the secrets of the art as few persons are capable of using its mysteries to advantage and without detriment. Did not my husband's words prove true? Erik hatched a plan to pry the secret from Jeppe, and convinced Sofie to aid him. He knew Jeppe went to the pond to bathe daily, and on this day, once Jeppe was in the water, he sent Sofie to him while he hid behind a tree close by.

I don't know what all happened. Next day, Erik was gone from Hveen, and Jeppe didn't come back to Uraniborg for a week's passing. Ach, Tycho was in a state! He began receiving letters from Erik's debtors demanding payment, and Sofie avoided him altogether.

Time passes, and Jeppe seems the only grown person who cares to take any heed of me. I say to him, "Jeppe, why you choose to sit in the kitchen with a simple wife when this place abounds with great minds, is a pleasant mystery to me."

He spoke clearly his answer: "To prefer a window to a door, a pond to an ocean, is like the bee taking small stones into his feet to fly safe against the storm."

SOVEREIGN VOICES

THE MASQUE OF BLACKNESS

The storm will howl and the curtain rise to reveal the daughters of Niger huddled within an enormous shell. The shell appears to float upon painted wooden waves that harbor gruesome sea monsters and mermen. Then I, William Parsons, will rise from the sea. Look on this grimace! Are you afeard? Do your knees quake in the presence of Oceanus, Titan of the sea? Who else could play the part? I'm the only giant in King James' court, aren't I.

What say you of my costume? For a man of my dimensions the cloth is sparse. I discern the purpose—to display as much of my strength as possible save pitching the ladies into swoons. Played truly, Oceanus would don nary a thread. If I played it true, the married ladies would retire after the masque and kick their puny husbands out of bed, wouldn't they.

'Twas Inigo Jones done me up as Oceanus; he devised the costumes and scenery. There he stands yonder with Ben Jonson, author of the masque. God, give me patience, if they change my lines and movements once again, I'll quit the show. Rather than bickering like two old hens, they should be jumping with joy. Ha! They'd fairly chime with coins. The majesties spare no expense on entertainments.

At last, King James enters the hall; the masque will soon commence. Tonight we celebrate Twelfth Night and honor the appointment of Prince Charles as Duke of York. Have a peek through the curtain; he's the dark-haired boy dressed in gold satin, bows upon his boots. Note his sober expression. Such a fine laddie. He sits at the king's right hand. On the left is Villiers, a dandy with the muscles of a girl. He is indeed the glass wherein the noble youth dress themselves. A pretty young man, the current court favorite. Oftentimes whilst I guard the royal bedchamber, 'tis Villiers who tickles the king's fancy within. He best keep in mind the last favorite, who now weeps "foul" from a tower cell.

Queen Anne partakes in the masque as a daughter of Niger, her alabaster face and limbs painted black. 'Twas her desire that she and her ladies appear as blackamoors. Poor Jonson had to script words that made sense of blackamoor women presented at the English Court. Here's the gist of the plot: The daughters are in despair after hearing of the superior beauty of nymphs in other lands. So they set sail in quest of a place where they might be cured of their blackness.

Only through the superior strength and power of Oceanus, who guides their shell, does this unhappy group land in England. Then, from behind a cloud, the goddess of the Moon happily declares her prophecy fulfilled: The daughters of Niger have arrived at Britannia, a land governed by "a bright sun," meaning King James, "whose beams shine day and night and are of force to bleach an Ethiop and revive a corpse."

Betwixt we two, I'd be happier lifting an ale with the yeomen of the guard. Good fellows each, and ever at the ready to engage in games of strength. All considered, the stage is not an unpleasant change from my duties as royal porter. Least I'm paid handsomely here, for at Cow Lane End, Bartholomew Fair, I was lucky to earn tuppence a day. 'Twas at the fair King James hired me after receiving great pleasure from walking neath my outstretched arm. Among my possessions is a handbill of that year which reads: *Miracula Naturae.* Being that Giantlike Young Man, Aged Twenty-Three Years last June; Born in Ireland of such a Prodigious Height and Bigness, and every way proportionable that the like hath not been seen in England in the memory of Man. He is to be seen at Cow Lane End in Bartholomew Fair, where his Picture hangs out.

VELAZQUEZ

What a remarkable subject he'd be. Look—my easel quakes as Parson walks through the hall. I gauge his height at seven feet. His skin would appear sickly white if not for the numerous freckles. That bush of hair is closer to orange than red, wouldn't you say? As is the moustache he gnaws between his large square teeth. His eyes are small and copper-colored like fox eyes. Have you heard the bawdy tavern songs he sings, swaggering through the streets? The man is full to busting with himself.

Could you guess one sight that takes the wind from his sail? A dwarf! When he encounters a court dwarf, he tugs his ear, mumbles, *Little people*, and turns his step in the opposite direction.

I'd like to paint the giant before he leaves Madrid, though I doubt he'd be still long enough for a sketching. Then too, permission is required from Charles, Prince of Wales, whom Parsons serves. The prince and his two companions, Villiers and Parsons, rode to Madrid in a mere sixteen days. Have you seen the horse Parsons rode? An immense animal, yet its every bone must ache.

The purpose of the royal visit is to woo King Philip's sister, the Infanta Maria, as bride. King James will be disappointed; his son-in-law Frederick, lost the Rhenish Palatinate to Spain, and this marriage would regain what was lost. Though Philip keeps Charles distracted, prolongs his stay, concessions and promises in mind, Maria will never be allowed to marry a Protestant.

Perhaps I could speak to Villiers about painting Parsons. He's the king's closest advisor and was recently made Duke of Buckingham. How would I pose Parsons? I ask my subjects to choose their stance and setting. Doing so, I paint them as they allow themselves to be seen. As court painter, most of my canvases portray the royals, but because the family finds pleasure in the company of dwarfs, I'm able to paint them also. Three of these portraits hang on the south wall. Would you care to have a look?

The first is Francisco de Morra, a boy of fourteen. He chose his favorite place, a window nook in the castle atop a pile of cushions with a spacious view of the hills. His shirt and robe are common cloth, soft and loose. He holds a deck of tarot cards given to him by his mother who dwells in those hills. Yes, he does look like a very young child. Except for the curve of his mouth?

Next is Don Diego de Acedo. His clothes are very fine, no? He's as meticulous in his appearance as he is with his figures. Twenty-five years he has served at court as Secretary to the King. Scattered before him are the tools of his profession: inkwell, quill, books and ledgers. You should meet this man, his intellect is most vigorous and his conversation stimulating.

Last is Don Sebastian de Morra who possesses a warrior's face. He sits upon the floor, his short legs thrust out before him, fists clenched at his sides, his dark eyes challenging. Even his beard and moustache are fierce, I think. But I explain too much. The court dwarfs offer sanity amidst pervasive madness. These men are known for speaking the truth, though sometimes cloaked in the guise of jest. This is an old tradition, kings having dwarfs and fools about, and Philip's court houses a great many. Once, when King Philip was visited by the Duke of Modena, he dressed two dwarfs as Castilian kings and sat them on the steps of the throne while Philip and his guest attended the bullfights. Understand that a king must be on guard as so much depends on his personal favor. Those close to him obscure the truth to maintain good grace. The dwarf can be coddled by the king without arousing jealousy among courtiers and can speak clearly without fear of retaliation. An enviable position.

DUKE OF BUCKINGHAM'S ESTATE, LONDON, 1627

VILLIERS' BAKER

While the nobility slumbers in feather beds, warmed by hot bricks and brandy, me and my girls will be half the night cleaning up this mess. Aye me, 'twas a fond pageant. Lord and Lady Villiers were hosts to King Charles and Queen Henrietta Maria and various members of the court. My kitchen was like a beehive these past two days.

A good soaking this cloth will need, thanks be to that little bugger Jeffery. He's a dwarf that's lived here nigh on three years. I know his pa, the local butcher; I buy meats from his shop. Oh, he's a big man with a big voice, a thickskin who fancies himself citified. He sold Jeffery to Lord Buckingham, and methinks Jeffery was happier to be rid of his pa's company than his pa was to be shed of Jeffery.

'Twas Lady Villiers' devisement to put Jeffery in a pie. Hang off! Course I didn't bake him inside of it. Yesterday, I bade Jeffery sit in my biggest pan for measurement. Why, sitting down he's nary a foot high. Usually I forbid that imp in my kitchen. Small as a babe he may be, but he's seventeen years. Forsooth, old enough to be stirred up. He plays the baby goose around my girls, and soon as they lift him, his fingers start roaming where they ought not be. Aye, he baits me. So, after measuring the pan, I baked the bottom crust, then baked the top crust separate. Before dessert was to be served, I filled the pie with fresh fruit, Jeffery climbed inside, and I laid the top crust over him. The pie was carried to the table and set down. Straight off Jeffery jumped out, making a merry dance, throwing grapes, tipping goblets, and squashing plums underfoot. Then he leapt into the lap of Queen Henrietta Maria and he took up the mirror she wore tied to her waist on a ribbon. He held it to her face and said: "I've seen you where you ne'er have been and where you naught will be, and yet within that selfsame place, you can be seen by me."

My, she was enthralled. Jeffery has a way with ladies, excepting little Anne Shepherd, Mistress Mary Villiers' dwarf; she'll have naught of his rakish ways. Well, that's all one now; he's gone off with her majesty to live in the palace. I watched from the kitchen door as they departed; that Jeffery didn't look back once.

BOAR'S HEAD TAVERN, DOVER, 1632

COURIER TO LOUIS VIII

There goes Hudson, the greatest courier in all of England, Scotland, and Ireland combined—keenest eye, steadiest hand, quickest of foot, most expert on horse. Observe his level stride away from the tavern, after four ales, mind you. Half my size, yet I need to sit a spell before my ride.

See the tavern maid there? The comely mademoiselle with a bum like to a shelf. After Jeffery and I exchanged messages from Louis and Henrietta Maria, Jeffery bid me hail her and order two ales apiece. She makes her eyes wide, scowls her lovely brow, shakes a finger, and admonishes me, "Sir, you're not thinking of putting ale to this sweet babe's lips?" She leans over and chucks Jeffery under the chin, her obvious endowments fairly popping from her blouse. Jeffery smiles his crooked smile, looks at her with angelic eyes, and says, "I'd rather put my lips to your sweet titties, love."

Had I spoken those words, my face would bear the crimson mark of her hand, but she giggles at Hudson and pinches his cheek. I ask him, "How do you get by?"

"'Tis my duty in life to make married men cuckolds without making them jealous and to make mothers of maidens without letting the world know they had any gallants," was his reply.

If you think him a harmless little joker, best think again. He takes his profession seriously. I've witnessed him shoot three men dead while riding at full gallop. No wonder my king's sister keeps him close at hand.

✧

VAN DYCK'S STUDIO, COURT OF KING CHARLES I, LONDON, 1633

RICHARD GIBSON

If you must comment, whisper to me most softly. Van Dyck's subjects are Queen Henrietta Maria and Sir Jeffery Hudson. The portrait's nearly complete; he paints the single dark curl fallen loose upon her shoulder. How I stare, but I'm anxious to learn from this master while I have the opportunity. The man conferring with him is my teacher, Peter Lely, a court painter and a fine artist in his own right.

Observe Van Dyck's mastery in rendering the gold curtain; see how the crown, set upon a pedestal, blends into the drapery folds and reflects no light. A sporting portrait, the queen has set aside her diadem for a bold feathered hat and hunting dress. Truth be told, she dislikes the hunt; the portrait's purpose is to please the king. Does not her smile seem bemused? A smirk rather than a wide grin. Chances are good Jeffery kept her well entertained throughout the posing. She does love Jeffery and her marmoset dearly. Van Dyck has set the monkey on Jeffery's arm. The little beast paws Jeffery's hair in this portrait and Jeffery's expression betrays his desire—he'd like to throttle the ape.

Jeffery's known for his good nature and his jesting. We became friends straight off, through Jeffery's efforts, I must say, for there's no shy bone in his body. When first I came to court, I kept to the studio like a snail within his shell. I have no bit of trouble speaking by way of my brushes and paints, but among people, I struggle for words. Jeffery found me out and would have none of my shyness. He took my arm, pulled me without, and sang in a lusty voice, "Here comes a

85

pair of very strange beasts, which in all tongues are called fools."

I stopped short and told him I cared not to be insulted. His face drew into surprise, "Shakespeare's words, not mine, my friend. Besides," he winked, "we both know why we're here. You may be the best of painters, but you'd not have been brought to court if not for your lack of stature."

I know Jeffery speaks true, but I'm not one to look a gift horse in the mouth. As a boy, my parents were good as any parents can be, but I had an itch to journey beyond our pastures. At fourteen years of age, I traveled to Mortlake and came to be a page for the widowed Lady Boughner. When she discovered my artistic abilities, she arranged for me to have drawing lessons. I owe much to that kind lady. In my pocket I carry her portrait, a miniature I painted while in her employ. Before her death, she wrote a letter recommending me to the court of King Charles, where Sir Peter took me under his tutelage. I have learned much.

What has Jeffery learned? I would not dare speak for him. I tell you something for certain, by looking upon his boyish face on Van Dyck's canvas, you'd not guess the history of this dashing man who did me the great favor of making me his friend. His childhood was not so pleasant, but it's not my place to discuss his private matters. I will say this, there are but two ways of spreading light: to be the candle or the mirror which reflects it. He is the candle that burns constant. 'Twas Jeffery introduced me to Miss Anne Shepherd, pronouncing her too tame for his fancy. Anne's mistress, Lady Mary, was taken in at court after her father, the Earl of Buckingham, was assassinated, and she brought Anne also. There's much intrigue afoot inside the palace walls, and Jeffery's in the thick of it. Though he's smart and quick as a whip, twice he's been captured and ransomed while serving the queen as courier.

HUDSON'S SHIPMATE

Leave him rest. He's exhausted. Sit a while, you look a mite green. I prefer standing with wood under my feet and sea wind in my nostrils. Ah, 'tis good to be aboard an English ship again, a beautiful woman she is, decked out and wide of girth, rocking me in her sweet arms home to England. England—last time I set eyes on her green shores I was working as a hand on the *Dreadnaught,* as fine a ship as Mr. Phineas Pett ever built. That's where I met Jeff, eleven years ago, in the year 1649. We'd put in at Brest, unloaded cargo, and picked up passengers to cross the Channel. I noticed Jeff straightaway. Not only was he the smallest man I'd ever laid eyes on, but he was wearing a velvet suit and leather riding boots up to his knees. The first mate thought Jeff was out for a cabin boy job and gave him hell for being dressed so fancified. Jeff put him to rights in a wink! He pulled a wee pistol out of his vest, shot the feather off the mate's hat, then tossed him a bag of coins.

Hardly had we put up sail when a Turkish corsair came alongside. Ain't nothing strikes fear in the heart like the Turk pirates: heads wrapped in cloth, bare to the waist, dagger tween the teeth, scimitar swinging overhead, and howling like banshees. You'd not believe how quick they took us. Aye, the renegades of Elizabeth's reign taught the Turks well. But they learnt to fit out vessels better than the English, better for pirating.

An Aga captain of the janissaries took command of the *Dreadnaught,* and we ended up in the Barbary city of Tunis, a walled stronghold for pirates. Strung together like fish on a line, we were marched to the jails. Me and Jeff were put in a cell with six other men. The odor was sharp as ripe cheese. I was scared out of my wits, but Jeff was calm as could be. He laid his cloak on the dirt floor and curled up for a snooze. Next day, the pasha came around to survey his loot and the prisoners. Oh, the way he was got up! Big as a whale, wearing silk breeches that puffed out around his legs like balloons. Gold chains on his neck, gold rings on every finger, and a gold belt set with jewels. Jeff struts up to the bars, sticks his face between them, saying he's worth his weight in gold, that Queen Henrietta Maria will pay his ransom, and whack! A janissary's club comes down on Jeff's head. If Jeff'd had a side arm, there be one less Turk in Tunis. The pasha points his fat finger at each man and jabbers in his heathen tongue so I don't know what fate's in store for me. Found out soon enough. Being strong and able-bodied, I was sent with a crew to build fortifications around the city. Aye, 'twas backbreaking labor, but I fared better than Jeff.

Day after day, Jeff kept at the guards, saying his ransom would make them rich. A Frenchman in our cell, who spoke the Mohammedan tongue, repeated Jeff's words. Cursed dog janissaries laughed and turned their backs to us. Me and Jeff still shared a cell, though I saw less of him than the other slaves on account of I was there only at night, when Jeff was usually taken away. 'Scuse me for spitting, there's a bad taste in my mouth. The guards were overly fond of Jeff. Janissaries are the pasha's private thugs, been so for hundreds of years, only soldiers that get paid regular wages. You'd think men would line up to join. Ain't so, cause they're flagellated to make them strong-willed, made to live in barracks, no wives, no women allowed. A Christian slave with a pretty face ain't sent to labor. For once in my life, I blessed the scars on my ugly mug. Jeff's not only fair, his body's like a young lad's.

Under the worst conditions men can endure, the best salve is friendship. Talk of home kept our memories alive and our hopes from failing. I'd led a simple life on the sea, and I've no talent for turning a colorful phrase, but Jeff knows how to draw men out and spin a tale from threads of talk. When Jeff spoke of home, so clear was his describing, 'twas like looking in a magic mirror that grants wishes.

As I told you, before the *Dreadnaught* was captured, we'd put in at Brest. Guess how Jeff came to be departing France? He killed a nobleman! But let me start with what took him to Paris. Jeff was a companion to Queen Henrietta Maria, wife of King Charles. When civil war broke out, Jeff fought as Captain of the Horse against Cromwell's forces. In 1644, scared she'd be killed, the Queen went to Paris, and she took Jeff with her. That same year, King Charles was beheaded in London and Jeff quarreled with a nobleman named Crofts. Crofts had made uncouth remarks about Jeff's good fortune with the queen, and Jeff challenged him to a duel. Crofts showed up at the field armed with a child's toy gun. Jeff was right properly insulted, and he demanded another match for the next day. This time, Crofts brought a pistol, and Jeff took aim from atop his horse. After shooting Crofts dead through the heart, Jeff was obliged to leave Paris. That's when he booked passage on the *Dreadnaught*.

Our luck took its first turn nearly a year ago, when the pasha was strangled by a rival. The new pasha cleared out the janissaries and took inventory. He had no use for slaves lingering in cells, and many pretty boys were run through. Jeff would've been too, but this time his talk of ransom fell on greedy ears. As fate would have it, Charles II was back on the throne, and his mother, Queen Henrietta Maria, returned to London. I guess you know the ransom was paid, cause here we are, Jeff and me, headed for home.

I'd be a rotting corpse in Tunis if not for Jeff. He told that second fat pasha I was his uncle and the ransom was for the pair of us. Don't know what England will have in store after all these years. Got no family and no wish to return to the sea. Ain't complaining—hell, I'll work the docks. I've still got strong arms and once I get some English food in me, I'll gain back my belly. Jeff says his ordeal with the Turks caused him to grow to a height of three feet six inches, and that's too tall for a court dwarf. But knowing Jeff's character as I do, he'll not be far from the throne.

COURT OF KING WILLIAM III, LONDON, 1689

SIR PETER LELY

So a Dutchman will occupy the English throne. The common people are thrilled that our new queen Mary is "embraced in Protestant arms." Her father, James II, is an impatient, arrogant, silly man. As sovereign of our country, he had little interest in the arts or sciences, was oversexed and a poor judge of character. Perhaps the memory of his father's fate on the block urged him to surrender the throne after a mere three years to his son-in-law, without a whimper of protest. I care naught of these matters excepting William and Mary's reign brings Richard Gibson back to England.

When Richard first arrived at court, we were both young men. He was so quiet, I worried he was dim-witted. I soon learnt his quiet exterior masked a creative intensity that none of my pupils since have possessed. Richard was neat and orderly in the studio, listened to suggestions, and took criticism well. He was obsessed with landscapes—panoramic views on huge canvases. A difficult feat for a man his size, and the paintings were of poor quality. I held my tongue for several months, watching him climb ladders, come down and cross the room to view the scale, climb again—it exhausted my spirit. Finally I asked Richard why the giant landscapes were so important and if, in his heart, he believed them worthy of his talent. One week later, he showed me a miniature he'd painted of his first patron, a Lady Boughner. It was exquisite. From that point on, Richard refined his gift of portraying the human face with delicate excellence. Why, the great master Van Dyck requested one of Richard's miniatures; there is no higher compliment.

I recall the day we observed Van Dyck paint Queen Henrietta Maria and her dwarf, Jeffery Hudson. Dedicated to his Catholic queen, Hudson spent years enduring the tortures of the Barbary bagnios in payment for his loyalty. Nine years ago, at the age of sixty-four, he was imprisoned during the Popish Plot. I know this news will sadden Richard, for they were friends in those more innocent years.

Monarchs and religions come and go. Richard and I prospered through the changes by remaining loyal first to our craft, and in doing so, we've become wealthy men. After King Charles lost his head, Richard was commissioned by Cromwell. When the monarchy was restored, Richard was appointed court miniature painter, as well as painting instructor to James II's daughters, Mary and Anne. Mary became wife to William Prince of Orange, and in 1678, Richard and his wife Anne accompanied her to the Hague, where they've lived these past ten years. Before their departure, I painted this portrait of the Gibsons.

How pleased I'll be to see them again. They have five grown children, among them a daughter who shows promise as a painter and a son who is sculpting. Will Richard recognize me? Have I changed much? I shall know the moment I set eyes on Richard; the truest of mirrors is an old friend.

✦

HANOVER, GERMANY, 1710

QUEEN ANNE'S EMISSARY

While attending to the queen's affairs in Germany, I called on one Matthew Buchinger, a monster of reported prodigious talents. He has performed for many crown heads of Europe, and word of him had reached her Majesty. It's my duty to find distractions for the queen, who is nearly an invalid and has suffered sorely throughout her life. In her advanced years, her enjoyments are good meals, good gossip, and playing at cards. Due to her corpulence, she must be moved about on chairs propelled by pulleys. She dislikes taking fresh air, so amusements need be brought to her.

Arriving at the Buchinger home, I was greeted by a gaggle of children and escorted by the eldest daughter to a drawing room, where Matthew sat before a table engaged with pen and ink. He had neither arms nor legs, but out of his shoulders grew two fleshy protrusions, not unlike fins of a fish. Lacking legs of any sort, his feet appeared to be stuck onto the base of his trunk. He jumped from his chair with a warm smile and a "How do ye do." Quickly, the room filled with his offspring, giggling and pushing, carrying instruments and props. Mrs. Buchinger followed with an unusually dour expression. She was reed thin and her wig needed dusting.

Matthew stamped his feet and the children quieted and sat upon the carpet. His show began with a demonstration of expertise at games: cards and dice and skittles. Next, he performed witty tricks with cups and balls. An accomplished musician, he played tunes upon the hautboy, dulcimer, trumpet, and bagpipe. At the performance's end, Matthew asked his wife to serve brandy and cakes. She replied, with slurred tongue, "Sir, you're so all-fired handy, fetch them yourself."

The poor man's cheeks grew bright, but he implored his wife, "Dear Lady, please bring refreshments to our honored guest, agent to her Majesty Queen Anne."

The shrewish wife snapped, "Think I give a whit for that old fat cow or her lackeys? Here I am stuck with all these brats, out of the seven only one's my own, while her majesty grows fatter, guzzling spirits, gorging on sweets, not a royal urchin in sight . . . when our Georgie takes the throne, I'll serve up a feast!"

Barely had she loosed her words when Matthew hurled himself at her, and using his head like a battering ram, knocked her to the floor. He jumped on top of her and beat her with his flippers as she begged for mercy. A gentle hand tugged my sleeve; Matthew's daughter escorted me to the door with profuse and sincere apologies, something I wager she's accustomed to. I gave her my card and asked that her father contact me forthwith as I was leaving on the morrow.

That was over a year's passing. I should be most pleased if Matthew would agree to visit the court, especially as the queen's health is failing. I'm certain she'd find him as fascinating as I did. However, he has not written a response to my many letters.

LETTER TO HILDA

5 May, The Year of Our Lord 1716
London, England

Dearest Daughter,

My greatest hope is that this letter finds both you and your husband in good health. Please accept the money I've enclosed to buy a cradle for my forthcoming grandchild. You must send word immediately upon the child's birth, and I shall come to visit. I'm a rich man, if not so rich in gold, certainly rich in blessings—I shall be a grandfather and a father once more in the same year! I believe this eleventh child shall be my last; your new stepmother has declared it so.

A workingman is a happy man and I have shortage of neither work nor happiness. Kings and queens of Europe's past have shared in their quests for the unusual, for dwarfs and giants and monsters, but in London, all ranks of people pay out coins to gaze upon monsters like your dear father. Though I'm not so much an oddity here when compared to most who exhibit at Bartholomew Fair. Some are such blatant fakeries they'd make you laugh, though you'd not laugh at the preserved bodies of the dead. Too many others are invalids who have the misfortune of being in the care of mountebanks.

I'll tell you of but a few and you'll think me a jester. There's the Northumberland Monster, a creature having the head, mane, and feet of a horse, with the rest like a man. Immediately after birth the creature was scalded to death by advice of the town schoolmaster. There are two girls joined together by the crowns of their heads. When one turns her head the neck of the other turns also. Many people come to see them and give three stivers apiece. The Painted Prince, who can be seen every day at the Blue Boar's Head in Fleet Street, claims he's from a far-off island kingdom. I have my doubts about that, but I do not doubt he is a wonder to behold. His body is stained with paints; the forepart shows engravings, the back parts afford a lively representation of diverse parts of the world, and much more I cannot write to my daughter. In Covent Garden by Rose Tavern is a Living Fairy, supposed to be a hundred and fifty years old. There's an hermaphrodite at the King's Head; and giants and giantesses from all parts of the country. Oh, there's a fine man that is much popular with the crowds as he elicits laughter from all. He's called the Bold Grimace Spaniard. His story is that he was snatched from his cradle by a savage beast and wonderfully preserved till some comedians passed through those parts, and, perceiving him to be human, pursued him to his cave and caught him in a net. He lolls out his tongue, nearly a foot in length, and turns his eyes in and out at the same time; he makes his face small as an apple; extends his mouth into the shape of a bird's beak, and his eyes like to an owl's; he licks his nose with his tongue, like a cow, and turns his mouth into the shape of a hat cocked up three ways.

So many strange and wondrous people I cannot list them all. I perform at the Hart's-Horn Inn in Pye-Corner during the fair, playing upon my instruments, doing my tricks, and drawing with pen and ink. I must tell you of a woman I met at the Brandy Shop over against the Eagle and Child in Stocks Market. She comes from Acton, my birthplace. Although she was born after I left, she knows many of the families I knew in my youth. She's called Dwarf of the World, and is so small, she's carried in a little box to any gentleman's house, if desired. I care not for her uncle, who profits so greatly from her condition.

There are many German folks in England since George of Hanover was crowned. I'm soon to meet him at court! On Wednesday last, I drew to life the face of a lady named Ehrengard Melusina von Schulenberg. As it turns out, she is a close acquaintance of the King. He was greatly impressed by my drawing, and has invited me to perform at St. James Palace on the night of 25 May. Say a prayer for me on that day.

My sincerest love,
Your father, Matthew Buchinger

✧

COURT OF KING GEORGE I, LONDON, 25 MAY 1716

PRINCESS CAROLINE

How like my father-in-law to present this type of entertainment before the court. He cackles like a hen when Buchinger dances, yet misses the wit of his puns. I do not deny the talent of Buchinger, but a wiser, more thoughtful ruler would take this entertainment in private. One ought to seek out one's own pleasures and not subject others to this preference, which they may not share. I've a preference for the paintings of Van Dyck; four hang in our gallery. My husband, Prince George, and I enjoy them at our leisure. As my teacher, Gottfried Wilhelm von Leibniz taught me, our happiness is based upon our natural sensibilities. The more we follow our natures, the more we come to find pleasure in the happiness of others, and it's this that forms the basis of natural benevolence, and of charity and justice. Difficult indeed to keep these teachings in mind when I look upon King George. He's stated his opinion of the arts on several occasions: "I hate all boets and bainters."

Buchinger is neither, but he draws exceptionally well with pen and ink. He's possessed of intelligence as well for he drew "The Maypole" kindly if not accurately. Need I point her out? She's one of the king's two mistresses. The other is Charlotte Sophia Kelmanns, the huge woman squeezed into the chair against the wall; she's known as "Elephant and Castle." To view her uncorseted is to know terror. Ehrengard, the skinny one, is ten years George's senior. She and the king cut paper patterns with scissors most evenings, according to court gossip. I heard of one Englishman who described the king's mistresses as, "Old trulls such as would not find entertainment in the most hospitable hundreds of old Drury."

My husband's mother, the beautiful Queen Sophia Dorothea, grows ill and mad with grief, imprisoned in the Castle of Ahlden. Twenty-two years she's been so kept, divorced and denied the sight of her children. George was eleven years old the last time he saw his mother; he nearly drowned trying to swim the castle moat. What was her crime? True love in the arms of another—a Swedish colonel of the Dragoons, who disappeared after the queen's imprisonment. Truth be told, his mutilated body is buried under the floorboards of Herrenhausen, the king's country estate.

Is it any wonder the English people scoff at the king behind his back? Look well on Matthew Buchinger, see his wife there with her babe, pride flushing her face. Note his grace and his style. Now look upon King George and his company and tell me which is man and which is beast.

MATTHEW BUCHINGER II

Father drew this self-portrait in 1732 in Cork, Ireland, two years before his death. As eldest son, it came into my possession. I placed it on the mantel where I can look upon his face before I retire and wish him a good night.

Father drew countless portraits that flattered his subjects, but this one—a truer portrait he never drew. His eyebrows arch upward in an amused manner as do the corners of his mouth, and in between them that great bulbous nose. Yes, I have it also. I do not have my father's talents, but thanks to his generosity, I have a fine farm and a happy life.

How many strokes of the pen would you estimate were drawn upon this vellum? How many hours of patiently working his nubs across the paper, sitting on his large, callused feet? You'd not think this possible unless you had seen how gently he caressed his son's head.

Examine his wig in the portrait and pay close attention to the curls. Ah—now you see them, words worked into the curls, six of the Psalms and the Lord's Prayer. I'll help you; begin here where my finger points:

The Lord is my shepherd; I shall not want. He maketh me to lie down in green pastures: He leadeth me beside the still waters. He restoreth my soul: He leadeth me in the paths of righteousness for his name's sake. Yea, though I walk through the valley of the shadow of death, I will fear no evil: for Thou art with me; Thy rod and Thy staff they comfort me. Thou preparest a table before me in the presence of mine enemies . . .

POLTAVA, UKRAINE, 1709, CAMP OF PETER THE GREAT

THE BOYAR

After nine years of war, we celebrate our victory over the Swedes, and ten Swedish generals sit in places of honor at the tsar's table. True, they are prisoners of war, but Tsar Peter raised his cup to them and proclaimed, "I drink to the health of those who taught me the art of winning victory!" By the beard of Christ, he turned over his sword to Marshal Rehnskjold as a token of esteem, along with his permission to wear it. Do you think the Swede will be taxed for the honor of wearing the tsar's sword? Suggest it and you'll hang in Moscow Square. Yet I must pay one hundred rubles a year to wear my beard, and there, seated next to the tsar, is a Swedish grenadier with a flowing yellow beard—and by God, the grenadier's a woman. The stack of bronze medallions before her are like the one I carry at all times. Each medal bears the inscription, "The tax has been collected," and a picture of a beard above the motto, "The beard is a useless burden." The tsar gave her those, laughing with glee and tugging at her beard with his fingers and his teeth. I should not be surprised by Peter's antics after my years of service to the crown, but this is a grave insult to Russian men.

Consider the number of shaven chins present. Only the proud and rich wear this noblest attribute of manhood, and in doing so, we chance incurring the tsar's wrath. Ten years ago, Peter published a ukase forbidding all but members of the clergy to wear beards. This occurred after his visit to Cracow, where he met with Augustus II, the new king of Poland. Upon his return, Peter received the boyars with fond greetings and was telling us of his conversations with Augustus, when he suddenly raised a pair of scissors and cut the beard from Generalissimo Schein. He disfigured each boyar in the same manner, roaring his great laugh, beards flying through the air, hair covering the floor. We stood bare-naked chinned and ashamed as young boys, filled with the fear of God's wrath. Patriarch Adrian had recently spoken against changing the face of man; the Savior Himself wore a beard, as did the holy apostles, the great prophets, Constantine the Great, Theodosius the Great, and Vladimir the Great. Tsar Peter wears only a moustache, in the European fashion. The patriarch said to shave one's beard is not only a horror and a dishonor, it is a mortal sin. He urged Orthodox men not to give in to that diabolical inclination. He asked from the pulpit, "Where will you stand at the time of the Last Judgment? With the saints whose faces are adorned with beards or with the shaven heretics?"

Five days later, at a royal banquet, the tsar commanded a twenty-five gun salute and ordered Valakoff, his favorite dwarf, to attack the beards that remained, which he did with zeal, contorting his body and face as he fiendishly snipped. Now, if a bearded man comes to an office, his request is denied, he's obliged to pay fifty rubles, and if he's unable to do so is sent to Roggervik to work off his fine. Tsar Peter was not content to change only the face of Russian men, but our dress also. His latest ukase requires boyars, courtiers, and officials in Moscow and other cities to dress in the Hungarian and German fashion, the outer caftan reaching down to the garter and the inner one shorter. He who protests openly will soon be free of his beard along with his head.

The most offensive injustice is that the finest beards in Russia are found on the chins of peasants. The tsar's tax is determined by social status: one hundred rubles for noblemen, sixty for courtiers and tradesmen, thirty for lackeys and coachmen, and a half-kopeck for peasants. The peasants pass through the city gates, attend mass, and go home with the proper beards of true Christian men, while the boyars, second only to the princes of Russia, are skinned one way or another. Or is it a greater injustice that a Swedish woman's beard should so delight the Tsar?

VALAKOFF

No need for my antics tonight. Peter's captivated by the bearded female soldier. Her hair is as pale as his is dark, and her eyes are so blue the tsar's black eyes swallow them. Oh, watch this. Peter's head twitchs—the first sign of the sickness. How extreme will this fit be? Will he frighten the girl out of her senses? See his features jump about, the eyes fill with demented rage, his lips pull away from his teeth like a black bear cornered by hounds.

Peter grips her arm! Ah, the girl shows her mettle, not a flinch. The fit passes as quickly as it came, and the girl has gained more than she can guess. Once, when dining with Queen Anne in England, Peter had a violent fit. The queen, completely undone, attempted to rise from her chair, which is no small task considering her girth. The tsar, trying to reassure her, grabbed her arm and gripped so tightly that the queen let out a yelp. If not for her layers of fat, I believe he'd have snapped her arm in two. He shrugged and said, "Russian women do not have such delicate bones."

Peter's sickness began when he was twenty years old and had been especially vigorous in his playful pursuits. He was so close to death that Prince Boris kept horses at the ready in case Sophia should seize power. Peter's a man of iron—he cheated death—but since that brush, he has fits when overly tired or excited. To combat them he takes a medicine powder made from magpie stomachs and wings. Doesn't appear to help much, and I should know. I've been with Peter all of his life.

I was eleven years old and living in the Kremlin when Peter was born. Tsar Alexis had freed my parents from serfdom as a reward for producing a dwarf. My first duty was to drive Peter's coach, a miniature copy of Alexis' gilded European carriages. Four dwarf ponies drew it along, and little Peter sat inside, waving to the crowds that gathered whenever we ventured out. Back then, there were twenty-four dwarfs at court. Now, there are over one hundred. Russia is lousy with dwarfs; there's no better country to dwell in if one's a dwarf! Surely you know it's a tradition for kings and queens to keep dwarfs and giants at court. Every Infanta of Spain is accompanied by a court dwarf, the uglier the better, to emphasize whatever beauty the royal lady may possess. To keep up with the royals, the nobles fight over dwarfs. We're bona fide status symbols. Ask any nobleman on the street and he'll tell you a pet dwarf is better than a talking parrot or a dog that performs tricks.

Have you seen our giant? We have only one. King Frederick William of Prussia's got most of the giants on the continent, over one thousand, calls them his Blue Prussian Battalion. Saw them with my own eyes once, when Frederick's son, little Fritz, gained his own company of giants. Frederick had a big celebration, and Peter and I went to inspect the troops. Fritz's grandfather, King German George of England, was there too. He favors his mother Anne, in bulk.

Want to know the difference between the kings of Prussia and of England? Well, I'll tell you. Both have giants at court, in Prussia they're used as a display of might and in England they're used in domestic service to bolster the image of sovereignty. In both roles they're slaves behind the fancy facade.

Frederick sends his agents to grab giants from Sweden, the Ukraine, Ireland, Wallachia, wherever he can find them. He pays enormous amounts of money when necessary, but more often uses devious methods to entrap giant men and kidnap giant women. He hopes to cultivate a cheaper, homegrown crop. A few years ago, Frederick heard of a giant carpenter living in Julich. He sent an agent there with a cooked up story; he needed a coffin for a soldier who was too large for a standard box. When the job was done, the agent said he didn't believe it was large enough. The carpenter replied, "I made it to your exact specifications. I am six feet six inches myself and I know I will fit inside it." He lifted the lid, climbed inside, and stretched to his full length. Wham! The agent and his men slammed down the lid and nailed it shut. The poor sap was shipped off in a carriage to Potsdam, but suffocated before the carriage reached Frederick. The king displays the giant's bones in a gallery closet.

Peter sent him several Russian giants, but keeps his sweet Nicholas, the only man in Russia taller than the tsar. You can't miss him—he's standing behind Peter's chair as he always does. Peter brought him back from a trip to Calais. Guess the former trade of that flabby colossus? He made pastries! Seven feet of doughy flesh and a brain the size of a pea. Once, at a synod party, (I must tell you about the Drunken Synod), Peter dressed Nicholas in a diaper and bonnet, and I led him in by strings tied around his wrists. Most often, he struts about in his Preobrazhenski regiment uniform, which pleases Peter to no end. He takes him everywhere he goes and heaps gifts upon him as he would a mistress. "Child of my heart," the tsar calls him. Knowing Peter as I do, the novelty of Nicholas will wear thin, as do most of the tsar's passions.

Peter and I share a kindred spirit—we're both revelers of prodigious capacity. This we recognized at our first meeting and commenced to shake the shit out of life. Speaking of which, let me enlighten you on the synod as I promised. Peter had not reached his twentieth year when he formed the Drunken Synod. We'd enjoyed many notorious parties, but Peter, clever man that he is, wanted something permanent, official, and irreverent. The synod formed to celebrate Bacchus, and at the head of this company he placed the greatest drunk of all, his former tutor Nikita Zoltov whom Peter dubbed "Prince Pope." Zoltov received a salary of two thousand rubles, a palace, and twelve servants, stutterers every one! For the ceremonies, he wore a tin miter and carried a tin scepter while making delightful speeches, mixing obscenities with Bible passages. He blessed those that knelt before him by striking them on the head with a pig's bladder. Then he presented an icon for them to kiss, naked Bacchus, and they'd kiss his prominent prick. Oh, how old Zoltov could dance, staggering, belching, farting, with his holy robes pulled up between his legs. The twelve stuttering cardinals served under the Prince Pope, as did a company of mock bishops, archimandrites, deacons—amazing guzzlers and gluttons. Peter played archdeacon; he drank, but kept a clear head, goading the synod to degrade themselves still further as he wrote notes on their conversations.

New members donned the red cardinal robes and were taken to the Vaticanum, the palace of the Prince Pope, to pay homage. The initiates were ushered to the consistory where the throne of His Very Holy Buffoonery stood behind piles of casks. Zoltov would ask not, "Do you believe?" but "Do you drink?" Then he would say, "Reverendissimus, open your mouth, swallow what's given to you, and you'll tell us wonderful things." After consuming goodly amounts of vodka, the synod marched to the gallery to begin the conclave. Peter, dressed as a Dutch seaman, led the way beating a drum, Zoltov behind him, seated on a cask drawn by four oxen, surrounded by monks, goats, pigs, and bears.

Beside each couch in the synod gallery stood a barrel cut in two; one half for refreshment, the other for pissing and shitting. You see, it was forbidden to leave the couch until the end of the conclave, which lasted three days and three nights. Dwarfs and buffoons kept the cups full and provoked members to ribald comments. All were dressed in costume and vied with each other to make faces. Soaked in sweat, panting, eyes bulging from their heads, the synod company would insult each other, slap heads, belch, fart, weep, roll on the ground, vomit on their costumes and wigs.

Since the wars with the Swedes, the synod's been retired. I wager the red robes will be dancing again when we return to Moscow, and I wouldn't be surprised, judging by the way that grenadier empties her cup, if the synod inducts its first maiden.

HEDDY

We've stopped here in Kiev from the march to Moscow, and at last I have a rest from the tsar. His mistress, Catherine, lives here. Russians come to the camp to look us Swedes over. Most always, because of my beard, people think I'm a man, but on the tsar's order, my uniform jacket and two top shirt buttons are left unbuttoned to reveal my bosom. When the Kiev women see me they cross themselves, and the men glare.

We stayed too long at Poltava; the stench of dead bodies finally moved the tsar to end his celebrating and break camp. Two days into the march, Peter ordered our detachments to execute maneuvers so he might observe how the Swedish army operates on campaign. Peter applauded, whistled, and paced up and down as we performed. It's hard to dislike a man who shows such admiration for his prisoners of war. Keep in mind our troops, led by King Charles, had beaten Peter's army at Gradna and again at Franstadt two years earlier. If we'd stuck to the coast, we could've held our territories; a grave mistake following Peter into the heart of Russia. His Cossacks burned the towns they traveled through, leaving us ruins that offered no food, no shelter from the cold.

The night of the day we left Poltava, I was taken to the tsar's tent. I'm constantly on guard, as all good soldiers are, but I wasn't concerned. The tsar had shown himself to be amiable enough at the banquet. There was that moment he gripped my arm to show off his strength, just as my brothers did in our youth. I reasoned he'd summoned me to his tent to discuss military matters. He stood, arms at his sides, hands opening and closing as if the air were solid. He ordered my escort from the tent, then leapt upon me, seized my jacket, and attempted to rip it from me. I was momentarily stunned, but when his hands found my breasts, I snapped into action.

Let me explain. I have six brothers, four elder, two younger. We're each one year apart in age. That should tell you plenty. But you're interested in how I came to be in the Swedish army. To begin, my father's a general; retired recently, he lost a leg at Narva. My mother is a kind woman, and though she's strong in body, she's delicate in spirit. Hard enough her sons before me were unruly little demons. With my father away on maneuvers much of the time, she was left to manage them by her own devices. And they proved to be unmanageable. They ran wild, playing war games, tearing up furniture with their swords, chasing the village dogs, setting fire to barns, breaking each other's noses. Upon my birth, Mother's heart filled with joy—a daughter, a girl to pamper and dress prettily, curl her hair and teach her the feminine graces. Alas, her joy died when my chin sprouted yellow hair before I took my first steps. Mother spent the next year in prayer and gave birth to another son. The following year she spent in a state of bewilderment and birthed yet another son.

In those two years, while Mother wandered about the house, her eyes distant, mumbling her prayers, baby at her breast, my brothers took me into their care. I was tied to trees, held captive in closets, patches of hair yanked from my head, my eyes blackened. Their favorite torture was to hold a pillow over my face and at the moment I needed to gasp for breath, one would snatch the pillow away just as another broke wind over my face. My brothers taught me to fight, and as I grew, they took pride in watching their pupil apply their lessons to my younger brothers and to children stupid enough to tease me about my beard.

One by one, my older brothers were recruited into the Drabants, the elite royal cavalry guard, cadets who become army officers. On their visits home, I'd sneak away with a uniform and put it on. I'd sniff the dark blue coat and inhale the wonderful scents of leather and horse and dust. The brass buttons were heavy as jewels and just as bright. I'd pull on the yellow breeches and the heavy riding boots and clomp around my room, making salutes, thrusting an invisible enemy with my stick sword. I made up my mind to join the Drabant Corps, and when I set my mind to something, I'll not give up until it comes to pass.

I almost did it; my months of practice nearly paid off. Under the watchful eye of King Charles, I rode over the royal field with the other hopefuls, performing maneuvers, besting them all. Then the Drabants took the field. My brothers could've given me away—they had no idea of my brash plan—but that old pride flashed in their eyes and they kept the other Drabants from getting a chance at me. I thought all was lost when one of the cadets, who as a boy had been a nasty, foulmouthed teaser, and out of whom I beat the nastiness on several occasions, recognized me and shouted, "A girl, a freak of a girl tries to pass as a soldier!"

Everyone stopped. Horses were reigned in, and heads turned to stare. I wanted to knock that villain from his horse and thrash him until he cried for mercy. Instead I rode my horse at full gallop straight to the king, jumped from my saddle, looked Charles in the eye, and said, "Let me be a warrior for Sweden's sake."

The king called forth one Drabant after another to test my skill (thank the Lord he didn't call one of my brothers), and when I had beaten seven, he stopped the trial. I waited anxiously one full hour before being summoned. For the first time in my life, I felt nervous. I knew the king's opinion of women, for my brothers had spoken of this. Six princesses had been proposed to Charles for marriage, he declined each one, and he always slept alone. Charles preferred his soldiers to be unmarried men who thought only of duty, who saved their strength for battle rather than the pursuit of women. He said that married men with children were less likely to advance courageously on the battlefield.

Charles addressed me directly. "I am impressed with your expertise and your dedication to our country. However, it is impossible for you to be accepted into the Drabant company." My heart sank. "Ordinarily I would never consider allowing a woman into the army because of the distraction and temptation to the men. However, your beard gives you the appearance of a man, and makes you sexually repugnant," he said. "Therefore, you have my permission to join the regular army cavalry." The year was 1700, the same year the Great Northern War began.

Nine years later, a survivor of many battles, I found myself wrestling on the ground, fighting off the advances of Russia's tsar. No man had ever approached me in this manner. I'm not sure whether King Charles was correct in saying I didn't appeal to men, or that because I had six fierce brothers in the army, no soldier dared touch me. I'd thought about mating, but a soldier's life is not conducive to it. King Charles was my hero and my example, and the only man I would have willingly given myself to completely.

As I said, when Peter's hands groped my breasts, I snapped into action—I clipped him a good one on the jaw. I was generous; normally, I'd have gone right for the opponent's nose and broken it with one blow. Peter fell on his back, and I tried to scramble out of the tent, but he grabbed my ankle and pulled me to him. He embraced me so tightly I could barely move. He seized my hair, pulled my head back, and beheld me with an inquisitorial gaze. He said, "Exquisite creature, need I wrestle you or woo you all night to look upon both your blond beards?"

The wrestling contest didn't last long. Though I put up a fight, my body's small, and my success in battle comes through quick action and expertise with weapons. Before the night had passed, I was a maiden no more. Since then, I've been brought each night to the tsar's tent. A table is set with food and drink. The tsar asks me questions about my family, my village, the battles I've fought. He tells me of the new Russian capital he'll build by the sea on the lands he won from Sweden. All the while he laughs, gestures, paces, and showers me with radiant smiles. But always the evening ends the same as the first. I hate being beaten at any contest of force. The act itself is neither agreeable nor disagreeable, simply part of nature's design. Besides, I'm a prisoner of war, surrounded by the Russian army and attended by three burly guards. What choice have I?

SAINT PETERSBURG, 1714

LEIBNIZ AT THE DWARF'S WEDDING

When there are many roads available, one has the freedom to choose among them, the choice being determined by the fact that one would be better than another. Even when only one road is good, as when there is a bridge across a deep and swift river, one still makes a choice between the bridge and the river—though, of course, the choice is not much in doubt. But if one were in a narrow street between two high walls, there would be only one way to go: and this situation represents necessity. We can see from this that it is not the so-called "indifference of equilibrium" that constitutes freedom, but the mere fact of being able to choose among a number of alternatives—even though they are not equally feasible or attractive for the agent.

When the priest asked the bride whether she had not made any promise of marriage to another besides her bridegroom, she answered, "That would be very pretty, indeed." However, when he asked whether she would have the bridegroom for her husband, she uttered her response in such a quiet, resigned voice she could hardly be heard. This occasioned a good deal of laughter from the company. It is my understanding that the tsar arranges marriages between dwarfs in hope of producing more dwarfs for the royal houses.

I had been invited to the new capital city of Saint Petersburg by Tsar Peter to speak on educational reform. I came prepared with a proposal for an academy of science, and I intended to present my ideas clearly, but the tsar had little patience with me. Constantly interrupting my speech, he accused me of treachery one moment and praised my intellect the next. He turned and addressed the giant Nicholas, who stood behind him, or the dwarf Valakoff belched as I paused to begin a new point, and Peter roared with laughter. Instead of discussing education in Russia, I found myself a guest at two weddings in two days.

The first marriage was that of the tsar's niece Anne to Duke Frederick William of Courland, and the second, which I believe was intended as a mockery of the first, was celebrated with exactly the same ceremony and pomp as the marriage of the royal couple. The smallest dwarf led the procession, and he was followed by the bride and bridegroom dressed in expensive finery. Next came the tsar attended by his ministers, princes, boyars, Valakoff, Nicholas, and a bearded female in a Swedish army uniform. Then followed the troop of dwarfs, matched in couples, seventy-two in total. The tsar, in token of his favor, held a garland over the bride's head according to Russian custom. When the ceremony was complete, the company traveled along the Neva by boat to the palace of Prince Menshikov. Dinner was served in the spacious hall where two days before I had dined in honor of the duke's marriage. In the middle of the hall several small tables had been set with miniature dishes for the newlywed couple and the other dwarfs. The normal-sized guests were seated on a balcony surrounding the hall to afford a good view of the festivities. The tsar and his company seemed delighted by every action of the dwarfs. They pointed and howled with laughter at a dwarf with a hump on his back, another with a huge belly, and another with a head of prodigious size. After dinner the dwarfs danced lively Russian dances, except for the bride. She sat silently, her food untouched but for her tears, which fell copiously upon her plate. At a very late hour, Tsar Peter declared the celebration complete and ordered the couple carried to his own bedchamber. This was done by the giant, Nicholas.

A CARDINAL REPORTS ON
NICHOLAS' NUPTIALS

Buh-buh-by order of his holiness, pah-pah-Peter, the ah-ah-ah-Archdeacon of the duh-Drunken s-s-Synod, I gah-give this report buh-buh-before the s-s-synod on the nuh-nuh-nuh / Shit! wedding of Nicholas the giant to lu-lu-Lucia, the lah, lah, large and lah-lah- luscious fah-Finnish giantess on the tah-twentieth dah-day of juh, juh, January in the yah-year s-seventeen fah-fifteen.

Wedding geh-geh-guests were pah-personally invited buh-by myself and three other mah-men who cah-cannot s-s-speak as cah-clearly and eloquently as I. The bah-bah-bridesmen, s-stewards, and wa-waiters were men s-s-so old and dah-decrepit, they could bah-barely s-s-stand or walk. The fah-fah-four running fah-fah-fah / Shit! s-s-somebody fah-fill my cuh-cuh-cup, my throat's as dry as a s-spinster's cuh-cuh-cunt.

Now, where was I? Ra-right, fah-footmen, the fah-fattest fah-fellows in Russia. Nah-Nicholas, duh-duh-dressed as s-s-Samson, wa-was carried to the cha-cha-church on a puh-platform, puh-pulled by a s-s-sled, to the fah-fah-four corners of which wah-were tied as muh-muh-many bears, which, bah-being pah-pah-pricked with goads by dah-dwarfs, made a ha-ha-hell of a nuh-noise.

At the altar of the cha-cha-church, the huge cuh-couple were juh-joined in muh-muh-muh-muh/ Shit! wuh-wedded buh-bliss buh-by a pah-pah-priest a hundred years old. S-s-s-since he ha-has lost bah-both eye-s-s-sight and mah-memory, tah-two candles were ha-held buh-before his eyes, and the wa-words s-shouted into his ears. After the nuh-nuh-knot was ta-ta-tied, the procession moved to the s-s-s-tsar's wah-wah-winter pah-pah-palace for the wedding fah-fah-feast.

Nah-nah-need I report there was mah-much drinking and

dah-dancing? Nah-Nicholas did nah-not dah-dance as a ha-ha-happy bah-bridegroom ought—he was tah-too bah-busy sta-stuffing his mah-mouth with s-s-sausages. Afterward, the tsar and tsarina cah-conducted the bah-bride and groom to the nuh-nuh-nuh—Shit! wedding chamber on the ga-ground fla-fla-floor of the gah-great wah-wooden pyramid of the fah-Four Frigates. The bah-bah-bed was bah-bah bedecked with casks of wine and bah-brandy, and the tsar and tsarina dah-dah-drank a tah-toast tah-to the giant cah-couple bah-before they withdrew and sha-shut the dah-doors. Bah-but mah-members of this sta-sta-stinking s-synod, on edict of our archdeacon, pah-Peter, had dah-drilled holes in the walls of the pyramid s-so we all wah-watched Nah-Nicholas s-s-stuff his s-sausage into her s-s-second mah-mouth. Jah-jah-judging from the ruckus within, we expect a s-s-second gah-generation of gah-giants.

THE MUSEUM OF CURIOSITIES

Please come in and warm yourself at the fire. It's rare to have a visitor of late, so many gone to fight the Turks in the Crimea. Join me in a drink, will you? Forgive me, I'm Nikita Bourgeois, curator by appointment of Catherine II, Empress of Russia. My papa was curator before me, and his papa before him. I stand seven feet and two inches high. By the age of eight, I was taller than my pa. He wasn't born a giant like his parents, and the tsar was displeased. So Grandpa Nicholas was sent away from the palace and made curator of this museum. There he stands in the corner, my grandpa, Nicholas Bourgeois, a favorite of Peter the Great. After his death, Peter ordered him stuffed and enshrined here. His heart, stomach, liver, and kidneys are preserved in those jars beside him. Say, would you like a tour?

The Museum of Curiosities was built in 1713 by order of Tsar Peter. He issued a ukase instructing the provincial governors to seek out and send to St. Petersburg any oddity, human or animal, living or dead, to be found in their territory. There were rewards: so much for a living monster, so much for a dead one, so much for a human being, so much for an animal.

Here are his earliest acquisitions: the body of a man without genitals; an infant with two heads; and here's a five-footed sheep. When I was young, Papa told me Peter frequently walked among his collections, questioning those who were living and examining the preserved corpses. Papa said during the tsar's stay in Holland, he acquired a kit of surgical instruments in order to explore the mysteries of the human body. The physicians at our hospital were ordered to inform the tsar whenever they had a patient to operate upon. He dropped everything to attend the operation and made the surgeons explain as they proceeded. The tsar often used his lancet. None of the physicians dared criticize his methods. Ah, here is an example: kidneys of the merchant Borst's wife, who suffered from dropsy. During surgery, Peter removed from her twenty pounds of water. He was extremely proud of his accomplishment, but when the patient died four days later, he was outraged. He ordered an autopsy in his presence to release him from blame before the physicians. At the funeral, the widower Borst, with tears in his eyes, got to his knees and thanked the tsar for giving his wife four additional days.

Now here's a treasure—the tsar's famous bag of teeth. Oh, yes, he had a passion for dentistry too. The sight of a swollen cheek filled him with joy. Most of the teeth in the bag are those he pulled from servants and courtiers. Shall we move on?

We should start at the beginning. When I became curator, after my papa died, the museum was a mess: clothing strewn about, baskets of trinkets, cobwebs hanging from heads and arms, jars stacked one on top of another, spilling contents onto the floor, and the odor. Whew! Cloves stuck in oranges, that takes care of the smell—Mama taught me that trick. But bless my old pa, he kept a ledger with detailed descriptions. It took me a year to arrange the items according to history.

This cake press is the oldest item in the museum, and it was one of Tsar Peter's favorites. Carved into the wood is the image of Eliza and Mary Chulkhurst of London, England. It's dated 1134. This piece of wood, my friend, is over six hundred years old. The reason Peter acquired it is that, as you can see, the girls are joined together at the hip. I don't know how old they were when they died; I hope they lived a good long life. They were maids of twenty years or so in this likeness, wouldn't you say?

Here's Peter's prize possession: a copy of *Animaux, Monstres et Prodiges,* written by the French surgeon Ambroise Pare. The pages are worn from the Tsar's thumb, and it's old, written in 1575. That's why I keep it wrapped in linen inside this box. The book has drawings made by the surgeon of cases he'd seen: a man with horns, a woman with a nipple on her thigh, a child born without a mouth, a girl with a mass of hair covering her entire body, a man so thin he seems a skeleton, a man with testicles large as melons, a boy with spotted skin. Peter spent hours studying this book, occasionally shouting and slamming his hand upon the table.

Can you guess what this is? Because it's thin, the shape is not as good as it once was. A nose—it's a gold nose. Tycho Brahe, a Dutch astronomer, had this made after his nose was sliced off in a duel. I don't know the exact date, sometime around 1580, according to Papa's notes. My guess is the duel was over a woman—isn't it always a woman? A man who studies the stars must possess a romantic soul.

This handbill comes from Bartholomew Fair, 1615, publicizing the giant William Parsons. The fair is still held in London, England, and monsters come from various lands to display themselves and earn a few kopecks. Peter kept this paper because he intended to go there, but he never got the chance. There on the south wall hangs a painting of Parsons. He looks a merry man.

What I like most about the painting is he appears to be an ordinary man. You see, the horse he straddles has feathering above the hoofs—a draft horse which must have been huge. Horse and rider pose before a Spanish castle—everything in this painting is big.

Another box—a very small box, what could be inside? I'll show you. You lift it out, my hands are too big. Can you believe this tiny tooth came from the mouth of a grown man? Sir Jeffery Hudson, a dwarf at the court of Charles I and Henrietta Maria of England. Much is written about Hudson. He was a spy, a rogue with the ladies, and a lover of drink. Should have been a Russian, eh? The story is that the museum bought the tooth from a captive Turk who'd been a boy when Hudson was jailed in Tunis. His job was to bring water to the prisoners. Hudson often provoked the guards, and one day when the boy was present, a guard hit Hudson with such force this tooth was knocked from his head. The boy waited until the guard's anger had lessened, then took a jug of water to Hudson. He rinsed his mouth and spat out the tooth, which he handed to the boy through the bars.

Here is a piece of art fashioned by Hudson's friend Richard Gibson, also a dwarf. I won't handle small, delicate items, but you may examine it closely. It's a miniature porcelain painting, very popular at French and English courts in the 1600's. What size would his brushes have been? Like mouse whiskers, I guess. I don't know the subject, an English lady most likely. Look at the blush on her cheeks, the curls piled on her head, so tiny. Amazing, quite amazing.

And here's another artist's work. You think the drawing is merely a vase of flowers? Look closer. The petals are formed by words— they're German, so I'll translate for you: "The flowers appear on the earth; the time of the singing of birds is come, and the voice of the turtle is heard in our land." I don't know what the voice of the turtle sounds like. Have you ever heard a turtle make any sound other than a hiss? Well, I like the sound of the words. The phrase is taken from the Bible, but it doesn't sound very religious to me. The artist was Matthew Buchinger. He didn't have legs or arms, but feet on his trunk and something like hands on his shoulders. Word came to Peter that a self-portrait of Buchinger existed, and the Tsar would have it. He sent an agent to Hanover with a great sum of money, but the family denied such a portrait existed.

Oh, I see you bumped into Valakoff. Don't be frightened, he won't bite. Might pinch you, though. I'm fooling with you. Valakoff was Tsar Peter's favorite dwarf and drinking companion. You may know that Peter was the greatest of dwarf collectors. Queen Catherine, whose deceased husband was Peter's only grandson, does not keep dwarfs at court. But I'll wager you've seen more than a few on the streets of Saint Petersburg. Valakoff preceded Peter in death by one year. The tsar oversaw the preservation of the body, my papa said, with tears rolling down his face. And he kept Valakoff in his bedroom, much to the dismay of the tsarina. The very day of the tsar's funeral, Valakoff was delivered to this museum.

That's a beard in the jar. Why is a beard so unusual? It was cut from the chin of a woman! Her name was Heddy and she was a grenadier in the Swedish army of King Charles XII. After her capture at Poltava, she became a favorite of the tsar. Papa said she was a woman of unusual fortitude, and one of the only women to sustain the tsar's attention for more than a few years. The beard is all that remains of her in Russia. She had no use for this museum; I imagine she pictured herself stuffed and standing next to my grandpa. She thundered out of Saint Petersburg in the dark of night, riding the tsar's black stallion, followed by a roan mare bearing Heddy's two robust royal children. The tsar always appreciated a lusty joke. This is how he found the beard: Heddy had pulled back the covers on her bed, laid her nightgown on the sheet as if a body filled it, and set the shorn beard upon the gown where her thighs would meet. He could've sent soldiers after her; I guess her joke won her freedom.

I have one son, Stepan, who lives with my sister in Chesme. Here's a letter from his mama which I carry next to my heart. She sent it after her last visit, five years ago. I'd been taken ill and was much improved by her company. She wrote:

I rejoice that you have been healed by my little pillows, and if my caress facilitates your health, then you will never be sick. Darling, you have no fault before me; stretch out your great arms, I shall embrace you. Being kind, as you are, you have no cause to change yourself. I am extraordinarily contented with you and hour by hour adore you on par with the love that will be with you irrevocably. Dearest, dear darling, you are born for me, and our feelings are essentially the same; your soul when it flies toward me, then it is met midway en route from my side.

Why certainly, she's an educated woman. She is Catherine II, Empress of Russia. When we were lovers, I wished to be better for her, but she preferred me as I was. I know she has had many lovers since, and I know people say she chose me thinking all my parts were of giant size. Have you seen our empress? Her birth name is Sophie, that's what I call her. Sophie's figure is noble, her walk majestic, every feature proclaims her superior character. Her neck is lofty and her head finely shaped. Her forehead is large and open and her mouth is sweetly fresh. Her hair is chestnut colored and uncommonly fine, her skin is of dazzling whiteness and her eyes are hazel, but in the sunlight they have a bluish tint. Our son, Stepan, has her eyes. Her voice is like chiming bells, but can change quickly when matters of business arise.

I lost my heart to her after the coup, when she rode into Saint Petersburg on a white stallion. She wore the uniform of a colonel of the Preobrazhenski Guard, the same rank Peter the Great held. Her favorite attire is the uniform; she wears it always on horseback, and her skill in managing horses is remarkable. You would be amazed at the way she blends an ease of behavior with the dignity of her rank, making herself known with the meanest of her subjects, yet never losing a speck of her authority. She inspires at once both respect and affection. She loves to talk and it's impossible to follow her, she is so quick, so full of fire and spirit.

Stepan was born eight years after the birth of the empress's heir, Paul Petrovich. Stepan was secretly delivered and taken to my sister's home by courtiers. He's ten years of age now, a strong and bold boy who is tall, but not uncommonly so, and is as bright and witty as his mama.

Sophie once told me she thought of herself as following in the footprints of Peter the Great. She said she owed the crown to him because she would not have become sovereign without the changes he made. You see, Peter abolished the order of succession by seniority through the male line.

Think of what a heavy responsiblility it must be to rule an empire. I cannot say I'm sorry to have loved and lost her. I knew from the start I was a diversion, though a pleasurable diversion. Men in power would be dangerous lovers. Sophie told me she was haunted by the specter of a lover who would use her to gain political dominance. Her dedication to the Russian people left her exhausted and lonely, and she found some comfort in my arms. She gave me Stepan; what greater gift can a woman give?

Although she does not realize it, Sophie put the idea in my head of going to America. She speaks often of their revolution. She said, "Rather than have granted America her independence as my brother monarch King George has done, I would have fired a pistol at my own head."

I'd like to take Stepan to America. I don't know if I could earn a living there. This is the only occupation I've held. Would I be able to get along with American people? I admire their spirit, but these curiosities have been my people for years. They've given up their secrets to me. I've passed countless hours imagining the life each object represents, my mind a mirror reflecting their passions and sensibilities. They speak to me through their afflictions; "I am special, a miracle to behold, gaze upon me and remember my endurance."

Visit a graveyard and what do you see? Stone slabs with a name chiseled there, and perhaps a short sentiment. Does anything set them apart from their comrades beneath the earth? I'll miss my friends, but I wish Stepan to live in a country where he's not known as the bastard son of a giant and the Little Mother, a country where there are neither kings nor queens.

THE GREATEST SHOW ON EARTH

✧

THE PROFESSOR

P. T. Barnum, the Shakespeare of Advertising, having conquered New York City, is currently on a steamer bound for England with his latest prodigy, the twenty-five-inch general, Tom Thumb. The museum has been left in my charge during his absence. You can call me "the Professor," the moniker Mr. Barnum bestowed on me. My specialty is edification of the public on the scientific nature of our numerous exhibits, relics, and rare curiosities—hundreds of them packed into five stories of glorious mayhem. The man is a genius. How long did you wait in line? Did you notice the horsecars and stagecoaches tail-to-tail along Broadway and Ann?

Before Barnum bought this building from the Scudders, it was like a mausoleum, and I felt as dusty and moldy as its stuffed penguins. I began working for Mr. Scudder in 1811, one year after he purchased the Tammany Museum collection and enlarged it by acquiring numerous oddities from sea captains and adventurers.

I was a young man when first I roamed the halls of Tammany, intrigued by the "curiosities" assembled there. I'd come up from New Orleans as soon as I was old enough to break free, with Aunt Minnie's aid. I was born to parents of wealth and station—born with a hairy tail protruding three inches from the base of my spine. Whenever Mother laid eyes on me, she got the vapors, so Father moved Minnie into our home.

Polite society hides disgraceful deformities. Behind the locked door of my nursery, Minnie taught me to read and write, and as shelves were added to my room my world widened. Father walled in a piece of land adjacent to my room where a garden was planted, accessible only through the French doors of my prison. That's where my love of science began, with the heavy, fragrant flowers nodding their heads in the sun, the ambitious, prolific greenery that conquered the garden walls. Such an amazing variety of life the garden hid in its moist and muggy corners: iridescent lizards, blue-black beetles, walking sticks, bumblebees; birds whose calls I learned to distinguish and imitate. In the evenings, when the garden was dark, I'd turn to my books and imagine myself in New York City in wintertime. I'd skate on a frozen pond or sled down a hill, bells jingling on carriages, voices rising in harmony, caroling the season.

When I finally arrived here, however my tail was tucked 'tween my legs—literally and figuratively. For all her gumption, Aunt Minnie is still a southern lady, and consequently the problem of dealing with my "condition" in the outside world was not discussed prior to my trip. Along with the gold pieces, she gave me my first real suit of clothing and strips of cotton bandage, "to allow for a proper fit."

No book could have prepared me for the exhilarating chaos of New York City; the assault on my senses: machinery that belched, hissed, gouged the future into life—roads, schools, hospitals, industries—the possessed pace made me dizzy with excitement and exhaustion. By chance, I wandered into the Tammany Museum. I found contentment in the silent, three-dimensional exhibits: waxworks of villains and heroes; miniature models of Dublin, Paris, Jerusalem; an art gallery; dozens upon dozens of preserved reptiles, insects, mammals, and birds. One day as I stood before a stuffed goldfinch and imitated its call, Mr. Scudder happened by and paused to listen. He inquired on the species of the bird, which I related in Latin and expounded on its habitat and migratory patterns. After doing the same with each bird exhibit Scudder pointed out, I was hired as a guide.

Nineteen years later, we moved to this building, which was constructed over the old Spring Garden amusement park on the corner of Broadway and Ann. Scudder promptly added a living exhibits collection: an orangutan, an anaconda, an alligator, Apollo the card-playing dog, and Caroline Clarke, a twenty-year-old midget. By then, the city was bursting at its seams: omnibus, hack, horseless carriages flying through the streets, towering shops, crowded cellars, hotels, restaurants, coffeehouses, oyster saloons; the appalling misery and squalor of the Five Points district, where crime, drunkenness, and prostitution openly flourished. And people kept coming by the thousands. Is it any wonder I clung to the confines of the museum? Or that the museum prospered? Places of decent entertainment were few and far between.

Barnum's visits started three years ago. He was a frequent patron and hard to ignore considering his stature and presence; his expression was consistently like a man who'd just partaken of an excellent meal. He constantly stopped before the exhibit's glass fronts to check his appearance, adjust the tip of his hat, fluff his scarf. When he conversed with me, he enunciated well with a polished delivery. I was surprised to learn from Scudder that this man was P. T. Barnum, the same man who had pulled off two of the greatest entertainment hoaxes in the city. I'd followed the unfolding sagas in the press. The first involved Joice Heth, a 161-year-old former slave, purported to have been George Washington's nurse. After her death, an autopsy revealed her to be no more than 80 years of age. Newspaper readers were subsequently informed that Joice's anonymous exhibitors had rehearsed her in the famous "cherry tree" story and other Washington anecdotes, and had frequently been at pains to keep her from cursing. Her faked bill of sale was aged in tobacco water and needed redoing by the time the exhibition reached New York. Someone had discovered Virginia was referred to as a "state" in what was supposed to be a 1727 document.

The second hoax was the Feejee Mermaid, a wonder Barnum had purchased from a sea captain out of Boston who had purchased it from a Japanese sailor. I went to view the mermaid after reading a report in *Gentlemen's Magazine*. To my experienced eye, it was obvious the mermaid was the top half of a monkey sewn artfully to the bottom of a fish. "The naturalist" Barnum had hired to exhibit the mermaid was convinced of her authenticity, I'm certain.

When Barnum bought the museum, he offered me a job at twice the pay, assuring me I was "just the thing," convincing as a professor with my white hair and lean figure. If he hadn't made the offer, I would have asked to stay without recompense; this was the only life I could tolerate, and I confess to being caught up in his excitement.

The Barnum touch transformed this mausoleum into a perpetual carnival. He converted the empty roof into a garden ice cream parlor surrounded by pots of flowers and cedar trees. He sought out acts of greater variety, merriment, and drama. The transient attractions of the museum were constantly diversified—automatons, jugglers, ventriloquists, living statuary, tableaux, gypsies, fat boys, giants, dwarfs, a man monkey named Zip, rope-dancers, instrumental music, English Punch-and-Judy shows, Italian fantoccini, American Indians. He searched for new attractions with the fervor of a knight in quest of the Holy Grail.

To this day, he doesn't know of my condition. I prefer my role of Professor to that of Missing Link. I'd sooner cut my throat than return to a cage, no matter how gilded the bars.

PUNCH

11 March 1844, London: Benjamin Robert Haydon, painter, age 60, was found dead this morning in his studio by his daughter, Mrs. Green. Mr. Haydon was currently showing his "Banishment of Aristedes" at the Egyptian Hall. Mrs. Green reported that Haydon had suffered much from poverty and had twice been jailed for debt. He had hoped to profit from his exhibit, but appearing at the same time in the Egyptian Hall was the American midget, General Tom Thumb. After one week of showing, Mr. P. T. Barnum, (Thumb's sponsor) had receipts of three thousand pounds while Haydon's receipts amounted to thirty-five pounds. The following entry from Haydon's journal was noted by the Constable: "They rush by the thousands to see Tom Thumb. They push, oh! and ah! They see my

bills, my boards, my caravans and don't read them. Their eyes are open, but their sense is shut. It is an insanity, a rabies, a madness, a furor, a dream. I would not have believed it of the English people." This recorded, Mr. Haydon slashed his throat with a razor and then shot himself in the head with a pistol.

VICTORIA'S DIARY

23 March 1844

After dinner we saw the greatest curiosity I, or indeed anybody, ever saw, viz: a little dwarf, only 25 inches high & 15 lbs in weight. No description can give an idea of this little creature, whose name was Charles Stratton, born they say in '32, which makes him 12 years old. He is American, & gave us his card, with Gen. Tom Thumb written on it. He made the funniest little bow, putting out his hand & saying: "much obliged Ma'am." One cannot help feeling very sorry for the poor little thing & wishing he could be properly cared for, for the people who show him off tease him a good deal, I should think. He was made to imitate Napoleon & do all sorts of tricks, finally backing the whole way out of the gallery.

THE NEW ROYALTY

June 21 1847
London, England

My Dear Wife,

Three years have passed and it's time to come home! General Tom Thumb left America a diffident, uncultivated little boy, and he will return an educated, accomplished little man. He went abroad poor and he will come home rich. Great Scot, the crowned heads of Europe vied for our company. Oh, you'd have been proud of me, my dear, the way I orchestrated my campaign from the get-go by enlisting the Queen of England to play upon the snobbery of my British hosts. Reading in the British press of Victoria's predilection for oddities, I urged Edward Everett, u.s. Minister to the Court of St. James, to arrange an introduction of the General. The royal command was delivered a few days later, and the Queen was enraptured by our Tom.

When we arrived at Buckingham Palace, we were told how to conduct ourselves before the Queen; above all else we could not speak to or answer Victoria directly, but through the Lord-in-Waiting. That's not the end of it—we were to retire backwards when the audience was over. Tom was superb; let me relate the events that you may enjoy a laugh. We were guided through a long, gilded corridor lit with brilliant chandeliers, then up a spacious flight of stairs into the royal picture gallery where sat young Queen Victoria, Prince Albert, and two dozen members of the nobility dressed in the highest fashion. Tom, looking like a wax doll gifted with the power of locomotion, advanced with a firm step, bowed, and chirped, "Good evening, ladies and gentlemen!" The Queen rose from her chair, took Tom's hand, and led him through the picture gallery, which Tom assured the Queen was "first-rate." After an hour or so of his songs, dances, and imitations, we began our backward exit. You know how long my legs are—whenever the General found he was losing ground, he turned around and ran a few steps, then resumed the position of backing out, then turned around and ran, and so continued to alternate his methods of getting to the door, until the gallery fairly rang with the merriment of royal spectators. It was really one of the richest scenes I ever saw; running, under the circumstances, was an offense sufficiently heinous to excite the indignation of the Queen's favorite poodledog, and he vented his displeasure by barking so sharply as to startle the General from his propriety. He, however, recovered immediately, and with his little cane commenced an attack on the poodle, and a funny fight ensued, which renewed and increased the merriment of the royal party.

Twice more we were invited to the palace, and countless invitations came from royals throughout London. The London publication *Punch* dubbed Tom "Pet of the Palace." Youngsters danced "The General Tom Thumb Polka," and the music halls played songs dedicated to him. When we exhibited at London's Egyptian Hall, tickets were sold out for every performance; the Duke of Wellington attended several times. The Queen Dowager Adelaide sent Tom a miniature gold watch made especially for him, and he has been showered with many wonderful trinkets. So numerous were our visits to royalty, I found it necessary to expend nearly one hundred pounds on a court costume for Tom. But what really killed the public dead was the coach I ordered: painted bright blue and decorated with a coat of arms and the motto "Go Ahead." It measures twenty inches high by eleven inches wide. The interior is lined in silk and the windows are plate glass. It is drawn by two grayhounds, and children costumed in liveries and wigs walk alongside.

Imagine, my dear, your humble husband from Connecticut has kept company with Queen Victoria at Buckingham Palace and the Queen Dowager at Marlborough House. I have presented the General to the Queen of the Belgians, Prince Albert, and the Duchess of Kent. The Russian Tsar Nicholas took Tom in his arms and invited him to Saint Petersburg. We attended the bullfights in Spain with Queen Isabella, and in Brussels, we were entertained with a party given by King Leopold. I must say that if I was not a remarkably modest man, I should probably brag a little, and say that I had done what no American has ever before accomplished; but being remarkably modest, I shall say nothing, but wait for any other American to appear who has visited the crowned heads of the universe and on each occasion been received with smiles, cordiality, sociability, and royal favor.

I trust the Museum is prospering under the Professor's watchful eye. I am bringing home a marvelous new attraction, a family of British albinos whom I have dubbed The Night People.

ZIP AND THE LUCASIE FAMILY

Boss call em Night People, that crazy lily white family wif the pink eyes. This is what the man says when they's up on stage, that they's a separate race, these night peoples, and they lives deep down in the earth and onliest come out at nighttime when the light don't hurt they eyes. Shit, that family is darkies, like me, they just bleached out. Seen it before when I was a boy down in Georgia, leastways sumptin like it, onliest was a crawdaddy, hidin neath a pile a rocks in the river. Its shell was so white, I seen clean through it and its eyes was pink too, and I seen inside the eye right to its innards.

I know they was darkies cause the first time I seen em, Boss brought em round to my cage, and they get all het up, grinnin big lip grins and white nappy hair stickin out like big ole clouds, and the man jabbers some Afreecan nonsense at me. Course, I don't answer cause I'm not spose to talk to no one, if I do, I lose my job; I just growl and hoot at em and they jump back quick. Take a gander at this paper what peoples buy on me. Says I was caught by mens searchin for gorilla whilst explorin the River Gambia and fell in wif a race of beins never before discovered, that was six of us in a perfectly nude state, and we was rovin round the trees like oran-outangs. Says they capture three, but I was the onliest survivor, and that when I come here my natural position was on all fours, that I eats just raw meat, sweet apples, oranges, and nuts, but now I eats bread and cake and things. That picture, don't it make you laugh; I wears that wooly suit when I'm in the cage, the Man Monkey, it says. Drew my arms extry long, and was the Boss idea to grow my nails and shave my hade ceptin the topknot. You ever see a pointier noggin? Mama die birthin me, took too long; Granmammy says that why my hade look this way.

Nobody know where I come from, ceptin my sister, Lucille, and

the Boss, and he don't know the half of it, don't care to know neither. Just like talkin, I lose my job, and it's the bestest job I ever had.
I know the night peoples Afreecan talk cause my granmammy talk
that stuff; she weren't my real granmammy, but she was the oldest
slave on the place and we all call her granmammy, cause her job was
to look after and cook for the darkie chillrun whilst they parents was
at wuk in the fields. She had a big ole horn she blow at eatin time.
Marster told her she better fix plenty t'eat and have it ready on time.
There was a long trough that went cross the yard what we et outta,
vegetables and corn bread wif pot-likker over it.

When I was bout ten years old, Daddy run wif me and Lucille,
and we end up in New Jersey. Got wuk pickin for a farmer who
didn't ask for no papers. Daddy die and then the farmer die too
and his wife didn't want no troubles from government mens pokin
round after the funeral, so Lucille and I hit the road. Seem like this
city was a good place to come, so many peoples, not likely to care
bout a pointy-head darkie and a skinny darkie girl. We was onliest
here a few days when Boss found me on the street, and we made a
deal. And alls I got to do is dress in that monkey suit, make monkey noises, bare my teefs, jump and whirl round, and peoples
gather to look at me, and I gets to watch their faces, hear em gasp
or laugh when I cut up. Might think it be dull in that cage alla the
time, but there's a parade passin by ever day.

Boss bring those white darkies up to my cage when they get to
actin up bad, and he tells em he'll lock the three of em in wif me
and I'll chew their fingers off. They's a man and his wife and a son
bout ten year old. Oh, they can act real fancified, wif that England
talk. But they can make a heap of dissatification round here; they's
crazy. I know the story, cause my hobby's listenin—when you
cain't talk, what else you got to do but watch and listen? The
daddy was born in Afreeca. The peoples of the tribe was scared
half out of their skins when that boy was born, and they want to
kill him straight off. But his daddy was the chief of the tribe, so

129

nobody dare hurt that baby. Few years later, in the next village, the chief's sister, who was married to nother chief, birthed a baby girl lookin the same way. So they was promised to one nother and married soon as they was wean from the teats. The pair of em was close to growed when an English ship came round those parts, and them daddies got their hades together and sold off those two chill-run. When they get to England, a man like Boss bought em, taught em to speak English, play the fiddle and the piani, and took em round to drinkin houses to entertain. By the time the Boss go over there, they'd had themselves that boy, that little white devil.

They looks like haints, and Boss dress em in black so's they seem even whiter. The museum folk, those of us who lives here, was scared of em when they come here. Specially after the tales the midgit told bout what happen on the ship. That family was usta stayin up all night long in the drinkin houses and sleepin durin the day, cause they cain't stands the sun. Well, that family does enjoy the juice of barleycorn, and it bring out the demons in em. The little General loves younguns, and struck up a shinin to that boy on the first day. Whilst the General was sleepin that night, the boy snuck into his room, tied him up wif a rope, stuff a sock in his mouf, and tote him to nother room where this family was sleepin wif their baby in a cra-dle. He strip the General nekked, did the same deviltry to that baby, and switch em, so's when Boss go to wake the General, there was a yowlin baby in the General's robe, and Lord only know what them parents thought findin the General in that cradle.

After that, Boss lock em in at nights, but they sing and whoop all night, so's the captain complain, and Boss says he set em out in a side boat iffin they didn't git civilized. Ever since then, the haints sneer and stick out their tongues ever time the General walk by.

130

JOHN CAMERON, LITHOGRAPHER

I'd made up my mind to despise the little "General" if I chanced to meet him, especially after preparing the lithograph from Nat Currier's drawing. In the large, center square, he's dressed in a suit and vest, standing on a chair which emphasizes his smallness. In the other poses bordering the square, he's dressed as the various roles he portrays in his act: a gladiator, an American Tar, Villikins, Napoleon. Brother, in one pose he's "My Mary Ann." The lettering reads: The Original General Tom Thumb, The Smallest Man Alive. 22 Years Old 33 Inches High.

The process of changing an artist's drawing into a finished lithograph is long and arduous. Most lithographers complain that it's hard on the back, lifting the stones, graining the surface, hours and hours with the crayons, brushes, and pads rendering the artist's work onto stone, bathing the stones in gum and acids, pressing, inking, and rolling. As you can see, my back is suited to my labor. With each step of the process, over and over again, I'd see Thumb's perfect tiny body, his charming little smile, dressed in those ridiculous costumes, and I felt ashamed for him and angry that people pay money to look at him, angry because I was sure he believed they loved him. Why, I haven't the slightest doubt people would pay to see "The Man With The Largest Hump," or "The Greatest Clubbed Foot," or "The Worst Harelip." Those masses that flock to Barnum's American Museum gawk and giggle at the monkey man, the fat woman, the giants, the dwarfs, those whom nature has taken to the extreme, then return to their homes shaking their heads and clucking, "There but for the grace of God go you and I."

I earn a good wage because I'm the best lithographer in New York City. My prints hang in barbershops, firehouses, barrooms, the homes of rich and poor alike. My name's not on them, only "Currier & Ives," but each time I see one tacked to a wall, or pinned to the side of a pushcart, I feel a sense of pride and accomplishment. Nobody knows nor cares that the print was produced by a hunchback.

The General didn't know either when he came to the factory. He walked in the front door with a print of his lithograph and asked to see the man who made it. I was up on the second floor working a stone, but I could hear his voice, thin and piercing. Old Jones up front told him Mr. Currier had done the print and he should go to the Nassau Street shop, but Thumb said he wanted to meet the lithographer. Jones sent him upstairs—it took him a long time to climb them—and reaching the top, he squeaked: "Mr. Cameron, Mr. Cameron, Sir!"

I thought he'd come to complain, so I curled my lip into a sneer and scowled my brow. People can't see my expression unless I turn my head to the side, and then they see only half of it. When Thumb stepped up to me, I realized he was looking straight into my snarling face. His eyes were round and watery, like a spaniel's. Undaunted, he took my hand and shook it vigorously between both of his. "First-rate, Mr. Cameron, first-rate," he said, then asked if I would be so kind as to show him how the print was made.

I walked to the table where an unprepared stone lay, and started explaining the process when he tugged on my trouser leg. "Would you give me a lift, friend?" This was an awkward moment for me; I don't care for touching and I can't abide being touched. But he said it as one would say, "Would you pass the salt?"

When I finished my explanation, and had answered his many questions, he took a flask from his vest and invited me to join him in a spot. A man after my own heart. Well, I'll tell you, the afternoon slipped away as we discovered our similarities. We were both natives of Connecticut, both members of the Masonic Order, and our fathers were carpenters. The General's father had built an apartment for him with furniture that fit his size and doorknobs he could reach.

It occurred to me then, seeing how large my cup was in his hands, that every object in my daily life would be unwieldy for the General. He commented on how fortunate it was for him to have met Mr. Barnum, otherwise he'd have been dependent on his parents for all his days. He wouldn't have seen the world capitals, met kings and queens, or have met "this lady." He took a photograph from his pocket and asked if he might engage my services to produce a lithograph of Miss Lavinia Warren.

MISS LAVINNY'S PUPIL

It's been an awful long time since Miss Lavinny left Middleboro School, nearly two whole years. She was the best teacher I ever had. She took her schooling here, and she was such a smart girl, they made her a teacher when she was sixteen.

Our teacher now is Miss Adler. When we came into school on the first day in September, we all just stared at her. She looked so big sitting behind the desk! She's even got big hair—it's red and keeps popping out of her bun every which way. Her eyes are light blue and small, and there's a pink circle underneath them. When she walks by me, I smell lye soap. She's got a big voice too; oh, she's not mean, she can hardly control the little boys.

Miss Lavinny looks like a living doll, like the costly dolls in Mama's catalog. James Winder is the smallest and youngest boy in school and he's taller than Miss Lavinny. When she talked, we had to be real quiet so we could hear her. When it's quiet, nobody acts up. Miss Lavinny has dark, shiny hair, braided on both sides and wrapped around her head. Her eyes are like two black buttons, and she smells like vanilla. She wore crystal bobs in her ears and carried a lace handkerchief in the sleeve of her dress. There was a sled outside her door, and we'd take turns pulling her to and from school. If the snow was deep, David Thompson or another older boy carried her into the schoolhouse.

She's famous now! She lives in New York City, where she works for P. T. Barnum at the American Museum, and she just got married to the famous General Tom Thumb. Oh, my goodness, I have it in my lunch pail! Here, it's the front page of the *New York Times*—that's Miss Lavinny's wedding picture. It says the day after the wedding, President Lincoln invited them to the White House. Look where I'm pointing, that's a quote from the General. I can read it aloud:

"After receiving the congratulations of all present, the President took our hands and led us to the sofa. He lifted me up and sat me at his left hand, while Mrs. Lincoln did the same for Lavinia, placing her at her right. Tad, their son, stood beside his mother and, after a moment said, 'Mother, isn't it funny that Father is so tall and Mr. and Mrs. Stratton are so little?' The President replied, 'My boy, it is because Dame Nature sometimes delights in doing funny things; you need not seek for any other reason, for here you have the long and the short of it.'"

MATHEW BRADY

The New York Excelsior Band—I've nearly forgotten how a waltz can lift the soul. There must be a thousand people dancing in the street. Look—up there, on the balcony, the miniature bride and groom are waving their good night. I took more than a dozen photographs of the General and Lavinia today, and each one was perfect. Everything was perfect. The soft, bright candlelight, the sweet scent of gardenias, the organ's muted tones, the intricate lace of the bridal gown, the cream of New York society dressed to the nines, their eyes fixed with bemused adoration on the tiny couple, the ornate wedding cake, the glitter of gifts, a set of Chinese fire screens from President and Mrs. Lincoln.

Forgive me, I do believe I'm ranting. I've just yesterday returned from Fredericksburg and have not quite adjusted to civilian life. Tom and Lavinia's wedding is the first festive occasion I've photographed in over a year. My studio's on Broadway, across the street from Barnum's Museum. Its galleries still display the photographs I took for my book, *The Gallery of Illustrious Americans*: presidents, senators, tycoons, writers, actors, scientists, and religious leaders. I cajoled and hounded them to pose. Barnum's people, on the other hand, came to me; I photograph them and they sell the photographs at their exhibitions.

I often ask myself why I left my studio, my wife, and a thriving business to follow the war with my cameras. I'm not paid, and when it is over, I'll be lucky to have two cents to rub together. I can only describe the destiny that overruled me by saying that, like Euphorion, I felt I had to go. A spirit in my feet said, "Go," and I went. I have not, for a moment, regretted my decision.

I was reminded of Barnum's "Wonders" as I focused on the faces of the Union soldiers at Fredericksburg. They were preparing to cross the pontoon bridges over the Rappahannock river. On the other side, behind a stone wall, crouched Lee's sharpshooters. The faces of both the wonders and the soldiers wore a look of resigned anonymity. In battle of any sort, physical or emotional, fighters lose their individual identity, an inevitable casualty. With the camera, by God, I can stop time. I can give them presence and immortality.

But tonight, everyone's smiling, grateful for a fairy tale in the midst of this horrible chapter in history. Mr. Barnum hired me to photograph the wedding; he knew I was financially strapped, and he offered me much more than I needed to cover my expenses. He's also been most generous in his contributions to the Union cause.

THE AMERICAN MUSEUM FIRE, NOV. 1865

THE FIREMAN

All them freaks is saved, but we had a divel of a time with the giant gal. On me mother's grave, I swear, that gal stands eight feet tall and weighs four hundred pounds. Only doors in the buildin that weren't aflame were too small for her to fit through, and the stairs woulda broke under her even if she coulda got to them. As if things weren't bad enough, wasn't a spare man, pump, or horse that wasn't fightin a fire elsewheres. Ya see, a band of Confederate agents, bent on doin damage cause our Union boys was thumpin them down South, slipped into the city and began settin fires: nineteen hotels, the Winter Garden, Niblo's Garden, ships on the North River, and this here Barnum Museum. Some snake of a reb flung a glass bomb on the grand staircase and the place went up like a tinder box. Now, this is for sure, he picked his target. Mr. Barnum ain't shy about his opinions; many's the time he spoke out against "southern slaveholders and their Copperhead sympathizers in the north." He paid for volunteers to serve in the Union army. And in that museum, he puts on dramas of a patriotic nature about war heroes. The wife and I saw one about the drummer boy, Robert Hendershot, a wee lad whose drum was shattered by a Confederate shell while crossin the Rappahannock River. Brought a tear to the wife's eye, I don't mind sayin.

We dinna think we could rescue the giant gal; we could see her, wailin and sweatin inside her room, and at her side was a man that looked like a walkin skeleton. We motioned for him to come out, but that skinny feller wouldn't leave her, just kept pattin her hand and tryin to comfort her with words that couldn't be heard over the cracklin flames and fallin timbers. Then, a group of the freaks pointed out a loft derrick nearby, and me and the men set it up alongside the buildin with a strong tackle. We used our axes to break a big hole in the wall by the gal's room. Took four of us to fasten that tackle around her, what with her flailin about, scared out of her wits. While eighteen men held the other end of the line, we swung her out and lowered her down to the street where crowds were clappin their hands and whistlin. I picked up the skinny feller who'd collapsed on the floor—he was light as a feather—and carried him outside, where he shortly recovered.

ALTA

New York, March 27, 1867

Dear Readers,

Now that Barnum is running for Congress, anything connected with him is imbued with a new interest. Therefore I went to his Museum yesterday, along with the other children. There is little or nothing in the place worth seeing, and yet how it draws! It was crammed with both sexes and all ages. One could keep on going up stairs from floor to floor, and still find scarcely room to turn. There are numerous trifling attractions there, but if there was one grand, absorbing feature, I failed to find it. Barnum's Museum is one vast peanut stand now, with a few cases of dried frogs and other wonders scattered here and there, to give variety to the thing.

There are some cages of ferocious lions and other wild beasts, but they sleep all the time. And also an automatic card writer; but something about it is broken, and it don't go now. Also, a good many bugs, with pins stuck through them; but the people do not seem to enjoy bugs any more. In some large glass cases are some atrocious waxen images, done in the very worst style of the art. Queen Victoria is dressed in faded red velvet and glass jewelry and has a bloated countenance and a drunken leer in her eye that remind one of convivial Mary Holt, when she used to come in from a spree to get her ticket for the County Jail. And that accursed eye-sore to me, Tom Thumb's wedding party, which airs its smirking imbecility in every photograph album in America, is not only set forth here in ghastly wax, but repeated! Why does not some philanthropist burn the Museum again?

Mark Twain

ISAAC SPRAGUE, THE HUMAN SKELETON

Mr. Barnum rebuilt his museum after the fire, but my dear friend, the giantess Anna Swan did not stay. She bid a tearful good-bye to me and my wife and my boys, and she boarded a ship for England with her new manager. We miss her greatly, as she had a true liking for people and people truly liked her.

She was only seventeen when she came to the museum, so Mr. Barnum placed her in the care of little Lavinia Warren, who was formerly a teacher. He also paired them onstage to accentuate their differences. When I think of those days, I get a picture of them after the shows, when the museum closed its doors and everyone retired to their rooms. I'd change out of my costume, which is short pants and a vest so customers can see my bones, into a wool sweater and flannel trousers. I get extremely cold because of my lack of fat. I'd walk to the kitchen for a late meal and pass by Anna and Lavinia's room. Their door was always open, as most doors at the museum were until midnight, and they'd invite me in with a question: "How did it go for you today?" "Has Jackie's cough improved?" "Did the woman with the hat that looked like a bird nesting in her hair come to your show? I could barely keep a straight face!"

All the while they talked, one would be doing up the other's hair for bed. You know how women make curls and tie strips of cloth around them? Well, it was a process to marvel at with those two ladies. When Anna put up Lavinia's hair, Lavinia would stand on Anna's dressing table, and Anna would wrap strands of hair around her little finger, then thread a strip of cloth through the curl. She'd be talking along, pause and say, "Tie," and Lavinia's tiny fingers would find the ends and knot them together. When it was Anna's turn, she'd sit on the floor and Lavinia would wrap Anna's hair around her wrist and tie off the curls with a strip big as her arm; she'd utter a little grunt as she tied each knot. That's how I remember them most fondly.

After Lavinia married the General and left the museum, Anna was lonesome. She came from a family of thirteen children in Nova Scotia, and she was a long way from home. You should ask my wife about Anna; they became thicker than thieves. Anna doted on our boys; she could pick them up and toss them around, make them squeal with delight. Soon Anna will have her own babe to cuddle. I received this letter yesterday.

November 16, 1871

Hello Isaac and Ruth,

First off, I miss you and send hugs and kisses to you and the boys. How I wish you could have been here for my wedding. Since I know Ruth will want all the details, I'll describe as much as modesty will allow. The ceremony took place in Saint Martin's in the Field, one of London's oldest and most beautiful churches (with a wide aisle!). My gown was made from white satin, decorated with orange blossoms. Ruth, it took one hundred yards and was trimmed with fifty yards of lace. Do you remember Lavinia's precious little gown? My wedding ring, a gift from Queen Victoria, is a glittering cluster of diamonds. She didn't forget Martin either. She presented him with an engraved watch that chimes on the hour. The church was filled with guests—Martin's and my family took up the first two rows. Did I tell you he has ten brothers and sisters? He looked so dashing in his captain's uniform from the Fifth Kentucky Infantry.

Four days after the wedding, we gave a private levee for the Prince of Wales. Also present were Grand Duke Vladimir of

Russia and Prince John of Luxembourg. In the past few months, we've appeared at many London theaters and in the grand concert hall of the Crystal Palace. If someone had told me when I was a girl mending my father's nets in New Anna that one day I would be the toast of London, a guest in royal houses, I'd sooner believe I could fly. When Lavinia moved to Connecticut and assured me (you know how she says things with such authority, you can't doubt her word) that the right man would come my way, I tried to imagine him, but my heart wouldn't let me. Now, here I am, deeply in love, a married lady. And he is seventy pounds heavier than me! This won't be the case for much longer—I am going to be a mother! After the baby is born and we're able to travel, we plan on returning to New York. In the meanwhile, won't you come over? Isaac, you can swim the Channel (ha-ha).

All My Love, Mrs. Martin Van Buren Bates

That's her joke. My greatest pleasure as a boy was swimming in the pond behind our house. When I was twelve years old, I started losing weight—fast. My parents blamed it on too much swimming, but after they forbade my swims and I still kept losing, they took me to several prominent physicians. Not a one of them could come up with a cause for my condition. However, they all agreed I'd continue to lose my flesh until I lost the use of my limbs, but I might live to be an old man.

During my sixteenth year, I remained steady at sixty pounds. I learned the shoemaking trade and worked in a shop until I was nineteen, at which time I purchased a small grocery. Then my condition took a turn for the worse; I started losing muscle as well as flesh and had to give up the store. The following year, my brother Aaron and I went to a circus that had stopped in Bridgewater. Aaron, who was a born tease, asked the doorkeeper if there was anyone inside as fat as me or with arms as big as mine. The man felt my arm, smiled, and let us in free of charge. When we came out, the circus manager was waiting for me with a job proposition, and I accepted.

One year later, Ruth accepted my proposition, proposal I should say. She worked in the circus cook house, and she'd give me extra helpings of everything, supposing I starved myself to be so thin. You know what they say about the way to a man's heart. Now she scolds me about eating enough for three people. No matter how much I eat, I stay right near fifty-five pounds.

After Timothy was born, we decided to take a shot at New York and paid a call on Mr. Barnum, who hired me straight off. Onstage, he paired me with a lady who weighed over six hundred pounds. I heard Mr. Barnum say fat ladies caused him nothing but grief because they were so helpless. During my lecture, I'd put up my fists and offer a thousand dollars to any man my size and weight that I could not whip. This always got a good laugh.

There was another fire at the museum in March of 1868. Mr. Barnum was sixty years old and took this as a sign to retire. Ruth and I went back to the North American Circus, but we may be moving once again. Recently I heard that the old humbug is talking about taking his museum on the road.

ZIP'S EULOGY

Boss had ideas bout when his time come. He pass on last year, April '91. Member the first time he got to feelin bad was when the museum burnt down a second time. Boss retire awhile, and alla us freaks scatter for jobs elsewheres. Twernt too hard to find cause wif Boss' success, ever big city in the country open a museum. None fine as Boss run.

Few years later, Boss decide to put a new show together and he call it P. T. Barnum's Museum, Menagerie And Circus, and we open in Brooklyn under canvas tents. Boss bill it as seven exhibits in one, cause there was the museum, menagerie, circus, a hippodrome, a caravan, I forgit what else. After one week, we took down them tents, load ever beast in cages, all the humans in wagons, and we went north, puttin on shows in Maine, Vermont, New Hampshire. Boss was right impressed with the number of people what came to see us by the railroad. So in '72 he decide to put the whole shebang on railroad cars. There was lots of stuff from the first museum that there just wasn't room for, so Boss give up his treasures to a new museum, the Smithsonian. The new show was called P. T. Barnum's Great Travelin Exposition, The Greatest Show On Earth. Them was good years, goin all over this big country. From time to time, Boss had a dizzy hade, and he take a bit off and go to England.

Then, in '81, Boss hook up with James Bailey and it was a good match. Bailey was a jumpy little man who chew on rubber bands, but he know circus. We just grew and grew, bigger tents, mo acts, mo animals and a whole lot mo money. Earn enough to buy me and Lucille a chicken farm in Nutley, New Jersey for the time I retires. Been with the show longer'n anybody here. The little General pass on in '83 and Boss took it hard. Two years later, Miz Lavinia married nother little man, an eye-talian count.

That crazy white family of darkies gone too. Mr. Bailey fire em. Travelin by train and as big as the show got, Boss couldn't keep a eye on em like before, and their mischief like to drive Mr. Bailey outta his hade. There usta be a giant lady too, Miz Anna, but she left after the first fire. I heared through circus gossip that she marry a giant man in England and they had a baby girl weigh eighteen pounds, but she die when she was born. They come back home and got some land in Ohio and the giant man built a giant house just like the General built a little house for him and his wife. They raise draft horses and cattle. Soon enough, Miz Anna was spected again. That poor big gal had the pains for three days then her muscles give out. The doc used an instrument to pull the baby's hade out, but the shoulders was too big. So the doc calls for nother doc to come and he don't get there till the next day. They finally got the baby out, he weigh twenty-four pounds and was taller'n Miz Lavinia, but he onliest live a day. Miz Lavinia go visit many times, so did Mr. Isaac, the skinny man what stuck by Miz Anna in the fire. Miz Lavinia still performin, but not with us and not all the year. Mr. Isaac retire to Cleveland in a house by Lake Erie. When Miz Anna pass on in '88, her husband, the captain, put a statue over her grave the same size as her with words from the Psalms that Miz Lavinia told me: "As for me, I will behold thy face in righteousness: I shall be satisfied when I awake, with thy likeness."

Boss was findin new acts all a time. There was the elephant Jumbo, camels, lions and acrobats, trapezers, fancy dancers. Few years back, Boss got a boy so hairy, he look like I usta with that hair suit on. And there's Mr. Morris, the rubber man, put me in mind of a coon dog the Marster had when I was a boy down in Georgia. He got even mo skin than that dog; he pull the skin of his chest up to the top of his hade. The bestest act Boss got was just last year and that was Prince Randian, the caterpillar man. You think this pointy hade strange to look at, that man got no arms and no legs! He wear a garment sumptin like a sock over his body and he move by wigglin his hips and shoulders, creepin along just like a caterpillar. Not only do that man read, he write too with a pen betwixt his lips. And you won't believe this—he roll a cigarette with them lips. He's a darkie too, but he come from Gee Ana.

When Boss die, Mr. Bailey cancel the circus at Madison Square Garden and paid for a train to take some circus peoples to Bridgeport day before the funeral. I wasn't invited, but I got there anyways by sneakin in where the trunks was and hidin betwixt em. I jump outta the train soon as it slow down. Business was shut down, buildins and houses was draped in black and the Boss' picture was everwhere. Ships in the harbor had flags halfways down. All to honor the Boss. Had my own way of honorin. Waited till it was good and dark, hear a clock chime two times, then I go to Boss' house.

Told you before that Boss had ideas bout when his time come. He want his services in the English fashion with onliest close family viewin the remains. I heared him say he don't want no heathenish ceremony, lettin ever Tom, Dick, and Harry rush in to gape on his corpse and sayin, "There's a black streak on the side of his nose and a spot by his ear." Boss put down in writin, and made his wife promise there be no undertaker cuttin on him and puttin fluids in him, just put his body on ice in the parlor with the lights low til the buryin.

Everthing was quiet at the house and I sneak into the parlor to where the Boss was laid out. I says, "Boss, you never did want me to say much, so I ain't gonna spoil nothin now, just wanna say thanks and good-bye." Then I took out my mouth organ and I play "Swing Low Sweet Chariot," quiet as I could play.

THE CONGRESS OF
STRANGE PEOPLE

THE BISHOP OF WINCHESTER

I'd been reading from the Gospel of Saint Luke when my assistant brought in tea and *The London Times*. On page two was an article titled "Uprising of the Freaks." It reported a meeting that had taken place in London on 6 January 1898. The participants were rather unusual members of the traveling Barnum and Bailey Circus, and the meeting's purpose was to protest the use of the opprobrious word "freaks" as a means of classification. After a lengthy description of their particular deformities, the article concluded with the group's appeal to the public for possible alternative names.

I never met Mr. Barnum, despite his frequent visits to England. However, I couldn't help but notice his advertisements, which referred to his unique troupe as "oddities." Much kinder than "freaks," but still unsatisfactory. When Mr. Bailey took charge, the word "Freaks" began appearing on banners and broadsheets, though it has been used by common people for some time.

I put the paper aside and turned again to Saint Luke, Chapter Fifteen, which contains the story of the prodigal son who returns home and is welcomed with rejoicing. I thought of the occasions these special performers had attended services at the cathedral. Each time they toured in England, they returned to my church, and I rejoiced in welcoming them back. This set me to thinking on the derivation of "prodigal," and I turned to my books on Latin. There I found the word "prodigium"—a combination of "pro," meaning "before," and "agiom," meaning "a thing said." The current English use of the word "prodigy," is defined as something so extraordinary as to inspire wonder. I can find no explanation of how this definition came about from the Latin, but my best guess is that a thing of wonderment leaves one speechless.

This was the answer to the newspaper's appeal: prodigies. Never have I witnessed a more extraordinary group of individuals than these circus performers who worship here. Never have I failed to be inspired by their strength and determination. Some would argue that people so afflicted ought to stay at home, shut away from public view. Some of my parishioners, especially those with very young children, have left their pews when the prodigies attend service, I'm sorry to say. Mind you, it's not the children that have a problem; quite the contrary, they look at the prodigies with marvel and awe, like they've sprung to life from the pages of their favorite fairy tale books. I can only speculate, but I believe their parents envision what the children cannot, that being, what the prodigies must grapple with every day as a result of their afflictions, and how they would feel if forced to do the same.

I'm very pleased that my suggestion was chosen from over three hundred responses, but I cannot take the credit; it was divine inspiration. I understand the group took their protest and new title to Mr. Bailey, who agreed upon the change. Last Sunday, a delegation of prodigies attended services and stayed afterward to convey their appreciation to me. I was especially happy to see Mr. Samuel Parks once again, and his wife, Ida. We spent a few enjoyable hours fishing on the Itchen. He's known professionally as Hopp the Frog Boy.

The first time I met Samuel, four years ago, I came upon him squatting on the river's bank with a line in the water. I took notice of his unusual shape, but more so of his bait. He initiated the conversation by advising: "Cornmeal balls, always your best bet, even British fish can't resist them," and he pulled his stringer from the water dangling six fat carp. Both of us avid anglers, we spent a good while in conversation on the merits of various bait and prized fishing holes. He wasn't with the circus at this time, but in the city exhibiting for the medical students at Winchester College. He told me he'd been touring the leading universities of Europe;

he was paid an honorarium to exhibit himself, as his condition was unlike any other human in existence. Samuel's face, hands, and feet are normal, but the rest of his body—legs, arms, and torso—is formed like a frog.

Samuel said his favorite book was written by one of my countrymen. I could've guessed it was Walton's *The Complete Angler*. He said one particular passage sprang to mind while he exhibited for the medical students. "Which passage is that?" I asked.

> "Thus use your frog . . . Put your hook through his mouth, and out at his gills; and then with a fine needle and silk, sew the upper part of his leg, with only one stitch, to the arming-wire of your hook; or tie the frog's leg, above the upper joint, to the armed-wire; and in so doing, use him as though you loved him."

✧

BARNUM & BAILEY CIRCUS, NEW YORK CITY, 1900

HOPP'S WIFE

I was studying nursing at Rush Medical school in the spring of 1893 when Samuel exhibited in the arena theater. Following a brief address by our director, Dr. Logan, Samuel was brought on the stage in a wheelchair. As is the case with such patients, Samuel wore only a cotton wrap about his loins. The students knew better than to make any vulgar sounds, even though his appearance was startling as Dr. Logan lifted him to the table. His resemblance to a frog was undeniable. If not for the unusual deformity of his limbs and his distended belly, he would be classified as a dwarf.

I was seated in the fourth row so I had quite a good view. I thought it was the effect of the lamps that made his eyes sparkle so and his skin cast a radiant sheen. And was it because he spoke in a theater that his voice sounded so resonantly? For a man of nineteen years, he demonstrated admirable maturity. Despite the doctor's prodding and poking, Samuel remained calm and cooperative. About ten minutes into it, I looked up from my notes to find Samuel's eyes fixed on my face. He smiled, a tentative half-smile. My smile in return was much bolder, a kindness to him, an assurance, I told myself.

At the end of the presentation, Samuel announced that he would be exhibiting at the World's Fair throughout the following week, and his eyes settled on mine just before he was wheeled from the stage. During the next five days, prior to the fair's opening, Samuel was often in my thoughts. I can't tell you any one thing about him that captivated me . . . while picking roses in our garden, I thought of his skin; watching a rainstorm from the laboratory window, I saw his gray-blue eyes; my head on my pillow, darkness surrounding me, I heard his voice and imagined how it would sound speaking my name.

On the opening day of the fair, Mother asked, "What's gotten into you, Ida?" because I spent two hours choosing a dress and pinning up my hair. I'd say "I'm leaving now," then find some distraction to keep me home. Finally Mother shooed me out by threatening to put my fitfulness to work on scrubbing the kitchen floor.

I was hesitant to enter the pavilion; hundreds of people were milling around the stage. But more honestly, I was afraid. Afraid these people would be horrified by the man who had captured my soul. Would their revulsion lift love's veil from my eyes? Would Samuel be wounded by their reaction? Would his wounding be intensified by my presence? Did he even remember me?

When Samuel appeared, two women fainted, and various moans and oaths were uttered. Then Samuel spoke, and those who had remained drew closer, their faces softened into childish wonder. I excused my way to the front, as close as I could get to the stage. Samuel saw me, and a smile spread across his face, and I felt light as a balloon. As the show concluded, he pointed to his watch and held up five fingers, his eyebrows drawn into a question mark. I nodded my agreement.

Six months later, we were married. We spent our first year touring the medical centers of Europe. In London, Samuel was invited by Mr. James Bailey to join his circus. We accepted for various reasons: the financial gains were quite attractive, we were tired of living out of trunks, and we wanted to start a family. It was Samuel who suggested the stage name Hopp after a story by Edgar Allan Poe. Samuel's an avid reader, and Mr. Poe is one of his favorite authors. Do you know his story, "Hop-Frog"? The tale takes place in the Renaissance era when kings kept fools and dwarfs at court. The main character, Hop-Frog, is, as the king says, "a triplicate treasure," for he is a dwarf, a jester, and a cripple. Hop wins the love of a beautiful dwarf girl and destroys the king who had abused them both. The actual title of the story is "Hop-Frog: Or the Eight Chained Ourang-Outangs." because Hop dresses the king and his seven ministers in suits of long, silken flax to resemble the beasts they truly are.

DIME BOOKLET ON JO-JO, THE RUSSIAN DOG-FACED BOY

Barnum and Bailey, The Greatest Show On Earth, provides this booklet to educate you on the history of Jo-Jo, the Russian Dog-Faced Boy. Jo-Jo is sixteen years of age. Thirteen years ago, a hunter in the forests of Kostroma in central Russia, saw two beast-like figures, one full-size and the other quite small. The hunter tracked them to their cave, but fearing it unwise to enter alone, he returned to his village and gathered a party of men. The hunting party went to the cave and captured the wild pair. Father and son were covered with an abundance of hair, especially on their faces.

They subsisted upon wild berries and small game which was killed with stones and clubs. The father was extremely savage and resisted capture in every way in his power. The father could not be civilized and was turned loose into the forests. The child was more easily subdued and all efforts to raise him as a normal child were provided by the Russian government, of which Jo-Jo is currently a ward. Even though he appears amiable enough, do not tease him, for when angered, he reverts to his wild state and will snap and bark. As the child was very small at the time of his capture, nothing could be discovered about the mother's descent.

✧

MADAME PAQUET'S TENT, PARIS, 1903

JO-JO'S MOTHER

Papa was given eight goats, two cows, six chickens, a bolt of purple silk, a jeweled dagger, and a barrel of vodka for giving me in marriage to Fedor, the dog-faced manouche. Could he resist such a treasure? Even after Grandma Rose read the cards on me and turned up the Seven of Cups: fool's gold, illusion. Next, three cards of Three: lies, things not as they appear on the surface. Did Papa heed the cards? Not that greedy pig.

Seventeen years ago our wagon traveled through Poland, further north than we'd ever been, seeking better fortune. As we neared the Russian border, our supplies were gone, and our stomachs growled. We would gladly sing and dance or read cards in exchange for a chicken or two. But the peasant farmers were stingy, suspicious people with no music in their hearts. When we made camp that fateful night, and my brothers borrowed vegetables once again from a nearby garden, I refused to eat them. I told Mama I'd rather turn into a stick and never have a husband than eat another bite of vegetable stew. No sooner had I uttered that oath than we heard the familiar jangle of tambourines and the singing of violins. Oh, how Papa's eye's danced when he saw that caravan—ten wagons full of fat gypsies. Their king, dressed in velvet and a fur cloak, approached Papa, his arms extended in greeting. We'd never met Russian gypsies, but we all speak Romany, no matter which land we come from. He said his name was Fedor, and he invited us to share their evening meal. Papa called us from the wagon: Grandma Rose, Mama, my three brothers, my little sister, Uncle Pierre, and me. Fedor kissed both my cheeks, held on to my hands, and told Papa how blessed he was with such a daughter. My eyes and my nose were on the feast being set out, and my stomach was so happy it commanded my feet to dance. Fedor eyed me like the wolf eyes the lamb. He took Papa aside, offered him a gold goblet of wine, and they walked off together as we gathered around their fire to enjoy the good food and good company.

I was stuffed and ready for sleep when they returned. Papa staggered with delight, and Fedor pumped his hand, slapping his back, calling him "Brother." Next morning I learned what had been sealed the night before. Papa said Fedor had been looking for a wife for his eldest son, also called Fedor, and I was to be the bride. I was a smart girl, even at fourteen, and I smelled a rotten egg. "With that great treasure, why does his son not already have a wife? How did King Fedor come by his fortune?" I asked. "Of all the gypsies roaming the earth, why choose a skinny girl with big teeth and coarse hair? Have you seen young Fedor?"

Papa said, "No, but what does it matter? You'll be rich, and your family will profit also. We'll meet your groom tonight at the wedding ceremony." Then Grandma Rose read the cards, and I was nervous, but excited too. As the sun set, our wagon hummed with preparations for the marriage. Mama got her best dress out of the cedar trunk and took in the seams to fit. Grandma put her white lace shawl under her mattress to press the wrinkles out. I washed my hair in the rain bucket, and Mama combed it smooth as she could. As she pulled the comb through my tangles, I peeked through the curtain and saw the king standing with a young man, their backs turned to me. With all my might and concentration, I willed them to turn around so I could see the face of my husband-to-be. As if a hand had touched his shoulder, the young man turned toward our wagon. I let fly a shriek—my groom's entire face was covered with hair; only his eyes and lips were hairless. I threw myself into Grandma's lap. Papa raised his fist to silence me. I told him I'd run away before I'd marry that creature, but he said if I did, he'd find me and beat me and take me back to my husband.

Did I learn to love him? Pah! Sleep with dogs and you wake up with fleas. I did love the money and the fine things it bought. That's how old Fedor got so rich, from the money people paid to gawk at my husband. But a girl can take cold nights alone for only so long, and one year after our marriage, I gave birth to a son. By the time he was a year old, he was as hairy as his dog-faced father. Our caravan was in Germany, and a man of science named Virchow came to see the two generations of hairy gypsies. Guess what he said?

"If someone were to breed these people he could develop a race which would present an entirely different appearance from the rest of mankind."

His words were like ice in my heart. I'd be beaten and damned before becoming mother bitch to a race of hairy freaks! I ran away, got as far as Paris before my money ran out. It wasn't long before I found a new husband, Jean Paquet. I'd seen him playing the concertina, strolling among the outdoor cafes, and I caught his eye. With each year, I grew more beautiful, and my children are beautiful too. I make plenty of money reading cards. I don't know where Fedor is and I don't care to know. He and the boy were in Paris five years back. I didn't see them! I stayed out of the city until they were gone, but I saw a handbill with a drawing and the words "L'HOMME-CHIEN ET LE CHIEN FILS."

October 13, 1905

Jo-Jo The Russian Dog-Faced Boy is now appearing with The Ringling Brothers, Barnum And Bailey Circus. The circus was purchased by the Ringling brothers following James Bailey's death last year. Jo-Jo has been exhibiting in the major cities of Europe as "l'homme-chien," the man dog. This is his first American exhibition. The French moniker is appropriate. Dressed in a Russian cavalry uniform, Jo-Jo's appearance certainly bears a strong resemblance to that of a Skye terrier. His face is completely covered by a thick growth of silky yellow hair, which is specially abundant on each side of his nose. Here there are two little tufts, like a terrier's whiskers, while his mild, hazel eyes have a remarkably canine expression. The luxuriance of his hair is offset by the scarcity of his teeth. Of these he has only four, two in the upper jaw and two in the lower. Although the hair is most abundant on his face, his whole body is covered with scattered growth. You can view Jo-Jo at Madison Square Garden along with the other members of The Congress of Strange People.

✧

RINGLING BROTHERS CIRCUS, 1910

JIMMY MORRIS, THE ELASTIC SKIN MAN

When you were a kid and you made faces, I'll bet your mother said, "One day it'll stick that way." My mother never said that—she knew my face would snap right back, because Dad and Granddad had the same kind of skin. If she caught me at it, she'd take a hickory switch to my bottom. Mother was determined to keep me from showing off my peculiarity, which is very tempting when you're a kid. You get respect from the other boys in school, you can make girls scream and run, you can scare off bullies from other neighborhoods. And, I was soon to discover, you can make money. It was my best buddy, Andy, who first revealed the potential of my condition when he bet another kid a nickel that I could pull my cheeks out to my ears.

Growing up in Queens, I learned the games, the cons; I'd win some, then lose it at the dog-fights or poker or dice—I'd bet on anything, and I'd do most anything to get a new stake. It's an old story. As Christ was dying on the cross, Roman soldiers rolled dice for his clothing. I could always count on my skin, count on people to pay to see me stretched to the limit. I led two lives: the dutiful son learning the barber trade from his father, and the boy sneaking off to dark, smoky rooms to scratch my itch.

One day a customer came into Dad's shop bragging about the fortune he'd made in one spin of the roulette wheel at the Saratoga Club. The very next summer I was in the stands at Saratoga Race Track, seventeen years old and decked out in a double-breasted suit, derby, and spats. In my pockets were a flask of bourbon, a leather cigar case, and a gold watch. By September, when the resort closed for the season, the watch was gone, along with every cent I'd won.

If I'd had a lick of sense, I'd have gone back to Dad's shop, but I knew I couldn't make enough there to get me back to Saratoga come summer. So I spent the winters showing at dime museums in the Bowery, and there were plenty to choose from. They were short on cash and long on flash. On the first floor there'd be a penny arcade, funny mirrors, machines to test your lung power or your strength, peep shows. I'd be upstairs in the Ten-In-One with attractions such as the Minnesota Woolly Baby; Kii Kii and Quebo, the Congo Glass Dancers; General Rhinebeck the Military Midget; Joe Berliner, the Human Fire Alarm; Layman, the Man of a Hundred Faces. There were self-made freaks like tattooed men along with fake mermaids and headless women, and otherwise normal people who swallowed swords, jammed spikes up their noses, or hammered nails into their flesh.

When June came around, I headed for Saratoga on a train, my satchel full of cash. There was lots of talk about Coney Island, across the harbor from Manhattan. Sodom by the Sea, it's called by some. Boss Tweed's behind that, him and his heelers. The "pic-nics" are usually arranged for the benefit of pickpockets, prostitutes, panel-girls, rowdies, three-card monte games. Plenty of guys around with money in their pockets and larceny on their minds: professional bounty-jumpers, fly-by-night entrepreneurs grown fat on fraudulent army contracts, land speculators loaded with loot from the Pennsylvania oil boom, all enticed to Coney and parted from minor sums of money. Sure, there were some classier joints at the east end of Coney Point, like the Manhattan Beach Hotel and the Brighton Beach, but West Brighton was one rough spot.

Mr. Canfield's Saratoga Club is a bit of heaven on earth. You couldn't find a palace in Europe with more class than Canfield's club. Opulent is the word. The rich came in from as far as Atlanta to dine on chef Jean Columbin's pâtés, truffles, grouse, Lynnhaven oysters, to drink Barolo wines and White Seal champagne. I saw J. P. Morgan, William Vanderbilt, Bet-a-Million Gates, Diamond Jim Brady, and Miss Lillian Russell. Least I saw them when I was winning. Sometimes they'd play roulette or faro on the first floor, but more often, they were upstairs in the private suites, the only place card games were allowed.

Five years I lived that way, rags to riches, riches to rags, before I got shed of the gambling bug, thanks to John Ringling. Now and then he'd go down to the Bowery dime museums to check out the competition, see if any acts were genuine and interested in moving up in the world.

As a member of the Congress of Strange People, I make $150.00 greenbacks a day, and the only one who can poker me out of it is Prince Randian, the Living Torso. My first day with the show, he bet me a dollar he could shave his face faster than I could shave mine. Well, there was a safe bet, the man has no arms or legs. Would you be surprised to learn I lost?

THE LIVING TORSO

Prince is my true name, Prince Randian. I am not a prince, just my name is Prince. People in Guiana have similar names, like Queen Victoria, Prince Albert, King George. I have four older brothers: Matthew, Mark, Luke, and John. I was to be named Acts, but because I was born this way, my mother feared the wrath of God if she named me after the Bible. "Randian" is the name my grandfather Yukuma gave me, an Obeah-man of the Arawak tribe. Obeah is the doctor of the tribe, who can cure with herbs and spells. My grandfather raised me 'til I was near ten years old.

I have never seen my brothers or my mother, Esmay, or father, Buddy, that I can remember. This story was told to me by Yukuma. Buddy wished to set me in the Demerara River and Esmay would not put me to her breast, but neither could bear the sin of murder. Yukuma settled the matter when he come walking into Georgetown from out of the bush and took me back with him.

My earliest memories are sights and sounds of the jungle as seen from my hammock: giant green leaves glistening with rain, vines and flowers in every bright color you can imagine, butterflies bluer than the sky, pale green spiders in webs of gold silk, and birds every-where making chatter with the monkeys that swung over my head. In the hammock, I was safe from the dangers of the jungle, Yukuma nearby to kill a curious snake and to pick bugs from my skin. I was fortunate to learn my early skills from the Arawak. They cook meals in the pepper pot— stew with red peppers and vegetables and what-ever meat or fish is caught that day. Bowls are dipped into the pot and the meal is eaten with farine, a bread made from the cassava root. Was easy enough to tip the bowl with my lips and bite chunks from the bread. Because I was expected to do for myself, I learned all I could do. My neck grew very strong.

I was ten years of age when Yukuma died. The new Obeah did not want me to stay in the tribe as he feared Yukuma's spirit had passed into my body. I was taken to the village of Coomacka, to the Maria Henrietta Mission, which was run by the London Missionary Society. Pastor Seaton was the head of the mission, and under his tutelage, I learned to speak and read the English language as a proper Christian should.

There was twelve children besides me, orphans of many shades: five Coolies, a brother and sister who were English/Coolie mix, one Chinese girl, three Negrah children, and one Portuguese boy, Alphonse. Alphonse became my best friend and protector. Children, well, they got it in them to attack what is weaker and different than themselves, like dogs, you know, one dog can be gentle and friendly, but in a pack with other dogs, it is something wild.

Alphonse was also my teacher of things the Pastor didn't teach, like playing cards and spitting for distance. One time the Pastor catch me and Alphonse playing cards, and he said, "If you can hold cards between you teeth, you can certainly hold a pen." Soon after that, I learned to write the English language.

Alphonse was crazy for girls. This is one of the tricks Alphonse played. When a pretty girl was coming along, I would wriggle into her path and set to moaning. When she bent over to answer my distress, Alphonse stood behind, looking up her skirt. Being a few years younger than him, I didn't understand his interest at the time. I asked him what was there to see under those skirts, and he said, "The sweet naked truth." When I lived with Yukuma, nobody wore clothing; Pastor Seaton introduced me to clothing by way of a stocking that covered all of my body excepting my head. At first I hated it, chafed me the way a collar chafes a dog, but I got used to it, and I wanted to be like the other children, so

I didn't complain. And I went along with Alphonse's tricks because he was my friend.

At fourteen, the yearning came into my body as it do with boys of that age, and then I understood Alphonse's interest. This was the time in my life when I most miseried pon not having hands. I had seen Alphonse in the night, using his hand, hear him moan, "Dios," and roll to his side. I wanted to ask if he was sick or hurt, but something in my head told me to keep still. One night, he caught me watching, and he asked, "How do you do it?"

"Do what?" I asked. He pointed at his swelled organ.

"Guess it work the same as yours," I said.

"But, how do you relieve it?"

I was so shamed and confused and angry, I turned my back to him. I felt his weight pon my cot, but I wouldn't face him. He rolled me to my back, lowered the sheet, wrapped his fingers around my only member, and introduced me to eye-popping pleasure. After his work was done and he was back pon his cot, he said, "I got to find you a woman."

Alphonse never did find me one; he left the mission to work in Georgetown a few months later. I found my own woman. I was fifteen when Sarah came to work for Pastor Seaton, sweeping up and tending after the little ones. She was thirteen and sweet as Demerara sugar crystals, and I was lonely as a fish out of its school. Pastor Seaton threw the pair of us out when Sarah's belly grew. We lived with Sarah's aunt in Georgetown until an Englishman in a fancy suit came looking for me. He was an agent for Mr. P. T. Barnum, who learned of me from a doctor that once visited the mission. It was hard for me to believe his story that people would part with money just to look at me. Well, I'd never earned a cent in my life; Sarah was working as a housemaid at a sugarman's place. When the agent told me how much money I could expect in one year, I took up the pen in my teeth and signed the paper with my lips smiling.

Next thing you know, me and Sarah and our baby boy Matthew were in New York City. I was put in the sideshow of Mr. Barnum's Greatest Show On Earth. During my performance, I rolled a cigarette with my lips, and shaved my face with a razor fixed to a wooden block. I earned extra money by signing picture cards, which bore my photograph pon the front and my life history pon the back. Mr. Barnum named me the Living Torso, and called my wife Princess Sarah, claiming we were royalty of the jungle tribes of Guiana. That little deception made people more curious he said. As the years passed, Sarah blessed me with three more sons: Mark, Luke, and John. We didn't have our Acts either—our baby girl is named Olive.

There was another dark-skinned performer, but he was born in this country. Mr. Zip, now, he is a funny funny man, make me laugh 'til my eyes tear up. He's also very good at cards and playing the mouth organ and fiddle. After Mr. Bailey died and the Ringling Brothers took over the circus, Zip would imitate John Ringling, who fancied cigars. When they try to give him cheap cigars for the act, he push them away and insist pon the same cigars as Mr. Ringling smoke. He's been with the sideshow business longer than any of us; he's over sixty and still pulling in the crowds.

It's been eighteen years since I left Georgetown, and I'm thinking this is a good time to settle my family in one place. There's an island close by New York City called Coney that I've heard about from other members of the sideshow. People go there in the summertime to see the three amusement parks: Steeplechase, Luna, and Dreamland. There's beaches and horse racing, rides and restaurants, theaters, and at night, everything is lit with thousands of glittering lights. Many of my circus acquaintances have gone there to perform: Mrs. Lavinia and Count Magri, Jo-Jo The Dog Faced Boy, The Elastic Man, Hopp The Frog Boy, and Baby Irene, the fat lady, have all gone to Coney Island, and Mr. Zip says he's ready to give it a go.

THE BARKERS

Welcome to Coney Island, lay-dees, gentlemen, and children. Watch your step as you disembark. The Iron Pier in front of you is the gateway to a universe of dee-lights. Visit an Es-kee-mo village, a garden in Japan, the Alps of Swit-zer-land, the canals of Venice! See Mount Pey-lee erupt, see the Johnstown flood, the tidal wave that destroyed Galveston! Go under the sea in a gen-you-ine submarine or ride the whirligig! Feed an elephant, ride on the hump of a camel.

Hold on to your hats and ride the Loop-the-Loop, thirty feet of ex-hil-eration and breath-taking thrill!

This way for the Streets of Cairo! One hundred and fifty Oriental beauties! The warmest spectacle on earth! Pre-sen-ting Little Egypt! See her prance, see her wriggle! See her dance the Hootchy-Kootchy! Anywhere else but in the ocean breezes of Coney Island she would be consumed by her own fire! Don't rush! Don't crowd! Plenty of seats for all!

Pink lemonade, sweet and pink, smooth on the throat. Quench your thirst with pink lemonade.

Now, ladies and gentlemen, if you please, step into Lilliputia and see the world's tiniest people. Note the yardstick—an accurate, an exact, a perfectly calibrated instrument against which to measure the height of these minuscule humans, some of them members of the foreign titled aristocracy! Each and every one of these little people, ladies and gentlemen, is a full-grown human being!

Popcorn—fresh and hot!

Ride the Steeplechase Horses! This way to the track. Pick your mount and hold on tight! They may be wood, but they move like lightning. This way to Steeplechase's famous Horses!

Here it is, ladies and gentlemen, the world's largest Ferris Wheel. Guaranteed to make your eyes pop!

Steamed clams and lager beer—hot and cold! Treat your tummy! Step up to the clam bar!

Shoot-The-Chutes, the world's only aquatic toboggan ride! Climb into the boat and get set for sure-pop sock-ola excitement!

Yes, look well upon this group of savages, ladies and gentlemen! They are the dread Igorots, fierce head-hunters from the Philippine Islands! And what you see before you is but a miserable tithe of the vast anthropological, educational, thrilling and altogether unimaginable sights that will unfold before you as you pass through the Igorot Village!

The greatest novelty mystery act in the world! How can you believe it, even when you see it happening before your eyes? Just think this over, ladies and gentlemen, the time consumed in making the change from bag to trunk is one! two! only three seconds! We challenge the world to produce an attraction with greater Mystery, Speed, or Dexterity than Harry Houdini!

Bring your Sweetheart to The Barrel of Love. Talk about love in a cottage! This has it beat by a mile.

Climb the tower to The Dew Drop and come whirling down, fifty feet, around and around! Don't worry, a soft cushion awaits you at the bottom.

It gives me the greatest pleasure at this time to introduce a little woman who comes to us from an aristocratic plantation in the Old South and who is recognized by our finest doctors, physicians, and medical men as the foremost unquestioned and authentic female

Bearded Lady in medical history. Ladies and gentlemen, Lady Olga!

Ride the Which-a-way! You won't know which way is up. North, south, east or west—the Which-a-way is the Best!

Nathan's hot dogs. Follow the crowd to Nathan's. If doctors eat our hot dogs, you know they're good!

Here, ladies and gentlemen, sits Baby Irene, the Fattest of all the Fat Girls since the Dawn of History! Special girders are required beneath her platform, and special girdles must be constructed to contain her fabulous avoirdupois. Six hundred and seventy pounds of golden good nature! No one else can make this claim!

BABY IRENE

A gol-durn baggage car! That's why I came to Coney. Got too fat to ride in the regular cars, so John Ringling said I'd have to travel in the baggage car. Brother, he didn't mind me putting on extra pounds for the show—paid me extra for each pound I gained, then tells me to ride with the baggage. So I told him he could kiss my rosy behind, and I joined the Coney Island Freak Show.

Yeah, freak show. No Congress of Strange People here. A Ringling clown, Tod Browning, thought up that name. For a while, Ringling's freaks went by the name "Prodigies." That's when they were over in Europe a long time back. "Prodigies" didn't go over too well back home—your average Joe didn't know what it meant. I'll guarantee every American knows what "freak" means.

Hey, I don't give a good gol-durn what they call me. Been called a lot worse. If rubes want to pay five cents to have a look at me, laugh at my fat hanging outta this little-girl costume, that's fine with me. I'd laugh all the way to the bank, if I could get my fat fanny to the bank. What am I supposed to do? Cry? Don't have a tear left.

Time was, men on the street would tip their hats to me. I was a real looker, one hundred pounds and curves where a lady ought to have them. At nineteen, I got work at a shirt factory in Brooklyn and met Eli. Eli was young, strong, and handsome and knew it better than anybody. He said I was the prettiest gal on the whole West Side; swept me off my feet, that's a laugh, huh? We got married by a justice of the peace. Four months later, I was in the family way.

After Albert was born, stead of losing weight, I started gaining. Eli made mean remarks about my size, but I didn't care, cause Albert filled my days with happiness, and Eli doted on him too. I tried eating less, to please Eli, but I kept getting bigger. The doctor told me Albert's birth had thrown my glands out of whack. Just because somebody can explain why a thing happens to you don't make it any easier to live with. I wasn't sure I believed him neither; I ate next to nothing and all I lost was my energy and my patience. See, Eli was staying out all night, coming home smelling of whiskey and perfume. One night, I waited up, ironing clothes 'til he got home, and when he did, I called him on the carpet. He said he had to get drunk before he could screw a pig. Might as well have punched me. I leaned against the wall, one hand on my chest; the other fell on the flat iron, I grabbed the handle and flung that iron at his head. Knocked him flat out.

I was up early next morning—hard to sleep on hunger and anger. Eli was snoring on the sofa and Albert was snug in his crib, so I went to the market as I was out of eggs. When I got home, Eli was gone and so was Albert. It was June; there was a square of sun on the rag rug, a milk jug full of pink peonies on the table, a newspaper on the chair, sweat on the pump handle, my apron hanging on the wall peg, my string of blue beads on the counter-top. I passed in front of the hall mirror and I was scared to look, scared that I wouldn't be there. But I did, and I saw the flushed face of a fat woman hugging a paper bag.

I searched every street, every saloon, I cornered his cronies, not a trace of either of them. After a week I went to the police. They couldn't help much; found out he'd took a train bound for Chicago. Eli's got family in Kentucky, Utah, and Wisconsin—he could be anywhere, and I couldn't follow him because I was nearly penniless. The only thing Eli left me is this photograph of Albert; he was two years old then.

I wanted to die. What had I done to deserve this? I became a mother, the most blessed miracle possible, and then I lost my figure, my husband, and my baby. I had nothing left to lose, except my life, and if I gave that up, I'd give up the hope of ever seeing Albert again. So I quit fighting and started eating my way out of Brooklyn. When I hit 400 pounds, I went to the Ringling Brothers Circus and they gave me a job as the Fat Lady. Ringling traveled all over the country. In each city, I'd search every face in the crowd, stopping on little boys with dark hair and blue eyes. Is that boy in the red cap Albert? Is that Albert feeding peanuts to the elephant? Like to drove me crazy. Wherever Albert is, he's close to sixteen, and I doubt he knows a thing about me.

I gotta level with you, that story about the baggage car? Trumped up for the press. John Ringling's a good man, I just figured it was time to give up the search, and Coney was the right place for me. No more sleeping in stuffy trains, getting rained out in some burg where the kind folks throw food at you, wearing the same baby costume 365 days a year. I like the ocean, the quiet during off-season, my cottage behind Surf Avenue. I saved my money so I could afford to settle here year-round. Most of the freaks room in a boardinghouse on Sheridan's Walk from May to September, then have to look for work at the circus, carnivals, or dime museums.

There's something else about Coney. I've had years to sit and think about life and what it comes down to is how big or how small you make a particular situation. "Freak" is a small thing, a word, and in Dreamland's sideshow, we're all freaks. In the outside world, we're outnumbered, and what do you do when you're outnumbered? Look around New York City—there's Harlem, Little Italy, Chinatown, neighborhoods of Jews, Russians, Irish, Poles. There ain't enough of us to fill a neighborhood, but we got Coney. From the comfort of this small world of friends, everyone outside it has grown bigger. We can make them smaller with blank stares, or smile sweetly with contempt in our eyes.

Some of the old-timers don't like the word "freak." Lavinia and her Count will straighten you out in a hurry—they're midgets, they say, which is entirely different from a dwarf, and no one is a freak in their eyes. Actions speak louder than words, I say. They don't associate much with the "freaks," specially the ones they figure are self-made, like me, the tattooed lady, and the wild men of Borneo. They ain't wild, just a tribe Sam Gumpertz found on one of his freak hunts. The little people live in Lilliputia, a Dreamland attraction, a village where everything is tiny. There's a giant or two wandering around the village during show times for effect.

Gumpertz's newest draw is weddings. So far at Dreamland, I've been married over fifty times to three human skeletons. When the ceremony's over, I pick up my groom, give him a big kiss, and carry him offstage. One of them sang Sophie Tucker's song, "Nobody Loves a Fat Girl But How a Fat Girl Can Love." Course, the preacher's as fake as the ceremony. Giants marry dwarfs, the strong man marries a bearded lady, the armless man marries the legless woman. Brother, it packs 'em in. Imagine that! Someone would truly marry that thing, course it's a freak too, but isn't it something! Freaks fall in love. Hope they got sense enough not to have children and pass their afflictions on to the innocent.

THE THREE-LEGGED WONDER

Have you heard of eugenics? A fancy word for a monstrous practice. The belief is that each human is the result of the breeding of his ancestors. If a smart man marries a smart woman, they'll have smart children. If a stupid woman marries a stupid man, their children will be stupid. There's more to the theory. Eugenics supporters say that because modern societies protect the weak, survival of the fittest isn't working. The imperfect, the mentally and physically maimed will, if not stopped, breed at such a rate as to outnumber the better breeding stock. The solution? Sterilize and lock up these people in asylums. My parents took me to such a place fourteen years ago. I have smart parents. I think I'm pretty smart too, but I wasn't at twelve.

As a little boy in Sicily, I didn't mind my extra leg. I wasn't treated any differently than my eleven brothers and sisters. Actually, I should have had two brothers born along with me. Instead, I got parts of them. I have three legs: the leg growing out of the base of my spine is two inches shorter than my right leg, which is one inch shorter than my left; I have two sets of male organs, four feet, and sixteen toes. When you're young, your whole world is your family. You have a home, food to eat, clothes to wear, parents who love you and kiss and comfort you when you cry.

I was ten years old when we came to New York City. Papa had a job waiting at his brother's produce business. We lived in rooms above Uncle Sal's store, and from my window, I could see Central Park. My brothers and sisters spent hours and hours there. At first I tried to join in, but that's one big park and my extra leg slowed me down; kids pointed and laughed at me. Everytime I walked down the streets, I heard some grown-up say, "Isn't that a pity?" Or, "Look at that poor boy." So I stayed in my room, month after month, watching the boys play stickball, chase and tag, or ice skate on the rink, and I got more and more depressed. I wouldn't listen to my parents when they tried to reason with me.

One day, in answer to their chiding, I yelled at them in desperation and anguish, "I have no reason to live." Mama sobbed into her apron and Papa yanked me to my feet. He said, "Mother, get your coat, we're going to give Francesco Lentini a reason for living."

We took the trolley to a huge brick building surrounded by tall iron gates and with bars on the windows. Papa asked for my cousin Joseph who works there; he had keys on his belt that jangled as he walked. First we went to the children's ward. I saw little children who were blind, deaf, and dumb. Despite their problems, they had the spark of laughter that children give to each other. I understood what Papa was trying to do, but I also thought that if I lived with a dozen other three-legged boys, I wouldn't feel abnormal or unhappy.

Then we went to the Eugenics ward. Here were children and young adults terribly deformed and crippled, lying on the floor or scooting about. Some were silent and staring, others howled and tugged on our clothes. There were no windows, and the smell was sickening. The visit to that asylum, despite the misery I saw there, was the best thing that happened to me. From that time on I've never complained. I think life is beautiful and I enjoy living it. I learned something else from that visit, that I was one of the lucky ones not rejected by his parents. Most of us sideshow folks weren't. Parents who don't want a deformed baby put it in an asylum right away, where they stay until they die. If parents keep a deformed baby, they love it, sometimes even more than a normal baby. Fact is, lots of them are spoiled by parents who do too much for them. Hard for Mama to spoil me, though, with eleven other kids underfoot.

Soon after that visit, I got work in the entertainment business: Buffalo Bill's Wild West Show, then the Ringling Brothers, Barnum & Bailey Circus sideshow. I earned so much money, we couldn't believe it. To my family, I was a hero. The money was enough to buy a house in Manhattan and to bring Papa's parents over from Sicily. Every evening at mealtime, the family prayers included, "Thank you, Lord, for giving us Frankie and for bringing us to America."

I remember seeing Miss Liberty from the ship—try to imagine the impression she made on a little boy from Sicily. Her great torch in one hand and in the other the Declaration of Independence. I studied that document while preparing to become an American citizen. We hold these truths to be self-evident: That all men are created equal; that they are endowed by their Creator with certain unalienable Rights; that among these are Life, Liberty, and the pursuit of Happiness.

The eugenics supporters should study their own history; they should meet me and my family, come to our house for dinner. Then we'd go to Coney's sideshow and I'd introduce them to Olga. She'd give 'em what for!

LADY OLGA

Have a gander at this article, "Circus and Museum Freaks, Curiosities of Pathology." Doctors are behind this; they've organized, and mark my words, they'll be as dangerous as a bunch of politicians. Listen to what this medical man says about the sideshow: "Most of these humble and unfortunate individuals, whose sole means of livelihood is the exhibition of their physical infirmities to a gaping and unsympathetic crowd, are pathological curiosities." He continues by using medical gobbledy gook to label our conditions. Mine is hypertrichosis, giants have acromegaly, dwarfs are the result of pituitary defects, fat ladies and human skeletons have thyroid imbalance, and pinheads have microcephalous idiocy.

Here's where the good doctor's true design is revealed, at the end of the column: "These exhibits are sick individuals, deserving of our pity. Human oddities are not benign curiosities, they are pathological, in other words, diseased. Their proper role is not as public exhibits, but as patients of physicians, to be viewed on hospital rounds and in private offices by appointment only. The passing of the freak show is not a tragedy but rather a healthy tendency in the move to rid us of the morbid and unwholesome in our life."

Didn't I tell you, just like politician—line those pockets. I'm not bothered much by all that hot air. Yes, some people "gape" at us. If you were walking through a forest and came upon a purple tree, wouldn't you gape? What we see on people's faces when we look down from the platform is gut reaction, and who can explain that? It's like trying to define beauty. When somebody says, "Brother, that's beautiful," it's senses working; a diamond is beautiful to the eye, a rose is beautiful to the nose, Caruso's voice is beautiful to the ear. You don't analyze it—you react. Yet, how do we come by that sensual reaction? By exposure, yes, that's true, but also by association. Can you think of a single thing not associated with something else? After the crowd's first look—their gut reaction—association takes over and you can read their faces like a book, if you're literate.

The doctor says "the gaping and unsympathetic crowd" sees us as pathological curiosities. Well, some are curious; they look at the Seal Boy and wonder how he wipes his behind. Some laugh, out of defensiveness or because they think, *that Zip's the funniest man I've ever seen*. You can see admiration too, like when Prince Randian writes with a pen between his lips. Then there's the pensive pout—*what would I do if I was born like that?*, followed by the slow smile—*guess I'm not so bad off*, or the satisfied grin of the gloater. Once in a while we see looks of horror or hatred, but those are people who've never taken a good look at themselves, and they tend to stay away from the shows or don't stay long. So much for that doctor's bunk. Most of our audiences can't read anyway. The way I see it, folks come to Coney to have some fun, plain and simple. When I was growing up, there wasn't much in the way of entertainment, and people were starved for it. Traveling carnivals and dime museums were the answer for country folk, city people too poor to go to the theater, and immigrants who didn't understand English.

How did I get started? I was a little nipper of three, living in Wilmington, North Carolina. My father was a Russian immigrant. He made his living going from town to town repairing wagons. Oh, he was a great ox of a man with a black beard that covered him like a vest. My mother was half Irish, half Indian, and superstitious from both sides. I can't recall her face nor her touch; seems it was always Da's face over my cradle. By Da's account, my beard sprouted when I was near six months old. I was three when Da went to Raleigh on business and Mother took me to the Great Orient Family Circus. She went home alone.

I wish I could remember more about that family. I recall their skins were dark and they spoke differently, their wagons had wonderful bright paintings on the outside, soft pillows and spicy smells inside, and they were very kind to me. When Da returned home, he sent Mother packing and started searching for me. With the help of the police, he tracked me to New York City, only to find the circus had left for Europe.

While appearing in Berlin, I became extremely ill. The family took me to a hospital, and I remember they visited me, brought sweets and flowers. But my recuperation was lengthy, and by the time I was well enough to leave, the Great Orient Circus had moved on. I was placed in an orphanage. Upon my word, Da was a tenacious man. One day—I was five years old by then—I was brought to the orphanage office, and there was Da, weeping with joy. He'd tracked me across the country and across the ocean.

We went back to North Carolina, and with just Da and me on the place, I didn't think much about my whiskers. He quit the traveling repairs business and planted turnips, okra, lima beans, and such, and bought some livestock. I grew up like any other southern farm girl. But when I got to be in my teens, I noticed that boys my age shaved their chins. I did the same to mine. When Da saw me, he laughed 'til tears ran into his beard. Shaving didn't help attract local boys because my whiskers grew twice as fast as theirs.

It was our neighbor who turned my life around again. He was a farmer who spent the winters as a circus strongman. He told me if I didn't shave, I could cash in on my beard. Then he introduced me to his employer, the John Robinson Circus, and in '92 I was back in the business and stayed in. I don't mind telling you about my childhood years, it's all laid out in Ringling's Congress of Curious People pamphlet. However, my personal life is my affair, and I'll appreciate your refraining from questions of that nature.

I've been with the circus twenty years, and I wouldn't trade places with Queen Mary. You take some time and chat with these "diseased, humble, and unfortunate people" in the Coney sideshow, and if you feel a trace of pity, you're as stupid as the doctor who wrote this trash. I'll ice skate in hell before the medical profession convinces the public to pass by the titillation of the freak show. If we lose our audiences, it's because the shows have lost some veteran performers. The lure of profit in replacing them with fakes is too great for the promoters. I can't blame them leaving, the ones who could. The Great War took the men who could march and hold a rifle, and some didn't come home; we'll keep JoJo and Jimmy Morris alive in our memories. Age and the wish to retire took others, like Hopp, the original frog boy. Lavinia and Count Magri work Coney in the summer and run a general store and ice cream parlor in Middleboro, Massachusetts, off-season. Old Zip is still at it—played a week at Madison Square Garden, strutting around in a three-piece suit, a real monkey suit! Prince Randian is another old-timer who'll go the distance. Those who could sing or dance or play instruments have gone into vaudeville or moving pictures. Hard to keep em down on the farm after they've played the Palace or seen Hollywood.

THE PLAZA HOTEL, NEW YORK CITY, 1924

SIR

Violet and Daisy ain't receiving no visitors. They got a show tonight at the Palace. Hey, don't miss it, it's hot stuff. I can tell you everything you want to know about the Hilton sisters. Here's one of the pamphlets the wife and I put together: Life Story and Facts of the San Antonio Siamese Twins. Inside there's even an artist's drawing made from x-ray photographs that shows where their spines are attached. Costs a dime at the show, but, what the hey, this one's on me. The girls was born in Brighton, England, in 1908, and their mother died one year after their birth. Their father was an English army officer what was killed in Belgium in 1914 Shortly after, the wife and I adopted them. When we seen how bright and talented they were, we devoted all our time to their education and activities.

Violet and Daisy are sixteen now and their minds are supplied with those things what stimulate the mind and body with high ideals and healthful thoughts. If a young, unfortunate, jazz-crazed girl murders her mother, every effort is made to keep this sordid story from lodging in the minds of these little innocent girls. But instead of rehearsing all these tales of woe what make such fat fodder for mental morons, these girls are stimulated by higher ideals and nobler aspirations. At the mansion in San Antonio we've provided for them, the girls love to cook, sew, sing, practice the piano, romp, raise pets, play tennis, golf, and handball, go to the theater and the movies, read good books, and converse with cultured people.

In the pamphlet there's an interview with the wife, who the girls affectionately call "Aunt Edie." Edith spoke for the both of us when she said, "We have tried to show the girls every care and devotion and have been paid back with every ounce of love their little bodies hold. That in itself is enough. The girls radiate happiness for they say, 'We have all the good things in life that other girls enjoy, so what more could we ask?'"

DAISY HILTON

We have to get ready for the show and Sir will be knocking on our door any minute. Ah, that pamphlet's a bunch of hooey! Sir and Edith didn't adopt us. Mary Hilton, Edith's mother, left us to them in her will, along with her other property. The only thing on the square in that pamphlet is the when and where we were born. Mary was always reminding us that our real mother was an unmarried barmaid. They worked at the same bar in Brighton, and Mary says our mother abandoned us and it was out of the goodness of her heart that she took us in. Ha, I wouldn't be surprised if Mary stole us away from our mother. She knew a hot meal ticket when she saw one.

Starting at three years of age, we were on the road—Mary, her fourth husband, Sir Jones, me and Violet, and Edith. Edith was thirteen and mean as a skunk. We went to carnivals, circuses, and fairs in England, Germany, and Australia. Soon as we were old enough to learn, Mary got us tutors in piano, violin, clarinet, voice, and dance. She wore a belt, and if either of us didn't practice enough, or if she was simply in an ugly mood, that belt buckle would come swishing through the air. We both have scars on our backs and shoulders from "Auntie's" belt. Her fifth husband, Sir Green, told us we'd never get hit in the face because the public wouldn't be so glad to pay to look at little Siamese twins with scarred faces. Mary locked us in our room when we weren't having lessons. The room was small, with one bed and one chest of drawers—that was it, no rugs or curtains or knickknacks, except one whole wall was a mirror, like ballet dancers have. Mary said we should watch each other in the mirror so we'd know how other people saw us and correct anything that didn't look right, like the way we sat down or stood up, or if our walk was uneven, or our smiles too goofy. Instead, we'd play a game, "In The Mirror I See," and imagine into that room on the other side closets full of dresses and shoes, boxes loaded with toys, a kitten for Violet and a puppy for me, and children who could open the door and take us outside. We never saw anyone except our tutors, because Mary said people wouldn't pay to look at us if they could see us for free.

Edith met her husband, our latest "Sir," three years ago when we were in Australia. His name is Meyer Meyers, how corny can you get? He ran a balloon and candy concession at a circus there. Mary was close to sixty and having health problems. Seeing as how Sir Green had died, she let Edith marry Meyer because she wanted a man around. Edith and Meyer took over the booking, travel, and promotion arrangements. He convinced Mary that to make it big, we had to get out of the carnival and circus tours and into vaudeville—we had to go to the United States. To prepare us for the American stage, he hired people to teach us to play the saxophone and ukulele and to dance the Black Bottom.

Our first vaudeville tour was with the Orpheum Circuit, where we appeared with Eddie Cantor, Charlotte Greenward, and Harry Houdini. Violet and I whispered at night about how we couldn't wait to turn eighteen and be free of Mary. We were making over a thousand dollars a week and that old cow wouldn't give us a penny. We had our freedom fund though—I had a half-dollar and Violet had a nickel.

In Boston, Mary took real sick and died. Much as we hated her, we're more scared of Meyer. If Violet wakes up, don't mention him, okay? Least Mary protected us from him. She figured out what he'd been up to and took away his key to our room. Edith drove us to the funeral home. She didn't shed a single tear over her own mother, but I can't say I blame her. Looking down on her rouged-up old powdered face, I expected her to sit up and say, "What are you two lookin at? You got better things to do than stand around doin nothing!"

I squeezed the half-dollar in my pocket, nudged Violet, and said, "Let's run." We only got a few steps down the hall when Meyer grabbed us. Since then, we rarely have a moment's privacy. Meyer even makes us sleep in the same bedroom with him and Edith, even in hotels on tour.

Oh, but America's swell. The theaters are like castles: velvet seats, crystal chandeliers, a clean, polished stage, dressing rooms fit for a queen. We both love to perform. The audiences are so kind. And the stars we've met! Miss Sophie Tucker, you know her song . . . "Some of these days, you're gonna miss me honey." Eddie Foy and the Seven Little Foys, W. C. Fields, the world's greatest juggler, and Frank Fay, the funniest man I've ever seen. Have you heard his "Tea for Two" bit? It's a killer. We don't get to chat with them because Sir walks us to the curtain and waits in the wings 'til we're done. Once though, when a moving picture agent was talking to Sir after a show, we met Mr. Harry Houdini, and he talked to us for nearly half an hour. I asked him how he managed to get himself free from handcuffs and straitjackets and sealed chests, even underwater. He said, "Girls, character and concentration will accomplish anything for you. You must learn to forget your physical link. Put it out of your mind. Work at developing mental independence of each other. Through concentration you can get anything you want."

We thought about his advice for a long time, and we practiced. That's why Violet's been able to sleep through my chatter. But if I was startled, if for some reason my heart beat faster, she'd wake up, because we share a common bloodstream. Anyway, Harry was right about concentrating on independence from each other, so we decided to concentrate on getting independent of Sir and Edith. When we were playing in Newark last month, Violet read a review that said the Hilton sisters were dressed like children, their heads loaded with demure curls. I showed it to Edith and we had our first visit to the beauty parlor for a haircut.

Oh, there's the music for the Dancing Dolls, and we're on after them. I've got to wake Violet. Before you go, look at our bracelets—aren't they swell? Just like the ones Miss Sophie Tucker wears. We told Edith that she and Sir were making thousands of dollars off us, and we wanted bracelets. Through concentration you can get anything you want.

LUCILLE'S FARM, NUTLEY, NEW JERSEY, JUNE 1926

ZIP'S PASSING

Last thing I hear William Henry say was, "Sister, we fool em a good long time." Then he fell asleep. The nurses at Bellevue come in and check on him now and again, but he didn't wake up. He breathed his last the morning of April 24, 1926, at the age of eighty-three. Thought I'd go first, being as I'm two years older.

You know why he say that? Cause everybody thought he was a dummy, Zip the Monkey Man, Zip the Pin-Head. Yep, he fooled em a long time. William Henry never had any educating, but he was no idiot. He was simple and sweet as a child, but crafty as a fox too. He took care of me. Nobody ever had a better brother than mine. Left me this chicken farm. My children and grandchildren keep after me to move in with one of them. William Henry saw to it they all got homes and schooling; they live in the cities, but I like this farm. William Henry liked it too; past few years, he was living here all the time. He'd retired, 'cept for summers cause he was under lifetime contract to work Coney Island in the summer.

Funny, when you get this old, time jumps around in your mind and your eyes play tricks. William Henry'd be out in the yard admiring my rooster, and I'd look at his face and there'd be that little boy getting set to torment Marster's prize rooster, and I'd yell, "William Henry, Granmammy gonna whup you!" He'd say, "Lucille, Granmammy gonna reach her old arm down from heaven?" Or sometimes, at night, we'd be sitting in the parlor, the lamps turned down, and William Henry's head would start nodding, and he'd say, "Lucille, don't let me fall sleep." See, when we were running north, we took turns sleeping, me and Daddy and William Henry. I let him sleep; I was too scared to sleep anyways when Daddy wasn't awake, and William Henry'd crawl into my lap, put his right hand in my hair and my left thumb in his mouth, and that made me feel safer—don't know why, but it did.

Got a memory scrapbook so fat it's falling apart. William Henry knew I was partial to picture postcards and he'd send em to me from his travels with the circus: The Eiffel Tower in Paris, Big Ben in London, Saint Peter's church in Rome, German castles, snow-covered mountains. And I have newspaper items, oh, lots of em: William Henry in his fur suit when he was with Mr. Barnum; a boxing match with the Spotted Boy; his pretend wedding to a lady midget, which took place at Madison Square Garden with Mr. Alf Ringling as best man; his sixtieth birthday party (paper says "Feast Of Freaks"); dancing with a lady sword swallower. This here is my favorite and the last picture took of William Henry. He's playing golf at the Coney Island beach, dressed up in a shirt and tie and knickers, looking real fine.

I shoulda passed before him, but I was mighty glad to be present at his funeral. There were reporters and photographers in the hundreds, flashes going off like the Fourth of July. "The Dean of Freaks," Mr. Ringling called him at the services, cause he was in the business longer than any other circus performer in history. Pallbearers were the Strong Man, the Tattooed Man, and two of my

179

grandsons. There were honorary pallbearers too: Prince Randian, Lady Olga, the Doll Family, Baby Irene and her new husband, Pete, who asked me would it be all right if they did so. I said I was sure William Henry would preciate that. The church was full to bursting; people had to stand in the back. God bless him, I never knew he had so many friends, being as he kept quiet for all those years.

✧

SAN ANTONIO, TEXAS, 1931

THE HILTONS' ATTORNEY

The case made headlines in every major paper across the country: "Hilton Sisters Break the Silence, Siamese Twins Unfold Tale of Bondage." My phone hasn't stopped ringing since the trial. I had to hire a new girl just to make appointments. This was a case lawyers dream about, one that'll make your reputation and set you up as a savior.

Meyers, the girls' guardian, brought them to my office last April. I didn't know ahead of time they were Siamese twins; I don't frequent vaudeville shows. Meyers should have told me; maybe he thought I wouldn't take the case. I was embarrassed at first. They had to turn sideways to maneuver through the office door, then there wasn't anyplace for them to sit down. As struck as I was by their condition, after they settled in by leaning against the wall, I was more taken with their loveliness. Like a pair of orchids, delicate and exotic, pale skinned. Their dark hair curled in waves around their faces with eyes clear blue as a mountain stream. I couldn't stop myself from envisioning kissing one while the other looked on—hey, I'm only human. Isn't that every man's secret fantasy, two beautiful women all to himself?

I gained my composure quickly when Meyers said Violet and Daisy had been named as correspondents in a divorce suit. Their advance man's wife was suing the twins for a quarter of a million dollars. Meyers claimed the idea was ridiculous, that the guy was pulling a scam. I asked the girls if there was any truth to the allegation. So far, Meyers had done all the talking. Daisy looked to Meyers, then said, "Why, we've never even been alone with the man." Meyers smiled and nodded, so she continued. "We gave him a publicity photograph signed, 'To our pal, Bill, with love and best wishes from your pals, Daisy and Violet Hilton.'"

Meyers shot her a murderous look and gripped the arms of his chair. Both girls cowered and flinched, and I knew I needed to speak to them without Meyers present. I asked him to leave the room, and he refused. I told him the Hilton ladies were over eighteen and entitled by law to private counsel, and he left in quite a huff. No sooner had the door closed behind him than Daisy said, "We're practically slaves. Please help us get free."

After I'd heard their story, I knew I had a sensational case, but I'd have to proceed with caution. I told the girls to go with Meyers to their afternoon music lesson as usual. He waited for them in his car out front, and I was waiting out back. I took them to the San Antonio Hotel, where I'd engaged a room, and told them to order anything their hearts desired. The first things they asked for were dresses that weren't alike.

You could tell these sisters were real troupers; on the stand they played up my questions with sad eyes, and sweet, timid little voices. By the time they were through, there wasn't a dry eye in the jury box. The verdict was handed down: all contracts between Violet and Daisy and the Meyers were dissolved. The twins were awarded one hundred thousand dollars. A pittance compared to what those scoundrels stole from the girls over the years.

My modest fee from the case has allowed me to move to a larger office. Daisy and Violet are moving too; they're going to Hollywood to star in an MGM picture.

HARRY DOLL

This is my second picture for MGM, and my second for Tod Browning. Got his start as a Ringling clown, worked riverboat shows, then went into vaudeville as a minstrel singer. Now he's a big-time Hollywood producer. I'm razzin ya, he's a regular guy. First picture was *The Unholy Three*, released in '25. Did ya see it? Got socko reviews. *Variety* said, "It has everything—hoke, romance, crook stuff, murder, suspense, trick stuff, and, above all, is as cleverly titled as has been any production in many moons."

Title of this one is *Freaks*. I ain't gonna give too much away, you'll have to buy a ticket, but I'll tell ya, I play Hans, a midget who's played for a chump by a beautiful gal. On the level, it ain't like the old days when midgets were called General, Commodore, or Count. Tom Thumb was famous for saying, "I've kissed two million ladies including the Queens of England, France, Belgium, and Spain." I played the Palace, but I didn't kiss no queens. Why, if I woulda kissed a lady, even after she'd picked me up and cuddled me like I was some kinda lap mutt, I'd a got a sock in the nose or a hat pin in the arm and she'd scream, "Masher." If ya don't play it clean at the Palace, you're back to the Bowery with the rascals and the bummies. If you're a curiosity, you're back to Coney or the circus sideshow.

Got my start at Coney, me and Grace. Sam Gumpertz, who was running Dreamland, came up with the name the Dancing Dolls, and it stuck. Coney ain't so bad; we made enough money to bring our two sisters, Tiny and Daisy, over from Germany—the two that are midgets; we got four more that are normal size. We cut em in on the act and blew that joint for vaudeville. I'll tell ya on the level, Coney audiences ain't refined.

Our family name is Schneider, but we've changed it to Earles as a stage name, a joke on the old days. Anything's better than "Doll." If Daisy grows another inch, she'll be too tall for a "doll." I'd hate to lose her; she's sixteen and got a voice that'll knock your socks off. She loves it when people called her "the midget Mae West." She's in this picture too, so is Lady Olga, Pete Robinson, Prince Randian, Schlitze and Pip, the Hilton twins—we're taking Coney to every burg in America with a movie house and they're gonna love it all right, all right.

MGM COMMISSARY

Who do they think is going to pay to see this picture? You know what the title is? *Freaks*. I've been in MGM pictures for five years, and with Universal for three years before that. Right now, I've got a supporting role in *Miss Pinkerton*, a top-notch mystery. I'm telling you, *Freaks* is a sure flop. If show people can't tolerate them, you can bet John Q. Public won't. We'll be sitting here having lunch and find Pip the What-Is-It, a dwarf or the Siamese Twins sitting at the next table. Half the studio empties when they come in, because our appetites go out. So, Harry Raff, who is a great moral figure, got a bunch of us together and went to Thalberg to complain about the freaks. He laughed and said, "Forget it. I'm going to make this picture. We're making all kinds of pictures here. Tod Browning's a fine director; he knows what he's doing."

Can't bite the hand that feeds me, but the boy wonder is going to take a beating on this one.

FREAKS PROLOGUE

Before proceeding with the showing of the following HIGHLY UNUSUAL ATTRACTION a few words should be said about the amazing subject.

BELIEVE IT OR NOT . . . STRANGE AS IT SEEMS

In ancient times anything that deviated from the normal was considered an omen of ill luck or representative of evil. Gods of misfortune and adversity were invariably cast in the form of monstrosities and deeds of injustice and hardship have been attributed to the many crippled and deformed tyrants of Europe and Asia.

HISTORY, RELIGION, FOLKLORE, AND LITERATURE abound in tales of misshapen misfits who have altered the world's course. GOLIATH, CALABAN, FRANKENSTEIN, GLOSCESTER, TOM THUMB AND KAISER WILHELM are just a few whose fame is world wide.

The accident of abnormal birth was considered a disgrace and malformed children were placed out in the elements to die. If, perchance, one of these freaks of nature survived, he was always regarded with suspicion. Society shunned him because of his deformity, and a family so hampered was always ashamed of the curse put upon it. Occasionally one of these unfortunates were taken to court to be jeered at or ridiculed for the amusement of the nobles. Others were left to eke out a living by begging, stealing or starving.

For the love of beauty is a deep seated urge, which dates back to the beginning of civilization. The revulsion with which we view the abnormal, the malformed and the mutilated is a result of long conditioning by our forefathers. The majority of freaks themselves are endowed with normal thoughts and emotions. Their lot is truly a heartbreaking one.

They are forced into the most unnatural of lives. Therefore they have built up among themselves a code of ethics to protect themselves from the barbs of normal people. Their rules are rigidly adhered to and the hurt of one is the hurt of all, the joy of one

184

is the joy of all. The story about to be revealed is a story based on the effect of this code upon their lives. Never again will such a story be filmed, as modern science and technology is rapidly eliminating such blunders of nature from the world. With humility for the many injustices done to such people (they have no power to control their lot), we present the most startling horror story of

THE ABNORMAL AND THE UNWANTED.

FREAKS POST SCREENING PARTY

Daisy Earles: Anyone know who wrote that prologue? Where'd they come up with all that jazz? Calls Tom Thumb a misshapen misfit.

Lady Olga: Long-winded piece of trash, ain't it. Lavinia would turn over in her grave.

Pete Robinson: He wasn't misshapen, was he? Anybody know him personal?

Prince Randian: I did, and Olga too. He was shaped fine, just mighty small.

Harry Earles: Who's missing?

Olga: Schlitze and Pip fell asleep during the showing; they're in bed. And the Hilton twins.

Pete: Too refined for our company, those two. Only ones that got a private dressing room. Harry's the star; Mr. Browning said that's why he made this picture cause Harry was so good in *The Unholy Three*.

185

Harry:	They're okay. I knew Violet and Daisy from vaudeville, kinda shy, British, ya know.
Pete:	Suppose Daisy feels it when Violet gets kissed, like they did in the movie?
Daisy:	Sure. When the Dolls was playing the Strand, and the twins was there too, Daisy asked me what perfume I was wearing. I put up my wrist, she sniffed it, and Violet said, 'White Shoulders.'
Pete:	Well, Prince is British too, and he ain't shy.
Daisy:	Oh, you was scary in that storm scene, crawling through the mud with that knife between your teeth.
Pete:	Yeah, but he had one line in the whole movie, and I couldn't understand a word of it.
Prince:	Maybe you so skinny your hearing's thin. Hard to enunciate with a cigarette in my mouth.
Olga:	Careful, Prince, that's my husband you're kiddin with.
Daisy:	Pete, how does Irene feel about you playing Olga's husband in the picture?
Pete:	Can't say or do nothing to displease her since she found out we're in the family way. That's why she wouldn't take a part in the movie. They wanted her to play my wife—the fat lady and the human skeleton always gets a laugh. But she wants to take

186

er real easy, doc says she's up in years for mother-
hood. Her heart's tied up in this baby.

Harry: What about your new husband, Olga? He the
jealous type?

Olga: Save it for the movies.

Daisy: Yeah, Harry, you was the jealous bridegroom in
the picture.

Harry: Nah, Hans wasn't jealous, he was ashamed of the
way Cleopatra treated his friends at the wedding
party.

All: We accept her, we accept her, gooble, gobble,
gooble gobble, one of us, one of us.

Harry: (Imitating Cleopatra's voice) You dirty slimy
freaks. Freaks, freaks, get out of here, I say.

Daisy: Harry, you're such a card.

Pete: Know who else ain't here? Josephine/Joseph.

Prince: He's on a train, gone back to Coney. Man, he
took that punch in the eye, snapped his head
back.

Pete: He shoulda let the stuntman do it; that guy
musta showed him fifty times how to fake a
punch. That's Joey for ya. A scrapper. Once at
Coney, a guy got too fresh with Josephine, and I
seen Joey hit him one crack to the jaw, and the
guy was out like a light.

Harry:	Did it hurt ya, Pete?
Pete:	Whaddaya talking about?
Harry:	Remember our code? The hurt of one is the hurt of all.
Pete:	Oh, yeah. Brother, what's with that 'code of the freaks' shit?
Harry:	Gets to the audience. Separates them from us.
Daisy:	I thought the point was to show we're like everybody else, 'endowed with normal thoughts and emotions,' the prologue says.
Olga:	Now, there's the problem with this picture. In every horror story, which the prologue claims this is, the audience is on the edge of their seats, feeling like the victim until the monster's destroyed in the end. Then they can go home feeling safe and happy.
Pete:	But Cleopatra's destroyed in the end. Well, not murdered, but worse.
Olga:	Yes, but she's the pretty one. That'll confuse people. Beauty's always associated with goodness and ugliness with evil.
Harry:	Cleopatra is evil in the picture, and in the end, she's made into an ugly monster.
Olga:	There again, it breaks tradition. Take your fairy tales, Beauty and the Beast, the Frog Prince—

	always what's ugly is transformed into the beautiful, by magic or love.
Prince:	Is this not a story of a beautiful woman whose evil brings about the downfall of men? Is like the Bible story of Samson and Delilah.
Olga:	But in Bible stories, evil women are either murdered or they repent.
Daisy:	None of them's turned into a bird woman.
Olga:	That's where the egg basket breaks, the ending. The freaks are shown as normal, kind, and tolerant. Daisy, you come off as a bona-fide saint. Takes the threat of murder to one of their own to get them angry enough to do something. They could've called the cops, like normal citizens would.
Harry:	Or they coulda just killed her, out of revenge.
Olga:	That would've made more sense. Instead, the freaks are shown to be the monsters everyone thinks they truly are—the stormy night, creeping through the mud, armed with weapons, stalking the beautiful woman.
Prince:	That woman looked so funny at the end, I had to laugh. She looked like a half-plucked chicken with something stuck in her craw. And how was the freaks pose to make her into that? None of them was a surgeon. Black magic, maybe?
Olga:	She's an obvious fake, passed off as a mutilated freak. Everyone'll know she's a freak only for the

screen, but they'll also know the rest of us are real. Don't get me wrong. I'm thrilled about the picture. Might even help the sideshow business.

Pete: Well, it's sure helped the business of Pete Robinson. The whole country's in a depression, and I'm sittin pretty.

Prince: Me too.

Daisy: Me three.

All: One of us, one of us, gooble, gobble, one of us.

REVIEWS

VARIETY

July 12, 1932

Freaks: Metro production and release based on Tod Robbins story "Spurs." Tod Browning, director. At the Rialto theatre, N.Y. for a run, opening July 8. Running time: 52 minutes.

Planned by Metro to be one of the sensation pictures of the season, "Freaks" failed to qualify in the sure-fire category and has been shown in most parts of the country with astonishingly variable results. In spots it has been a clean-up. In others it was merely misery. It probably will not stay very long at the Rialto in spite of its distinct novelty. It has been sumptuously produced, admirably directed, and no cost was spared, but Metro heads failed to realize that even with a different sort of offering the story still is important. Here the story is not sufficiently strong to get and hold the interest partly because interest cannot easily be gained for a too fantastic romance. The plot outline is the love of a midget in a circus for the robust gymnast, her marriage with the idea of getting his fortune and putting him out of the way through poisoning and effecting a union with the strong man of the show. Her duplicity is discovered and the freaks convert her into a bird woman, making her one of their despised clan. As a horror story, it is either too horrible or not horrible enough, according to the viewpoint. It is gruesome and uncanny rather than tense, which is where the yarn went off the track. The result is a story which does not thrill and at the same time does not please, since it is impossible for the normal man or woman to sympathize with the aspiring midget. And only in such a case will the story appeal. The midget leads are Harry and Daisy Earles. Earles builds on his fine performance in "The Unholy Three," but he fails in the stronger scenes, when he seeks to gain sympathy through his despair. Nothing he can do probably would be taken as a serious appeal, but he does not quite rise to such opportunity as exists. Most of the dependence is placed on the freaks, and these form background, but not story. There is no sinister effect created by their watchful eyes as they spy upon the woman who has insulted them. There is never a suggestion of real danger, and even the author fails to explain the marvel of plastic surgery which converts the faithless wife into a legless bird woman. Summed up, "Freaks" is an inspiration too uninspiredly carried out, and which falls short of the mark in spite of several fine bits and the finest collection of human curios ever assembled outside the Ringling Brothers Circus.

New York Times: JULY 9, 1932

Movie Review: Freaks

The difficulty is in telling whether it should be shown at the Rialto, where it opened yesterday, or in, say, the Medical Center. The only thing that can be said definitely for "Freaks" is that it is not for children. According to one unverified story, women ran screaming from the theater, and the manager later complained that the film left him with a "cleaning job."

PRODIGAL VOICES

FRANK LENTINI

Cooking's one of my hobbies since I retired. You need to taste this sauce—Mmm—delicious. Know why it's so good? Fresh herbs; my wife grows them in those pots on the windowsill. You can see the lake from there. I swim every day, weather permitting, use my third leg as a rudder. Think I'm kidding, eh? You think I'm pulling your leg?

Fishing's my passion, rod and reel, fly, trolling, but the best fishing is with a hook and bobber for bluegills, sunfish, bass on a still, deep pond. Fish that way and you fish in time. I watch the bobber, it jiggles a little, and my memories are jiggled—then down it goes. Sit and have a bite; you can't get food like this in a restaurant.

I thought about going into the restaurant business back in '35. I was nearing fifty, our three boys were out on their own, and my daughter was married, so I figured I could afford a risk. Instead, I started my own Ten-In-One. See, in the thirties and forties, there were so many carnivals and circuses that they played every town, no matter how small. If there was an oddity in some burg, he'd go to the sideshow and ask to join up. More times that not, he'd been turned away from every job he'd tried for. In those days, circus life seemed glamorous and romantic to everyone. Stayed with it until '42. I ran a clean show—no fakes, all the attractions, myself included, were genuine oddities.

Did you get a chance to see the movie *Freaks*? If you didn't see it in '32 or '33, you missed it, because it was banned from theaters in every country in the civilized world. The actors, the oddities in the movie were genuine too, friends of mine from the old days. Where are they now? Let me think . . . Prince Randian, the living

195

torso. The outside talker would say, "The human caterpillar who crawls on his belly like a reptile." He's best remembered for rolling a cigarette and lighting it with his lips. Prince was one of the finest men I've known. He carried an air of dignity few people possess. His wife, Sarah, was devoted to him. He passed away in '36; died two hours after giving a performance at Sam Wagner's Fourteenth Street Museum.

Lady Olga, the bearded lady, what a character, bless her heart. She quit Ringling in '39 because they brought in a union. She settled at Coney, thought the salt air had a medicinal effect on her asthma. Also, she loved that roasted corn on the cob. She was well over seventy years old when she died a few years back, but the Coney folks will remember her striding along the beach, taking in deep breaths, a long scarf wrapped around her neck.

Irene and Pete Robinson have a place in Gibsonton, Florida. Far as I know, he hasn't gotten any fatter and she hasn't gotten any thinner. The town sits on a river and there's huge live oaks, real picturesque. A guy named Eddie LeMay, who ran a carnival cookhouse concession, built a restaurant in Gibsonton back in '24. Carnies started coming there off season, and now it's winter headquarters for lots of sideshow folk. The Robinson boy, Thomas, is a student at Michigan State College.

The Hilton sisters—now, let me think—after the movie *Freaks*, they went on the road with their own revue. During the thirties, they were the highest paid oddities ever. I heard they made as much as five thousand a week. They weren't so lucky in love. Daisy was engaged twice, but nothing came of either romance. She even dyed her hair blonde so her boyfriends could tell them apart. Violet was engaged to their orchestra leader, Maurice Lambert; it made all the papers, even *Time* magazine. Problem was, they couldn't get a marriage license because government officials claimed the marriage would be immoral and indecent. They tried twenty-one states before giving it up. Violet eventually was successful in getting a marriage license with a different fiancee. She and her husband, James Moore, were married in '36 at the Texas Centennial Exposition. Violet later said it was a marriage in name only, a publicity stunt that paid off and was quickly annulled.

Daisy finally got her groom in 1941, a dancer named Buddy Sawyer. Ten days after the wedding, Buddy left her. He said he guessed he wasn't the type of fellow that should marry a Siamese twin. Probably another publicity stunt, this time for his benefit. You know, if the press would've left those girls alone, maybe things could've worked out, but they hounded them with questions like "What's it like to have your sister along on your honeymoon?," and even more personal questions. Then too, I don't believe the twins ever learned the basics, about love and family, how to handle finances. From the day they were born, seems nobody cared enough to teach them, too busy making a profit one way or another.

As time passed, the public lost interest in their act; they weren't girls anymore, and they'd been seen in every corner of the world. They moved to Miami and opened a hamburger stand, which they called the Hilton Sisters' Snack Bar. They weren't in that business very long. Last I heard, they joined up with a traveling carnival sideshow.

Who am I forgetting? Oh, yes, Harry and Daisy Earles. They made another movie after *Freaks*. I know you saw *The Wizard of Oz*. Harry and Daisy and their two sisters played Munchkins. Since they couldn't get more parts in pictures after that one, they joined up with the Ringling Circus. I saw them last summer when the circus played in New Haven. They work from April to November and spend the rest of the year in Sarasota. They've got one of those scaled-down homes where everything is pint-sized—they call it The Doll House. And Harry's got a boat—*The Little Skipper*.

I guess the circus will always be around, but the sideshow is on the ropes. Started with the Great Depression: circus, amusement parks, carnivals were all hard hit, but after WWII, public opinion of sideshows changed. Too many people had been hoodwinked by grifts. People were desperate for money during the Depression years; some would do most anything to make a buck. You ask anybody in the business about the Blue Man or the Human Fountain, and they'll remember them both. The Blue Man's career started when he was prescribed silver nitrate for muscle problems. The drug gave his skin a bluish tint. He took more, got bluer, and made quite a profit at Coney. After he died, Sam Gumpertz found the silver nitrate in his trunk. Mortado, the Human Fountain, actually bored holes in his palms and feet to imitate crucifixion. Before the act, he put small sacks filled with red fluid in the holes. Then, on stage, he'd have an assistant pound nails through the wounds and the sacks would burst. After that, jets of water, hidden under the boards, were squirted through the holes. You could count on at least one fainter.

For a while, every carnival had a wild man or woman, dressed in animal skins, wild-haired, arms and legs covered with dirt, jabbering nonsense and growling. After the show, they'd clean up, go home, and eat supper with their families, just like any American Joe. I heard about a pair of Siamese twins at one carnival who had an argument on the bally platform, and one unlaced the girdle, and walked off alone. Half-and-halfs were popular attractions, especially with the men, because of the blow-off, a private show for an extra charge. They have their ways of fooling the public is all I'll say. Sam Gumpertz trailed after reported hermaphrodites for years before conceding that such an oddity did not exist in nature.

When the economy improved, so did the amusement parks: bigger roller coasters and Ferris wheels, bumper cars, shooting galleries; the sideshow couldn't compete. But the main reason for the fall of the sideshow is lack of exhibits. Doctors will claim they came up with cures or surgical procedures to eliminate freaks of nature. Truth is, in this country, it's become morally unacceptable for oddities to make a living by exhibiting. Old-timers like me, who retired on the earnings we made in the good old days, are set for life. What happens to the young ones? Not midgets, who have their own society, or giants, who inspire admiration, but those born with abnormalities like mine. Institutions? Locked rooms? The few seedy dime museums still operating in the backwaters?

SODDY DAISY, TENNESSE

THE MIDWIFE

Washed my hands don't know how many times. Sweet Jesus, I'm afraid there's a hex on these hands now. Been bringing babies in as far as Signal Mountain for most twenty years and never seen a sign of sin nor evil, but this be devil's work. Good thing she'd already bore one, or it would have killed her, sure.

"Ma'am, it's two of em in there," I said cause my hands could feel the arms and legs, and when a head crowned, I said, "Push hard." Out it come with a swoosh, mouth open and yowling, and I seen the other body was sticking out of that baby boy's chest. No head, just shrively arms, stout body, a boy too, but no head.

I dropped to my knees to pray to Jesus that Beelzebub wouldn't come carry us all away. Then I thought of that poor woman lying there, so I took it over to the basin. I was sorely tempted to hold its head under the water, but only the Almighty hath the power of giving life and taking away, so I washed it, saw to tying the stem, and wrapped it in flannel.

She was looking out the window, saying rain would be good for the beans, and the thing never ceased yowling. I took it to her. She unwrapped the blanket, held it to her breast, and her face in the light of the window was green, like when a tornado's coming.

WIL, THE GREATER TWIN

Even when we was small back in Soddy Daisy, I knew Bill was thinking and feeling. Go ahead and rub his arm, he'll raise it up like a cat for a scratch. I call him Bill; Wil and Bill, just between us. He didn't get a name from my parents. To this day, I know better than to take my shirt off in front of Daddy. I knew about Bill before we had that x-ray at the Chattanooga hospital when I got pneumonia. Doctor said there was "evidence of a rudimentary head" inside my chest. The promoter loved it—ten more lines to add to the spiel.

Bill likes Gibsonton. I can walk around with my chest bare, fish in the river, just lay down in the grass and soak in the sun. This here's the freak capital of the world, and nobody stares, even when he's having a piss. There's no hard edge to folks' voices. Back home, Bill was tense most of the time, especially when we was doing the dime circuses.

Things was better after we joined the carnival circuit, for me anyhow; I ran with a wild bunch. There was plenty of women—floozies, drunk and curious, eager to please for a buck or two. That stopped one night altogether. Bill was quiet, from the whiskey, I suppose. After I mounted her, he started in twitching and sweating heavy. I should've thought about him, but I get drunk and need to prove something. My heart was pounding with one thing on my mind. It wasn't until I heard her giggling that I saw she'd taken him into her mouth.

Came down to Gibsonton the first time last year when the carnival I was working closed down for winter. I'm bringing Mama and Daddy down for Christmas next month. Met a girl here. Her mama was a circus fat lady, but Etta's tiny as a thimble and sweet as mountain clover.

BILL, THE LESSER TWIN

A dimah look a dimah look mor'n one no yet two
Oh Lordy!
It don't matter it don't matter Bill
Lookey that Jesus holy Christ
Crying again, boy got morands and feets thanaresta us puttem
ta use
It don't matter Bill he can go ta hell
Great God almighty Landagoshen
That thang oughta be kilt
A dimah look a dimah look mor'n one no yet two

ETTA'S GRANDMOTHER

This clipping's from the 1940 New York World's Fair. She was the star attraction: "Pretty Patty, The World's Fattest Female." I named her Patricia Louise. She was a beautiful baby, twelve pounds at birth. People'd say, "You're so lucky to have such a big, healthy baby, what with the croup going around. She ain't gonna get sick with that appetite of hers."

Here's another one—the Panama Pacific Exposition in San Francisco; she was in Mardi Gras too. That was after she joined the circus. Before that, it was real hard. Kids teased all the time; sometimes I'd hear them outside the screen door on their way home from school, calling her "Fatty" and "tub of lard." I felt so bad—worse than Patty, I think. I mean, she'd slam the door when she came inside, and I let her get away with that, cause she'd be smiling by the time she got to the kitchen. How could I say no to her when she wanted a second piece of pie? I tell you, a mother can only do so much.

All through her high school years, she never had a date or went to a dance. After graduation, we sent her to secretarial school, and she did get a good job, but she kept getting bigger, and people would stare when they came into the place, and she got the boot.

You know, she was making $200.00 a day! Can you imagine that much money for just sitting? But, like I say, people loved her and loved to look at her. She had real pretty dresses and costumes with feathers and sequined hats; she smiled so big and wide, course, it was her job to look happy. But she weren't, even after she married Earl. She never said, but I know. Now Earl's a good man, I know he was good to Patty, and their union was blessed by having little Etta. But when you think she couldn't go nowhere outside that circus— no restaurants, no vacations, not even a pair of shoes to fit.

How would you feel if every piece of furniture was too small for you to sit in? That's pretty hard. And, in the end, she couldn't even get into the church . . . I'm sorry . . . I get to crying every time I think of it. I just can't talk anymore.

ETTA'S FATHER

Me and Etta decided to stay with the circus. Etta works in the office—she's got a head for figures—and I went back to concessions. That's what I was doing when I met Patty. Dot, the regular fat lady, was having surgery, and Patty came to take her place temporary. I was hawking the aisles with peanuts when she came into the center ring on a Belgian draft, dressed like a queen, white feathers all around her hair, silver robe trimmed with rabbit fur trailing on the horse' hindquarters.

Dot didn't make it through her surgery, so Patty was hired full-time. Smart move for the circus—Patty brought in twice the crowd. Ha, put on twice the weight in the bargain. Big in size, big in heart, my Patty. Don't know why she chose me. She said it was because I was strong as a mule, stubborn as a mule, and three times as ugly. Said you never could trust a man with a pretty face.

After Etta was born, things got tougher for Patty. Not because of the baby, I swear, there's never been a woman more suited to mothering than my Patty. But once Etta started walking, it was hard for Patty to keep up with her. That was the only time Patty tried to lose weight, for Etta's sake. Etta was just over a year old and playing in her crib. She had a red ball with bells inside that she was partial to. The ball bounced out of the crib, rolled into a closet, and Etta decided to go after it.

Patty was sitting in her chair across the room. She looked up just as Etta was swinging one leg over the rail. Patty couldn't move fast enough. Etta toppled over and banged her head on the floor. The cut wasn't bad, but it bled some. Etta was crying and she tottered into the closet after the ball. Patty was beside herself—she was too big to get into the closet, and there Etta sat, bleeding and screaming, hanging on to that damn ball. Patty started yelling for help; I was working at the time, but Pete was going by, and he came in, calmed them both down, and bandaged Etta's head.

I think she just plain worried some weight off. She'd "what if" me till I thought I'd go crazy. Etta didn't have any more accidents, and Patty got bigger. Had to move into a reinforced semitrailer, and have furniture special made to hold her weight. She'd fret over the cost, and I'd tell her, "Hell, honey, you earn it, I guess you deserve to spend it on the best."

What bothered her most about getting that big was needing to have somebody around all the time in case she'd fall. Ya see, she couldn't get up on her own. Then the tumors grew inside her knees. She wouldn't go to the hospital, scared I guess, after Dot. One day her heart started jumping. Took her over to the hospital in Tampa, but she was too big for the beds, and they had to turn us away.

The services were held outdoors in front of the Community Church. I know my Patty would have wanted it that way. It was a big funeral, proper for my big gal. Every one of our friends was there, and the flowers . . .

The Reverend's speech was short and not as personal as I'd like, but he didn't know her too well, us being on the road so much.

THE REVEREND

The Lord gave me strength to get through that abomination. Naturally, when the man came to me in need of clergy for his departed wife's services, I accepted. He seemed neat and clean, and he paid in cash.

I tried to make the best of it; holding funeral services out of doors is pagan, but the woman was so fat the coffin would not fit through the church doors. The sermon was shorter than usual, but what could I say? "I am the resurrection and the life, he who believeth in me, though he were dead, yet shall he live, and whosoever liveth and believeth in me, shall never die."

I know what I would like to have said: gluttony was man's first sin, the cause of our temptation, the very origin of damnation! Adam and Eve were driven from the Garden of Paradise because of that sin. The sickness, sorrow, and shame it breeds; farmers breaking their backs to provide food for our tables, while gluttons take more than their share, stuffing their gullets with imported delicacies. Saint Paul said of gluttony, "Meats for the belly, belly for the meats, but God shall yet destroy both it and them."

He destroyed that woman for her sin, for she sinned against God by ruining her body, His temple. She became an enemy of God by making food her golden idol; she dug her own grave with a fork and a knife.

Such a gathering of Godless creatures, misshapen by sin—too tall, too short, covered with animal-like hair. That poor daughter, a little slip of a girl, lovely beyond description, holding hands with that creature. When my Mrs. caught a glimpse of it sticking out from under his coat, she nearly collapsed. And that infernal tiny man, like a gargoyle perched on the shoulders of a giant, kept blowing his nose through the best parts of my sermon.

PETE'S BEST FRIEND

Wish I knew a way to cheer up Pete. It's been months since Patty died, and he's still down in the dumps. Well, he paints on a smile for the performances; we're both working as clowns now, and I don't like it one bit. Shortly after Patty died, the manager got a letter from the owners stating that the sideshow was being phased out.

I try to help, ask Pete to play a game of chess or take in a movie, and he seldom turns me down, but his heart isn't in it. Every morning, Pete would go over to Patty and Earl's place. Earl would be sleeping because he'd worked late; he was glad Patty had the company, and Patty was happy for someone to talk to. I couldn't drink her coffee, oh, boy, strong enough to take the hair off an elephant's back. But Pete, it got him going, he said.

Pete watched little Etta grow. She outgrew him by the time she was four years old. Pete wanted to know everything where Etta was concerned; how many inches she'd grown, how many pounds she'd gained, if she had any new teeth. He was there when she took her first steps. She'll be marrying soon, I just hope they don't leave the circus, the manager said he couldn't hire Wil, her intended. Well, Patty would tell Pete all about Earl's family, her own—mom and dad, brothers and sisters; Pete knew them all by name and would ask after them.

Pete and I never talk about family. We talk about the news, sports, and history. I'll tell you, Pete knows enough history to write a book. He's got more books than the public library and many are about unusual folks, like *Curious Myths of the Middle Ages*, *Pudd'nhead Wilson* by Mark Twain, *Pharaoh's Fool*, *Monsters and Prodigies*, *Giants and Dwarfs*. Can you believe some people think that because a dwarf is the size of a child, his brain is like a child's? Anyways, just one time Pete told me about his family, and the circumstances were actually quite funny. We were in New Orleans, and it was Mardi Gras. I'd been with the circus about two years, must have been about twenty-one years old then. After the show, we went out to paint the town red. We'd been sitting at an outdoor cafe, drinking rum and coffee for hours when a group of pretty belles went scampering by, and Pete decided he wanted to go after them.

Well, I can cover a lot of ground, even when I'm ten sheets to the wind, but Pete was having a hard time of it. So I picked him up, put him inside my coat, and started to run. And Pete's yelling, "Faster, faster, Sam, we're losing them."

Then I start really moving, and I forget about Pete; he's hanging on to my vest, his legs flopping against my hip, and he's white as a ghost. I stopped just in time for him to jump down and heave in the gutter. I handed him my bandanna to clean up with, and he gave me the soundest cursing I've ever had.

Later, on our way back to the grounds, we saw those gals going into a hotel. I kept my distance, just enough to see what room they had—waited a proper while, then walked to the room and looked through the transom; there isn't one made high enough I can't peek through. Then I lifted Pete onto my shoulders, and it was a good ten minutes before they noticed him and started squealing and we took off.

When we got back to the trailer, Pete told me about his sister, Geisella, and showed me her picture. She lives in Cleveland; she's two years older than Pete. He told me she's normal sized, but he'd had one brother and twin sisters that were midgets, and they died in the gas chambers at Auschwitz. His parents tried to protect them, but they were killed too. Pete told me about 10,000 dwarfs and midgets were exterminated by the Nazis. He said Hitler wanted to rid the race of physical abnormalities. I guess I was lucky being born in America.

Well, Pete's parents knew trouble was coming and wanted to get all the kids out, but four midgets were too conspicuous, so they put Pete and Geisella on a steamer to New York first. Pete got an idea

206

from a movie that Harry Earles starred in. Harry was German too and a midget, but he came to America after WWI. Pete's idea was to dress Geisella as a nurse, and Pete dressed himself like a baby.

After they got to the States, Pete worked as an aircraft mechanic. He could get into parts of planes that normal sized people couldn't. From the time he was eighteen till he was twenty-one, he crawled into those planes, working double shifts when he could.

Patty was his comfort, like a mother, I guess. Heck, Pete and I can misery together on how bad growing up was with all the desks and pencils too big or too small, clothes that never fit right, people staring, but it's just not the same. He misses Patty. I need to tell him I'm leaving the circus soon. I want to give my photography a try, maybe set up a studio with my savings. There's a couple of people I'd like to come with me, and Pete's one of them. I don't know if I can make a convincing argument for him to leave this place and take a risk on the outside. I think I'll get a letter off to Geisella.

CLEVELAND, OHIO

PETE'S SISTER

It was good of Sam to write. My poor Peter; I think, mostly, it's this time of year. It was in autumn that Peter and I received word from Germany about our family, and for Peter and me, every autumn is a reminder. It is most harsh for Peter, because he's a midget and feels he should have died too. All survivors feel guilty, Peter more than most.

There were three older than us, my twin sisters, Frieda and Anna, and another brother, Erich. We were all entertainers! Mama and Papa too. We girls played violin, Erich played cello, Papa the bass, and Mama the piano. Even though Peter was youngest, he was the maestro; the music he made with the violin was like nothing else you would ever hear.

He was the smallest too, no bigger than a toddler, even now. Oh! You can't imagine the pain we shared when I had to carry him in my arms, dressed in a bonnet and dress, onto the ship. So many tears shed; my sisters and brother insisting Mama and Papa go with us, Peter and I pleading to stay. It was not a question of money—we had the best of everything—but Mama and Papa never would have left the others. And taking four midgets out of the country would have drawn too much attention.

Peter has not picked up a violin since we left Germany. We lived together while he worked as a mechanic for the armed services. Then I received an offer to teach music at the conservatory here, and Peter joined the circus. At first I objected, but Peter told me that we held too much shared grief between us, and if he could not laugh, at least he could be surrounded by people who had laughter in their hearts.

He had promise you see. Peter was so intelligent that Mama and Papa sent him to a private school when he was ten years old. Math, sciences, literature, Peter eagerly absorbed them all. But where he really shone was in his writing. I have copies of all the poems he wrote in school. Here, here is one of his poems that was printed in our local paper along with a photograph of Peter and the headmaster.

> The bogeyman is not a ghoul with a mouth of gaping red.
> He does not hide beneath your stool or underneath your bed.
> He walks across the countryside carrying a purse of gold,
> searching houses far and wide for children to be sold.
> The littlest ones he puts in jars of various shapes and sizes,
> until their bodies, deformed and scarred, mold to the shape he prizes.
> But the children prized above all, I'm told
> are dwarfs and midgets who never grow old.
> Whether they stand further or nearer,
> their reflections are fixed within time's mirror.

THE HEADMASTER

I remember the day this photograph was taken . . . how many years ago? Now, what's to become of me? I'm not one of those fossils who retires to write scholarly papers and collect dust. All my belongings, all my memories fit in these two cardboard boxes. I want to stay here, this is my school.

Look in this box—first-place awards year after year in track and field, high jump, discus, javelin, rowing. Such strong, healthy young men. I wonder where they are now; what they are doing. Do they remember me? And this pathetic little boy. His parents sent me this article, don't know why I kept it, although I must say, I did cut a fine figure in those days, don't you think? Vaudevillians, those people, produced four disfigured children. Why didn't they stop after the first?

I have to admit, he was smart as a whip, but what kind of potential? If only his size could have matched his brain, I would have had a real champion.

MILWAUKEE, WISCONSIN

SAM'S SCHOOLMATE

Don't know what the big deal is. So he got somebody to put out a book of his camera pictures, and the town paper's gotta plaster his ugly mug all over the front page like he's some kinda local hero. Hell, he hasn't been around here since high school graduation. I mean, the guy's a weirdo, a freak.

Wouldn't ya think with a body that size he woulda gone out for sports? I lettered in three sports myself—football, basketball, and track. My name was in the paper every goddamn week of the year.

209

He lived down the street from me, so we was in grade school right up to high school together, and I'm telling ya, the guy was a real sissy. Us guys all tried, but he'd run away every time ya talked to him.

I recollect one time, in high school, we told him if he didn't come out for the football team, we'd put a love letter in Betty Donovan's locker and sign his name on it. Betty was homely as a mud fence, stupid as a cow, and bigger than most of us guys. It really shook ole Sam up, the thought of having Betty moon over him. We did it for his own good, just trying to help him fit in, ya know.

Well, he comes out on the field after school in those dumb clothes—always wore the same thing, a dark blue suit, white shirt and tie, for Chrissake. The coach yells at him to go to the locker room and get into proper dress, and he just stands there, staring. Some pip-squeak next to him says there weren't any that he could fit into. You know, the guy was close to seven feet tall by then. So the coach tells me to throw him the ball, see if he can catch, and I whip one over. The moron doesn't even lift his arms, the ball thuds him in the chest. He smiles and looks over at the coach kinda nervous like, and the coach tells me to try again. This time, I aim at his big head, I figure he's gonna raise up his arms to protect his face, especially seeing as he was a four-eyes, ya know. But by Jeezus—he don't, and wham! right in the face, knocks his glasses off and everything, and he just stands there smiling.

Some of the other guys were watching, and they started throwing balls at him too, and laughing 'cause he just stood there with that big dumb grin on his puss. Even the coach is laughing. Then that pip-squeak, don't remember his name, a nobody, didn't make the team neither, he picks up Sam's glasses and hands them to him. He puts them in his pocket and turns tail and runs like the devil. Some hero, huh?

You know how much they want for that book of his? Five dollars! Jeezus, if I wanna look at pictures, I'll get a copy of *Life* for twenty cents.

SAM'S FIANCEE

I know now it was a mistake, but I figured he'd find someone else by now. He will soon, what with his photography book in the stores. There's a picture of me and him together on page forty, taken right before he left the circus. It was too much to ask of me then, to leave the circus. Sam had lived most of his life with his family, in a regular town where people knew him and were used to his size. That's how the circus is for me—all the people here are my family, and outside, I don't fit in. Besides, I don't need to go out for anything—don't have to go to the market or cook meals, we have a barber that cuts hair and pulls teeth, and a nurse for ailments. Nora, one of the clown's wives, sews dresses for me, and traveling salesmen come around with brushes and whatnots.

I've been with the circus since I was five years old. I was as tall as Ma by then, and when a circus came into town and an agent offered Pa a contract, he packed my satchel, bought me a bag of peppermints, and kissed me good-bye. That was the first time I ever had candy, and the last time I saw my family. At first, I thought I was the worst-done-by, sorriest critter alive. But looking back, I don't blame Pa—dirt farmer with seven little ones to feed, and one real big little one. At the circus, I had lots of Mas, ones that weren't worn out and bone thin.

I was sixteen when Sam signed on, and I was smitten. He was nineteen and nervous as a long-tailed cat in a room full of rocking chairs. Pete took care of that. Pete's a midget, a real sweet and quiet man who had joined up about four years before. He brought Sam around to my tent to introduce us, and to help work on the act. The manager planned to bill us as "Sam and Sue, the Giant Twins." We were nearly the same height then, but I kept growing, and Sam stopped at seven feet three inches. I'd been used to standing on a step hid under my dress, but Sam was mortified when they put risers in his shoes. I guess we couldn't help but fall for each other, being together so much of the time, and I was the first giant woman Sam had met.

He was all the time trying to get me to go out, like to an ice cream parlor or to a Hollywood movie. He even managed to get me to a few—we'd sit in the last row so nobody would yell about not being able to see over us. I never could get comfortable out in public.

On my eighteenth birthday, Sam brought me a big box, all wrapped up with paper and ribbons. I untied the ribbons, lifted off the top, and out pops Pete, all dressed up in his fancy suit, and he's holding a little box. Inside that box was the prettiest diamond ring. I wear it still, here, on my pinkie.

We must have had one of the longest engagements in history. Despite the manager's urging that we tie the knot and produce a "giant baby," eight years passed with me putting Sam off. I told myself it was for Sam's sake, that he'd be better off with a normal girl. Sam's a true giant, which is very rare. Most of us in the shows are tall because of gland problems, and that means foot trouble and weak knees and hearts.

I'll be honest with you, I had no desire to become a mother. Not because I didn't love Sam, or because I thought the circus was-n't a proper place to raise a child. I'd been in the circus a long time, and I'd heard stories about women giants giving birth to babies twenty pounds and up. The babies rarely lived for more than a few days if they weren't stillborn.

I guess I thought Sam would stay with the circus and we could just go on being sweethearts forever. But after Patty, the fat lady died, the manager put Pete and Sam and me into a clown act. Sam started talking about going to Texas to open a photography studio. Death and change have a way of making people hurry up. He said, "Come with me, Susie. In Texas, everything's big, and there's no ice to slip on."

I should have gone. Myrtle Perkins is the smartest woman I know, and she said I should have gone.

MYRTLE PERKINS

A physician advised my parents not to shave my facial hair because this would cause my beard to grow back thicker and heavier. He was right. When I became an adult, I had to shave twice daily, sometimes more often than that. I went through my girlhood years with a hairy chin; nobody ever thought of disobeying their parents' wishes. And in those days—I was born at the turn of the century—the only way a bearded gal could make a living was in the museums or the circus.

I left home at age sixteen, which wasn't uncommon then. An unmarried girl of twenty was considered a spinster. The only thing I took from home, besides my clothing, was Father's razor. When I got off the train at Union Station, my face was as smooth as a baby's bottom. I looked for jobs that kept my hands busy so I wouldn't be touching my chin all the time. And jobs where the other workers were busy too, so they wouldn't have time to notice my two o'clock shadow. I worked in laundries and washed mountains of dishes in restaurant kitchens.

I keep my beard short now, trim it back with scissors. My hands are still steady at seventy, thank you Lord. I've been retired since 1960. I used to exhibit once in a while at a carnival or a town fair. I didn't need the money; I invested in real estate years ago, and I'm financially secure. I missed the people, the circus and sideshow folks, the lights, brass bands, sequins, feathered plumes, powder hanging in the air, the hoots and hollers of the crowds, the excitement . . . the excitement. That's what hooked me from the start.

The last job I had before joining the circus was at the Wink-N-Pup Bar. I washed dishes in the kitchen. The cook was a big, handsome man with a waxed handlebar moustache. Out of the corner of my eye, I'd see him watching me, but I didn't dare look back, else he'd notice my whiskers. Finally, after two weeks, I couldn't stand it anymore. I turned around, lifted my chin, and said, "All right, Mister, take a good look!"

I thought he'd discovered my secret; it was near midnight and my chin was bristly. You can imagine my surprise and relief when he said, "Thank you kindly, Miss. I've been trying to get a good look at that pretty face since you started here, but you've always got it hid in those blasted suds."

To make a long story short, Michael and I were married, and after saving and putting our money together, we bought a bar of our own. We called it "Mike and Myrtle's," and we made a good go of it until the real-estate boom, when taxes went so high we could hardly afford to stay in business.

One Sunday afternoon, we decided to take a day off and go to the traveling circus show. When the main performance was over, you had to walk by the sideshow to exit. We didn't plan on going inside, but I heard the barker say "Bearded Lady," and my curiosity got the best of me. We paid a nickel each and went inside. The woman had a very sparse beard, straight and rather short, and I said to Mike, "I could grow a better beard than that in three weeks' time." The barker overheard me, and said he'd take me up on it and give me a job if I wasn't fooling.

Next to marrying Michael, that was the wisest decision I ever made. We sold the bar at a loss and joined the circus. I'm not sure how Mike felt at first, seeing me with a hairy face; he didn't come to the shows for a long while. But after Shaun was born, everything was okay. Together, Mike and I saw the world, and we formed friendships that would last a lifetime. Our children traveled with us, Shaun and our daughter Margaret. We had a good life, even though it was too short. Mike had a fatal heart attack when he was just forty-nine. I left the circus for a year; couldn't stand it, everything reminded me of my Michael. I went to Florida and exhibited with Frank Lentini's Ten-In-One. Frank passed away four years ago, at the age of seventy-seven. Next to Mike,

Frank was the best-natured man I ever knew. He loved children; he'd take twenty minutes or more to answer a little one's question. He treated his people with courtesy and kindness, but I got to missing the travel and my friends in the circus. Time heals all wounds, it's true.

Shaun and his wife live on a ranch in Montana, and Maggie's a schoolteacher in Manhattan. Between the two of them, I have five grandchildren—there on the bureau is a photograph. My old friend Sam took that picture last summer when I had all the children here. He was up north visiting family; he always stops to see me when he's passing through. As I was saying earlier, it's the folks I miss, friends like Sam and his sidekick, Pete. My children were grown and had left the nest when Pete joined on. He was so shy and serious at first, tried to keep to himself, but that's nearly impossible when you work the sideshow. Patty got hold of him, and she could charm the spots off a leopard. Patty was the circus Fat Lady, and she married Earl, who worked concessions. She passed away, oh, around 1955. A shame she didn't live to see her granddaughter. That Earl dotes on her; I got a letter from him last week. He said Etta is still working in bookkeeping for the circus. They don't have to travel because the circus has a company headquarters in Sarasota. Her husband, Wil, works there too, in the stock department. Earl writes that Pete is the proud godfather, and sometimes they fight over who's going to baby-sit. I was so worried about Pete after Patty died. And then Sam left the circus, but he took a course in electronics and now he repairs televisions in an appliance store in Sarasota. I was worried about sweet Susie too. She was engaged to Sam, and when he left the circus, I couldn't talk her into going with him. She's doing fine. She married an animal trainer from Budapest and moved over there. I'm not so sure she was ever in love with him—she was just bound and determined to stay in the circus. In Europe, they don't have the reformers we have here who say exhibiting in sideshows is demoralizing.

What happened to the Hilton sisters, now that's demoralizing. I saw them perform the vaudeville show in Chicago just after Mike and I were married. The show was simply wonderful. I never saw them again, but I'd read about them in the newspapers now and then. I read their obituary last year. They'd been living in Charlotte, North Carolina, working at a supermarket as checkouts. You know how they happened to be in Charlotte? Well, in 1962, they appeared at a drive-in theater to publicize the re-release of the movie *Freaks*. The agent who'd arranged the appearance brought them to Charlotte and promised to pick them up, but he never showed—left them stranded with no money. The supermarket owner had to buy them dresses because all they had were show clothes. One morning, they didn't come in for work, and the next day, the store manager called the police. They were found dead on the floor of their apartment—Hong Kong flu. The article said Daisy and Violet had no relatives and hadn't made friends at the supermarket or in their neighborhood, that they wouldn't talk to anyone. Even so, many people went to their funeral. I guess the minister caused a stir when he asked, "How many of you came here to grieve?" According to the paper, he shook his head and added, "They were always looked upon as freaks."

I know, from a few sideshow friends who were in vaudeville, that Daisy and Violet loathed the sideshow business. Their way of dealing with their deformity was to deny it, which was easy to do when they were celebrities on stage, talented young girls making over five thousand a week in their prime. The reason they went on the carnival circuit was money. Same as for most of us, the freak show was a meal ticket. More for some; it was a relief from the loneliness of isolation, a place where they were accepted. And believe it or not, some were proud of their uniqueness. That era's gone, a shadow in an old lady's memory. The sideshow's faded into gray just like my beard. Pity, there's nothing so fascinates people as freaks.

✦

JOHNNY/JOHANNA

So you found me. Who brought you here? Alecto, Megaera, Tisiphone, with their secret stings and wreaths of serpents? Aeschylus, the tragic poet, having once represented the Furies in a chorus of fifty performers, caused such terror among the spectators that many fainted and were thrown into convulsions. The magistrates forbade a like representation for the future. Your ancient equivalent of the freak show.

What do you want? I've got a show in an hour and the makeup takes time. Let me guess. You want to know which is my true sex, what kind of equipment I've got and how I use it, if I'm married, if I have children, all those mundane concerns of righteous society. I am both man and woman; the breasts are real.

I do Marlene Dietrich in the act . . . Ich bin die fesche Lola . . . Dier Liebling der Saison . . . Here's an autographed picture. Most of the old queens in the show have photos of Mae West or Judy Garland, but nobody has Lola's. This picture was taken in Berlin in 1927 at the Femina Cabaret. God, what a city it was then! On the streets you'd see war profiteers, rakish in their orange and lilac suits, transvestites with red lips sitting in sidewalk cafes, skirts pulled up above their hairy thighs, the boys strutting in big suits and dirty sandals, and girls in transparent blouses and black stockings, skirts high enough to show their wares, the scent of perfume and perspiration. Marlene performed in cabarets and in the theaters. She walked around the city wearing a monocle and a boa, sometimes five red fox furs, or wolf skins. She always attracted a crowd. I met her at the Kammerspiele; both of us were performing in *A Midsummer Night's Dream*. She was Hippolyta and I was Hermia. She and I are both old now. Marlene is revered as an icon of the cinema, and I'm performing in Bourbon Street's finest female impersonator revue, the last refuge of an extinct species.

My mind inclines to speak of forms changed into new bodies. "Gods, breathe favorably to my undertaking for ye have changed yourselves, and them; and lead down a continuous poem from the first origin of the world to my times." From Ovid's *Metamorphoses*, the finest work of literature ever written. I left that reeking, bovine Indiana farm as sixteen-year-old Johnny, and in Berlin I became Johanna, the toast of the city's smart circles. I can't remember my earliest years; I don't know how my parents reacted to my birth. I do know my mother raised me as a female until I was six years of age, and that she kept the mystery of my anatomy a secret from the old man. Mennonites harbor many secrets. She was bathing me one morning when he came in unexpectedly, having torn his thumb putting up a fence. He entered with his hand raised over his head, his shirtsleeve soaked with blood. Mother screamed and rushed for a bandage. I watched her shoulders heave as she wrapped his thumb, and in my distress, forgot the promise I'd made to her and stood upright in the tub. I remember his sharp intake of breath, and Mother becoming stiff as a statue, then turning slowly to the sound of my whimpers.

"My daughter is a boy?" he said, first in disbelief, then in rage, "My daughter is a boy!" and his boot found the middle of her back. The next day, her flat features puffed with bruises, Mother shaved my head, burned my clothing, and dressed me in blue trousers, blue shirt, and black shoes. I became John, a good Mennonite boy.

I reached puberty at age fourteen, buoyant in a sea of sexuality, tossed through wet dreams, waking with erections, my budding breasts aching. When the old man discovered the bloody rags buried behind the barn, and knew it wasn't Mother's time, he snapped. I was confined to the stable, one arm chained to a beam; a single cot, a single dress, a comb to make me presentable. For the length of a year, I was the Saturday night entertainment for the old man's cronies. He charged them a dollar at the door. That bitch didn't lift a finger to stop him. She'd come in Sunday mornings, clean me up, and pray to her God. But it was my gods and goddesses who were listening, and my prayers that were answered: a shovel carelessly left leaning against the adjoining stall, its smooth, inviting handle within reach. After the deed was done, I took the key from inside his boot; he was facedown, the back of his skull pulsing gray and red like the hogs prepared for headcheese. As my final salute, I took out my famous phallus and pissed on his bloody carcass.

I sought refuge in a carnival freak show. Even though I was quite certain the Mennonites would keep the murder in the family, I couldn't take unnecessary risks. The carnival was constantly on the move. Don't get the idea that I found some kind of home there, among the freaks. I kept to myself completely, reading the Greek and Roman classics. My quarters had belonged to a tattooed man, a Greek who didn't return one night from a walk into town. His wagon had been cleared of everything of value to the carnival owner. Only maps on the wall and stacks of books remained. A treasure, the revelation of my heritage, my metamorphosis, my true and glorious self. Among those marvelous pages I found depictions of Pompeii wall paintings honoring the god Hermaphroditus. I saw The Sleeping Hermaphroditus, a Hellenistic tribute in marble to whom worshippers brought offerings of food and flowers on the fourth day of every month. It became my obsession to journey to Greece. Within a year, I had earned sufficient funds to book passage to London. From there, I took a train to Berlin, where my funds ran out. Being fluent in the language, and beautiful of face and physique, I had no trouble getting by.

As I said, Berlin was an incredible city, throbbing with intensity and passion. My passions were awakened as if I had dwelt all my life in the poppy-festooned cave of Somnus. One week, I would be my man self and seduce fetching frauleins, the next, my woman self, moaning with ecstasy in the arms of a sweet young boy. My escapades soon drew the attention of Karl, an icy-eyed, dashing pimp who catered to those possessing wealth and power. I rode in black taxis striped with gold, frequented cabarets with silk-covered walls, reveled until dawn when pyramids of champagne bottles clogged the narrow alleys. In a few short months, I had enough money to purchase a train ticket to Greece, but that grand dream diminished under the bright lights of the stage. One of my regular clients was a theater producer. After he learned I'd memorized many plays and could recite with the passion of Erato, Johanna, the toast of Berlin, was "discovered."

Among Berlin's theater crowd, those who refused sex with people of their own gender were ridiculed in smart circles. One dance club, The Golden Hare, was popular with visiting farmers. There were telephones on the tables for patrons to call each other. House rules required that if a man called a girl, she had to prove when she came to his table that she really had breasts. Many times a rube would find himself stroking the leg of an actor or athlete in drag.

I met Otto at the Golden Hare. A farmer! I was growing bored with the decadence of Berlin. Otto smelled of pine and wood smoke. His laugh was loud and generous, his eyes clear as the countryside, his hair fine like yellow silk on Indiana corn. Otto was proud of my height and my broad shoulders, and so infatuated he didn't mind that my phallus was as big as his. He told me that when he was a boy a neighbor had a bull that kept breeding even though it had been castrated. Otto explained that the bull had a hidden testicle, and by rights should've been slaughtered, leaving the cows to the best breeding bulls. But the farmer gave him extra feed, and men from neighboring farms would come to stare at the bull and stroke his ears. "You're like that bull, hiding a wondrous mystery beneath your skirts," Otto said.

He wanted to keep me all to himself, and when I learned I was pregnant, I gave up the theater and its trappings for my farmer. I wouldn't marry him, though; it wouldn't be legal. I moved to his cottage in the country and became a model hausfrau. There, I indulged my woman self, marveling at the changes in my body, the ripening of my fruits, the rounding of my breasts and abdomen. Four months into my pregnancy, my womb contracted in spasms. The infant slid onto the sheet, a rosebud torn from its stem in a rainstorm, petals curled and sodden. I watched Otto's back from the window as I wrote the farewell letter. He worked shirtless and his suspenders dug into his flesh. He was kneeling in the garden, tying young tomato vines onto stakes.

In Amsterdam and Paris I was Johnny; five years in as many cities I was Johnny. Then the dogs of war were let loose in Europe. Men were being "recruited" off the streets. Imagine they would have been content to discharge me after a night in the barracks? As Johanna, I made the crossing to America. Where was I to go to earn a living with nothing but ten deutsche marks and a tongue thick with a German accent? The only place I could go—the freak show.

Being a gen-you-ine "morphodite," I was never turned away. Occasionally, I was forced to blows with the fake half-and-halfs who came at me in fits of jealous rage after being fired once the managers saw me in the flesh. Any fool knows nature can't divide someone down the middle. The fakes would speak in a high, effeminate voice, then change to a baritone. Their scalps were shaven on one side. On the female half, their body hair was shaved and bleached, and the male half's muscles were developed by lifting weights. Some would inject paraffin on one side to fake a breast. I saw one guy who faked a vagina, and all he used was a long string of elastic. First he wrapped cotton around his phallus just behind the head, and tied a cinch knot over it with one end of the string. He pushed his gonads up into the abdominal cavity, leaving the scrotal sack hanging empty; pulled his phallus down between his legs then up tight between his buttocks and the remaining elastic was wrapped around his waist. The gaff made the appearance of a vagina; his empty sack was brought forward producing the lips. During his blow-off, I witnessed a man kiss it.

Surely you can understand why, throughout my many lives and loves, I often returned to the sideshow. I made more money from the blow-offs then I could make in half a year busting my nuts as a field hand. These divine hands were not made for common labor.

"If any gentlemen in the audience care to do so, for a small extra charge of fifty cents, they may step behind the curtain and examine Johnny/Johanna more thoroughly. In this private booth, she will strip for you and, if you so desire, you can examine her with your hands." The blow-offs *were* real gentlemen compared to my old man's pals.

I believe it was Hera who set me down in Indiana, gave me those cretins as parents. She has always been jealous of my true mother, Aphrodite. Notice this tattoo on my shoulder. The Caduceus, divine rod entwined with two serpents, given to my father, Hermes, winged messenger, god of science and commerce, patron of travelers and rogues, eloquence and cunning, guide of departed souls to Hades.

This is why I couldn't marry Otto or the love-struck Parisian chanteuse who slashed her wrists when I departed; they would have learned of my divine nature, of the many lives I've lived since Olympus, and I could not be responsible for their sorrow. It's a dangerous thing to go swimming in the waters of love. But if not for the spite of the gods on that hateful nymph who loved me so, this most perfect of all beings would not have been created.

I can see you're an intelligent person, not one of the gawkers, the hundred-eyed gawkers. I see envy in those hundred glassy eyes, misty with the beautiful dream of androgyny, Hermaphroditus awakened, the embodiment of their fears of being unmanned or unwomaned, and their guilt for desiring it. What do you see when you look at me? Though I'm dressed as a woman, you can sense my masculinity. How many times have you called to the less dominant side of your nature and wished you could be as helpless or as powerful? The gawkers are timid beasts, I can slay them with one look as my father slew Argus. It's the monsters you have to watch out for, the prodigies. As my mother, Aphrodite, in her infinite wisdom once said to me:

"Be brave toward the timid; courage against the courageous is not safe. Beware how you expose yourself to danger and put my happiness to risk, attack not the beasts that nature has armed with weapons. Your youth and beauty that charms will not touch the hearts of lions and bristly boars. Think of their terrible claws and prodigious strength! I hate the whole race of them."

I am a race of one; one of the immortals. So, If I make the lashes dark / And the eyes more bright / And the lips more scarlet, / Or ask if all be right / From mirror after mirror, / No vanity's displayed: / I'm looking for the face I had / Before the world was made.

BIBLIOGRAPHY

Drimmer, Frederick. *Very Special People*. New York: Bell Publishing, 1985.
Gade, John Allen. *The Life and Times of Tycho Brahe*. Princeton: Princeton University Press, 1947.
Hunter, Kay. *Duet for a Lifetime*. New York: Edward-McCann, 1964.
Jacobs, Joseph. *The Fables of Aesop*. New York: MacMillan, 1964.
Leibniz, G.W. *New Essays on Human Understanding*. Edited by Peter Remnant and Johnathan Bennett. Cambridge: Cambridge University Press, 1981.
Magri, Countess M. Lavinia. *The Autobiography of Mrs. Tom Thumb*. Archon Books, 1979.
McCullough, Edo. *Good Old Coney Island Days*. New York; Charles Schribner's Sons, 1957.
Morley, Henry. *Memoirs of Bartholomew Fair*. London & New York: G. Rutledge Publishing, 1892.
Ovid, *The Metamorphoses*. Translated by Gregory Horace. New York: Viking, 1958.
Pare, Ambroise. *Animaux, monstres et prodiges*. Paris: Geneve Droz, 1971.
Royal Archives. Queen Victoria's Journal. Journal entry for 23 March 1844
Sappho. *Poems and Fragments*. Translated by Guy Davenport. Ann Arbor, MI: University of Michigan Press, 1965
Sartre, Jean-Paul. *The Words* .New York City: G. Brazillier, 1964.
Saxon, A. H. *P. T. Barnum, The Legend and the Man*. New York: Columbia University Press, 1989.
Shakespeare, William. *King Lear*.
Shakespeare, William. *As You Like It*.
Troyat, Henri. *Peter the Great*. New York: E. P. Dutton, 1979.
Walton, Izaak. *The Complete Angler*. London/New York, F. Warne, 1878.
Yeats, William Butler. *A Woman Young And Old* : The Collected Poems of W. B. Yeats. New York: MacMillan Publishing, 1933.

Colophon

The text of this book was set in Adobe Garamond type with Zapf Dingbats. The title is set in Adobe Amigo. It has been printed on acid free paper and smyth sewn for durability and reading ease.